THE
WESTERN
LIGHT

ALSO BY SUSAN SWAN

SUSAN SWAN

THE
WESTERN
LIGHT

A NOVEL

Cormorant Books

Canada Council
for the Arts

Conseil des Arts
du Canada

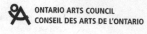
ONTARIO ARTS COUNCIL
CONSEIL DES ARTS DE L'ONTARIO

Canadian   Patrimoine
Heritage   canadien

Canadä

The publisher gratefully acknowledges the support of the Canada Council
for the Arts and the Ontario Arts Council for its publishing program. We
acknowledge the financial support of the Government of Canada through the
Canada Book Fund (CBF) for our publishing activities, and the Government
of Ontario through the Ontario Media Development Corporation, an agency
of the Ontario Ministry of Culture, and the Ontario Book Publishing Tax
Credit Program.

LIBRARY AND ARCHIVES CANADA CATALOGUING IN PUBLICATION

Swan, Susan
The western light / Susan Swan.

Issued also in electronic formats.
ISBN 978-1-77086-222-7

I. Title.

PS8587.W345W47 2012   C813'.54   C2012-903479-7

Cover design: Angel Guerra/Archetype
The cover image is a detail from *Related to the Octopus Tree, Georgian Bay*
© 1979 Charles Comfort; oil on canvas; height 50 cm.; width 65 cm.
(Private Collection.) Image courtesy of Joyner Waddington's Canadian Fine
Art. Used with the permission of the Estate of Charles Comfort.
Interior text design: Tannice Goddard, Soul Oasis Networking
Printer: Friesens

Printed and bound in Canada.

MIX
Paper from
responsible sources
FSC® C016245

The interior of this book is printed on
100% post-consumer waste recycled paper.

CORMORANT BOOKS INC.
390 Steelcase Road East, Markham, Ontario, L3R 1G2
www.cormorantbooks.com

In memory of Constance Rooke,
a friend to me and to all writers.

THE
WESTERN
LIGHT

WHEN I WAS IN MY FOURTH YEAR OF DOUBLE DIGITS, MY FATHER cuffed my cheek and said, "People are unpredictable. You never know what they'll do." I could tell by his tone that he meant it was true of him too. The year he admitted he was human like the rest of us, my father, Morley Bradford, was referring to John Pilkie, who had risen like a dark angel out of my father's neglect and threatened us with destruction. In those days, my father was a country doctor in Madoc's Landing, a tourist town on Georgian Bay, whose smooth-worn rocky shores are lined with thousands of pine islands and inside channels.

People were more stoical and more formal then. Men took their hats off when they entered a house and women wore white gloves for most social occasions and hats with popcorn veils. I was known as Mary (Mouse for short) Bradford and I addressed all adults as "Mister" and "Missus" and never by their first names, except when I joked about them with my friend Ben Shulman, whose father ran the psychiatric hospital in Madoc's Landing. Ben and I sometimes called our fathers "Old Man So-and-So" and we talked about "O.B.s" for "Old

Bags," and "B.O." for "Body Odour" and "N.C." for "Nut Cases."
I personally used "N.B." for "Non-Bleeder" and "I.T.T.O.N.B."
for "In the Time of Non-Bleeding," which was a fancy way
of describing my pre-pubescent state. Ben and I didn't say our
secret code words in public for fear of being mocked by other
children. Out of self-protection, I kept a lot of things private.
I saw myself as belonging to an earlier age of females, much
like the Paleolithic Age on the earth, and I had serious doubts
about getting a thing called "a period" even if I lived into a later
stage in my planet's evolutionary history. In the end, I grew up
like other women, although the person I was back in Madoc's
Landing is not the person I am now. For one thing, the world
has changed so much that what I'm about to tell you may as
well have taken place a couple of centuries ago.

In 1959, there were no free health care services. Doctors like
my father worked around the clock, the wide brim of his dove-
grey fedora shading his big, sad, healer's eyes. The Salk vaccine
had been invented, but it wasn't in common use and the threat
of polio sent families to the north, looking for germ-free air. This
reminds me that I should point out that the polio epidemic of
1953 left me with a crooked leg I called Hindrance and a powerful need to deny the obvious. Or is denial just another word
for optimism? In any case, it takes me a while to notice trouble
stirring. Seeing the glass half-full is one of my characteristics,
along with my narrow face and lopsided smile. M.B. Bradford.

PART ONE

DO YOU WANT TO MEET A KILLER?

I

BEFORE JOHN PILKIE WAS SENT TO THE PSYCHIATRIC HOSPITAL
in Madoc's Landing, my father and I lived a quiet life in our
two-storey brick house on Whitefish Road, overlooking the
Great Bay. My grandmother, Big Louie, had sent my mother's
sister, Little Louie, to look after me. According to Big Louie, our
housekeeper Sal couldn't bring me up properly, even though
Sal had been living with my father and me since my mother
died eight years before. My grandmother came from oil money
in Petrolia, Ontario, while Sal was a small-town nurse who had
worked in my father's office. The two women had different
ideas about raising me. For instance, my grandmother thought
I should do nothing but rest and Sal said I needed to exercise to
stop my leg from atrophying. To win her case, Sal would consult
one of Morley's dense medical textbooks before talking to my
father and convincing him that her way was the best.

Little Louie was pretty well useless in those conversations,
since she had gone to pieces after a dipsy-doodle love affair with
a married newspaperman. He broke her heart so badly my aunt
had to take a leave of absence from her reporting job in London,

Ontario. In those days on Whitefish Road, Little Louie didn't do much of anything, except sit around the house eating Macintosh apples and reading books. Her nickname made me laugh because Little Louie stood five-foot-eleven in her stocking feet, and her mother, Big Louie, was only five-foot-three. Little Louie resembled my mother, Alice, who had one of the pretty, heart-shaped faces common to the Vidal women. Before she died of brain disease, people had called my mother beautiful. What they called my aunt was nice-looking, and I guess that namby-pamby description stuck with Little Louie, even though she and my mother and grandmother all had the same yellow hair and large, heavy-lidded blue eyes. Little Louie hadn't grown into her looks yet, and my grandmother said my aunt's inferiority complex, which had been brought on by the beauty of my poor dead mother, would work itself out in time. My aunt dressed like she could care less. She didn't notice when her thick blond bangs needed a trim or if the seams of her nylons were crooked. And, even though she wore the pretty dresses that my grandmother bought for her, Little Louie often went around with her skirt hitched up in the back, or one of her sweaters inside out. Sometimes Morley called my aunt "Little Orphan Annie," and his affectionate, teasing tone brought out a mean fierceness in Sal's eyes.

MY AUNT LIVED IN OUR guest bedroom. She rarely made her bed, an antique four-poster with a gold lamé bedspread that came from Eaton's department store. She didn't remember to tie back the gauzy light-filled drapes that were exact copies of the ones in my grandmother's mansion in Petrolia. Such sloppiness drove Sal crazy, because she liked our house neat and tidy. So Sal would clean the bedroom when Little Louie went out and my aunt would accuse Sal of going through her things.

My father still slept in the bedroom that he had shared with my mother; the room hadn't changed since my mother died. Even her make-up table, with its glass top and pretty silver hairbrushes, remained exactly as it was when my mother was alive. It sat next to my father's Sheraton dresser, which sheltered a mountain of large white handkerchiefs and huge, bespoke shirts whose pockets had been especially enlarged so they were deep enough to hold Morley's custom-made spectacles. My father kept two books on his bedside table: a collection of essays by Michel Montaigne and a German grammar book, so he could understand his German patients who had come after the war. An old Palm Sunday bookmark, woven in the shape of a bamboo cross, rested inside the third page of Montaigne's essays, suggesting Morley had read this far at least.

2

MY FATHER NEVER ASKED ME MUCH ABOUT MY LIFE, AND I guessed he accepted whatever Sal told him with the same fatalistic wistfulness he accepted most things. Big Louie claimed that Morley was doleful, like the land he came from, and that I was doleful too. I was glad my father and I had something in common; and from Sal and my grandmother, I had put together a few facts about my father's life.

Morley had left his home on the French River and gone to medical school in Toronto on a scholarship when he was only fifteen. His mother, my grandmother Phyllis Bradford, had helped him and, in exchange, he had supported her financially for the rest of her short life. Before she died of breast cancer, Phyllis Bradford claimed that Morley followed in the footsteps of his late father, Duke, who used to say as he doled out cash to poor relatives, "There, but for the grace of God, go I." Duke had handed over so much money my Bradford grandmother claimed there wasn't enough left for their own children. Isn't that the confounding question? How much do you give away and still have enough for yourself?

After my father graduated, he took the position of a locum, or assistant, to an older doctor in Madoc's Landing and began working his eighty-hour weeks. When the older doctor died, Morley took over his practice. On Mondays, and every other day of the week, he started operating at eight a.m. at the town hospital. At noon, he came home for the lunch Sal prepared for him, took a half-hour nap, and was back in his office by one-thirty p.m. He saw patients until six p.m., when he came home for dinner and another nap. By seven, he was back in his office seeing patients again or making house calls. He called it quits at eleven p.m., but nighttime didn't necessarily mean rest for him. He was often roused from sleep to deliver babies or rescue victims of traffic accidents. There were no paramedics in those days, so my father was expected to pull people from burning car wrecks and sometimes perform surgery on the spot.

On Saturdays, he went to the office and followed the same gruelling schedule, except that he didn't operate. On Sunday mornings, he went to the hospital dressed in his Sunday best, a striped black director's coat and black trousers, to see how his patients were recovering from their operations. Then, if Sal and I were lucky, if there were no car crashes or boating accidents, he took the two of us on his Sunday calls in the countryside.

It was a punishing way of life. Sal said my father sometimes wished he had been a philosophy professor. His book of Montaigne's essays was left over proof of his old interest in philosophy.

As for Little Louie and me, our lives were slow and uneventful. Every morning, I rode to school in the hospital van with Ben Shulman and our archenemies, the gang of boys whose fathers were guards at the Bug House. (I wasn't allowed to say "Bug

House," although it was what everyone in Madoc's Landing called the Ontario Psychiatric Hospital.) Ben's father was their fathers' boss so that was enough right there to make them hate us.

Little Louie would be asleep when Ben and I left for school in the morning, and sometimes she was still sleeping when we came home for lunch. She was always up by the afternoon. And, per usual, she would be downstairs reading by our coal fireplace when Ben and I came in for our cups of Neilson's cocoa after school. Little Louie admired American writers like Sloan Wilson, the author of *The Man in the Gray Flannel Suit,* and Martha Gellhorn, who had been Hemingway's third wife. Little Louie wanted to be a well-known journalist, like Gellhorn, so my grandmother couldn't boss her around. For the moment, though, my aunt said she needed "time out." To justify her existence, she worked on freelance articles for Canadian magazines and newspapers. She called what she was doing "writing on spec" and she didn't act surprised when these pieces were turned down. Most editors preferred to assign stories rather than to buy something written without their direction, she told me.

When she first came to stay, my aunt was writing an article about socialized medicine, which hadn't yet come to Canada. Her married boyfriend, the mysterious M. Falkowski, was helping her, although Little Louie had told my grandmother they were "incommunicado." Maybe Little Louie thought that accepting his help on a magazine article was different than exchanging love letters, because M. Falkowski regularly sent my aunt dozens of articles about free medical care written by Canadian politicians like Tommy Douglas. He also sent up packages that contained books by Leon Trotsky and Karl Marx, although Little

Louie kept those tomes under a layer of cotton batten in her jewellery drawer. The name "M. Falkowski" was always scrawled in the left-hand corner of his envelopes as if he didn't mind anybody knowing who he was.

One afternoon, during the first few weeks of Little Louie's stay, I told my aunt that my father had considered studying philosophy; I said that Morley would like to discuss Montaigne with her. I knew that she, too, had studied Montaigne at university, and I swore that Morley had been secretly hoping he and my aunt could have a satisfying adult conversation about the French philosopher. To be honest, I had no way of knowing what my father was hoping, but I pointed out that his conversations with Sal and me were hardly fulfilling. "My father finds Sal and me dull as dishwater," I explained. "I'm too young to give him his money's worth and Sal is pretty well hopeless as far as philosophy is concerned."

Little Louie laughed and gave in. One evening, when Sal was busy in the kitchen, my aunt and I waited up for my father, our faces hopeful and serious.

"Anything wrong, girls?" He walked in, twirling his dove-grey fedora. His eyes fell on my aunt's books piled on the coffee table along with his copy of Montaigne's essays.

"We thought you might like to discuss Montaigne tonight ..." My aunt's voice sounded girlish and high.

Unexpectedly, my father laughed. I laughed, too, trying to go along. My aunt bowed her head, her cheeks darkening in a self-conscious blush.

"No, no. I didn't mean to laugh," my father remarked mildly. "Please excuse me. It's been so long since I read Montaigne. Let's see if I can remember ... wasn't it Montaigne who said every man bears the whole stamp of the human condition?" His tired, deep-set eyes looked thoughtful.

"I told you, Little Louie!" I burst out. "Morley doesn't have anybody to talk to about the things that interest him."

"What, Mary?" my father asked.

"If you don't want to talk about Montaigne," my aunt said. "We could discuss socialized medicine. I'm dying to know what you think about it."

The kitchen door slammed and Sal poked her head into the living room. "Did I hear you mention socialized medicine, Louisa?"

"Yes, why?" Little Louie asked.

Sal sucked her teeth noisily. "Doc Bradford doesn't believe in that communist hooey."

"Well, I wouldn't put it that way," my father said. "I think socialized health care will spoil a doctor's dedication to medicine."

"So there, Louisa," Sal retorted. I waited for Sal to stick out her tongue and say something nastier, but luckily for Little Louie the phone rang. Sal picked it up and said it was for Morley. Muttering apologetically, my father hurried out to take his call.

"I'm sorry, Little Louie," I whispered. "I guess my father doesn't have time to talk about Montaigne."

"Don't take it to heart," Little Louie replied. "You know that old saying, Mouse: shoemakers' children don't have shoes." I nodded my head solemnly. Oh, I knew that saying all right. You bet I did.

AN INTEREST IN BOOKS AND ideas was what I believed I shared with Morley, so I was preparing myself for the day when he and

I would sit down together and have long, soulful talks. After my night with Morley and Little Louie, I realized that day was still a long way off. In the meantime, I threw my efforts into my composition about my great-grandfather Mac Vidal, who had struck it rich when he hit an oil gusher in 1862. The Petrolia Chamber of Commerce was giving a prize for the best student essay about the early days of oil in southwestern Ontario, and my grandmother believed my composition could win the prize, although Big Louie had been known to overstate things.

My teacher let me work on my composition in class since I finished my lessons before the other children. She told my father she had never seen a harder-working child. I was doing it for him. As I wrote, I thought how impressed Morley would be by the way I had packed my composition with historical facts such as the mention of petroleum found in Genesis chapter six, verse fourteen, when Noah was commanded by God, "Make thee an ark of gopher wood; rooms shalt thou make in the ark, and shall pitch it within and without with slime." I was sure Morley would be surprised to learn that Noah's slime (the Bible sometimes called oil "slime") came from Hit on the Euphrates River, one hundred miles west of Baghdad, where to this day there are heavy seepages of petroleum.

Still, there was a problem with my plan to impress my father. In self-defence, I had developed two vocabularies: the one-syllable words I used at school and my private reading vocabulary made up of long words I'd learned from books. I couldn't pronounce most of the long words, since I never said them out loud in case the kids in the schoolyard called me a brown-noser. Sometimes, I tried out a word like "S-O-TERICK" (for esoteric) in front of my aunt and she tried to hide her smile when she corrected me.

M.B.'s Book of True Facts

My bedroom, the smallest in the house, was tidier than Little Louie's; I made my bed with hospital corners, exactly the way Sal had taught me. It was next door to my father's bedroom, although Sal wanted me to sleep in the bedroom next to hers. Sal's room had once belonged to the maid, and it still had the simple ironstone washstand that the maid had used and an old-fashioned sleigh bed.

Sleeping next door to Morley made me feel safe. But I could see the Bug House from my bedroom window. Of course, the Bug House wasn't really a house, but a group of buildings hidden behind a large maple sugar bush. It included Maple Ridge, a high security prison where insane murderers were locked up; a six-storey office building; the staff houses, with back kitchens and sheds; the nineteenth-century cottages that housed the harmless patients; and, last of all, the working farm where patients grew turnips and potatoes.

At night, a row of lampposts lit up the prison, which had started off as a reformatory for delinquent boys. The shadowy light falling on its large shuttered windows made Maple Ridge resemble a sleeping face. I used to complain that we were the first in line if a patient escaped until Sal pointed out that a house by the hospital was the very last place an escapee would visit because that's where the guards would look first.

I kept my crime scrapbook on my bedside table. Using LePage glue, my friend Ben and I pasted in news stories about bank robbers and criminally insane murderers. As far as Ben and I were concerned, reading crime stories was the best way to discover the frightening potential in your neighbours who could look as worn and ordinary as last year's rubber tires. The goriest crime stories were in the late night editions of the Toronto *Telegram*, printed on pink paper. After he read the stock listings, my father gave me the front section folded down to the stories about bank robbers like the Polka Dot Gang and Edwin Alonzo Boyd who once apologized to a female teller for dirtying her blouse.

On my bedside table, I also kept *M.B.'s Book of True Facts*. In my opinion then, a true fact was one you were glad to know whereas most facts lacked the sheen of that conviction. I was making a book of true facts because Sal had a low opinion of Canadians, her own people, and Little Louie wasn't much better. For instance, neither Little Louie nor Sal believed that Tonto (the Lone Ranger's companion) was a Canadian named Harold J. Smith who grew up on the Six Nations Reserve in Brantford, Ontario. Both Sal and my aunt laughed when I pointed out that the world's biggest cheese had been manufactured in 1866 inside a lean-to in Ingersoll, Ontario. On the trip to England for an exhibition, it stank so badly the crew had to toss it overboard.

In my bedroom cupboard, I stashed the books my grand-mother wanted me to read — classics like *The Bobbsey Twins*, which bored me silly — along with some ancient Baby Wet'um dolls, whose arms were still in the slings that I used to make out of Morley's linen handkerchiefs. When my mother was sick with the brain disease that killed her, I would tear the dolls apart and fix them the way Morley patched up his patients. I popped off their heads the way I used to pull apart the beads of my mother's plastic necklaces. My dolls were far harder to fix than I realized. Their heads didn't go snugly back into place and their broken limbs stayed broken. Only Morley could fix smashed up bones.

But he couldn't fix my mother. Nobody could. And that's how I ended up with Little Louie as a companion eight years later.

3

THE MORNING JOHN PILKIE CAME TO MADOC'S LANDING I WAS in my aunt's bed, reading her the front-page story about him in *The Chronicle,* our local newspaper. My aunt lay next to me eating apples and smoking one Sweet Cap after another. It was two weeks before Easter Sunday, and only thirty-one days after my all-time faves — Richie Valens, Buddy Holly, and the Big Bopper — died in a plane crash near Clear Lake, Iowa. The Cold War was ongoing, along with the Hula-Hoop, although we didn't see much about either in the newspaper that day. While Little Louie listened, I read out the headline: "Mad Killer Pilkie Comes to Town." The town newspaper often referred to him as Mad Dog Pilkie, as if he was a dog with distemper. That's how people talked in Madoc's Landing. There was a kind of poetry to it, and John Pilkie had more nicknames than most. Sometimes the newspapers called him "The Hockey Killer" or "Gentleman Jack Pilkie" on account of his debonair clothes.

I was still on the first paragraph of the news story when Sal yelled at us to get moving. Morley was taking us to the train station to pick up my grandmother, who was coming early for the Easter holiday — coming not only for a visit, but to inspect the job that Little Louie was doing on me.

"Did you hear me?" Sal shrieked. "Time's a-wasting!"

Neither Little Louie nor I answered. We were too absorbed in Kelsey Farrow's newspaper story. Kelsey said that John Pilkie and three other insane murderers were being transported by train to the psychiatric hospital in Madoc's Landing. According to Kelsey, the murderers were travelling under armed guard. They were in civilian clothes to avoid attracting attention, although how they planned to do that was anybody's guess.

The three other killers travelling with John Pilkie were: a Latin teacher, who split open his wife's head with an axe after she asked him to change his shirt for dinner; a potato farmer, who had stabbed his field hand for giving him a dirty look; and a seventeen-year-old boy, who shot his mother dead when she wouldn't lend him her car one Saturday night. John Pilkie's crime was mentioned too, although by that time he was better known for his escapes than for the murder of his family. Kelsey listed John's escapes in the newspaper as if he were a creature with supernatural powers:

The Escapes of Mad Killer Pilkie

1. Disappearing from a work crew while haying a field.
2. Scaling the twenty-foot wire fence around a Vancouver psychiatric ward.
3. Unlocking his cell at the Whitby psychiatric hospital using a key he had carved out of a jam jar. *The Chronicle* claimed he held some paraffin wax in his palm when he shook the

hand of a guard holding the key, and made a copy from the wax impression.

4. Slipping out the back door of a hospital chapel before the service ended and (this was the amazing part) watching the departing churchgoers from a tree.

"That killer is a regular Houdini!" my aunt exclaimed. She blew three smoke rings from her Sweet Cap cigarette and waited while I tried to poke my finger through her wobbly creations.

"John Pilkie used to be Canada's Most Wanted Man," I confided after the rings floated away. "That's what Kelsey said."

"Mouse, we don't have a 'most wanted list.' It's something the Americans invented."

"Well, I guess Kelsey wants Canada to sound as interesting as the United States."

My aunt laughed. "Then Kelsey has his job cut out for him," she said, reaching over me to get another apple. "I wouldn't believe everything Kelsey writes. Sometimes newspapers shade the facts. I'm a reporter, remember?"

Undeterred, I showed Little Louie an old news story about John Pilkie that had been written by a Toronto journalist, and not by Kelsey Farrow. On the day she was murdered, Peggy Pilkie, John's wife, had sprinkled kerosene on the bedroom floor to kill cockroaches. That night, in a fit of temper, John threw a lit match on the oil-soaked boards and ignited an explosion called a flare fire. His wife was heard to shout that John would pay for his crime. She couldn't make her way through the flames to save their baby girl, and the child died in the hospital of smoke inhalation. Mrs. Pilkie herself died a few hours later of shock and severe burns to her legs and torso.

I still shudder when I think about it. To set your wife and baby girl alight is unimaginable now, and it was even more unimaginable then. The courts said John Pilkie had been abandoned by reason and sent him away for life to a mental institution.

Accompanying the article was a black-and-white drawing that depicted the former Pilkie home in Walkerville, a Windsor suburb named after a local liquor baron. A large X marked the second-storey bedroom where the fire began. Next to the drawing was a photograph of a young John Pilkie and a dark-haired woman leaning on a crutch. Its caption said: "As a girl, Pilkie's young wife suffered from polio." I had forgotten that John Pilkie's wife had polio. It made me feel uneasy and somehow implicated. Did he kill her because she limped like me?

"Why did he leave his wife and baby behind to die?" I asked.

My aunt pointed to the last paragraph. "It says here that Pilkie suffered from a paranoid delusion that his wife was an enemy out to hurt him. That means he thought people were out to get him even if they weren't."

So he was overcome by a crazy notion. Maybe John Pilkie wasn't a true killer, I told myself. A true killer would know it was his own wife and child he was burning up. But I kept my doubts to myself and told Little Louie about the day I read my first story about John Pilkie. The story's headline read: "Hockey Killer Stopped in His Tracks"; it described Pilkie's capture in Montreal. It claimed he might still be at large if he hadn't come down with pneumonia and gone to a Montreal hospital where a doctor spotted his Ontario hospital underwear and phoned the police.

On the same day, my grandmother, Big Louie, had walked into Sick Kids hospital carrying a vial of convalescent serum for me made from the blood of recovered polio patients. I told my grandmother about Mad Killer Pilkie making headlines, and my grandmother said John Pilkie sounded like a knock-off man who didn't want to work for a living.

"It's as if Big Louie already knew that he was going to be sent to the Bug House, and she wanted to stop me from liking him," I told Little Louie.

"So Mom was right. You got better." Little Louie grinned. "And now the hockey killer is coming to Madoc's Landing. She must be tickled pink."

From the stairwell, Sal yelled up at us again. "Louisa, if you don't make Mary do what I say, I'm telling Doc Bradford."

"Shut up, you big B-I-T-C-H!" Little Louie muttered, spelling out the letters without saying the word. When she saw my face, she shouted back, "Okay, okay, Sal, we're coming!" Little Louie pulled on a pair of old jeans and a torn turtleneck sweater and I put on my best tartan kilt and clean white blouse with a Peter Pan collar; then she helped me on with my Boston brace. If you've never seen a Boston brace, it was quite a contraption. I wore an abbreviated version, custom-tailored to me. The top half fit around my pelvis and buckled up under my clothes. The second part was the long metal bar used to stretch and strengthen my left leg, which didn't move as fast as my right leg, the one polio hadn't touched.

A Useless Conversation with Hindrance

Me: I hate it when the kids at school whisper, "Here comes Peg Leg."
Hindrance: You'll just have to lump it, won't you?

Me: Over my dead body.

Hindrance: Say that enough, Mouse, and your wish will come true.

NEXT, I PUT ON MY blazer and the Lone Ranger hat Morley gave me. It had a black braided chinstrap. I refused to wear my winter coat or galoshes, because Little Louie said it was spring so she wasn't wearing hers.

"Where's your coat?" Sal yelled as I rushed past. "Upstairs," I shouted over my shoulder. Our springer spaniels, Joe and Mairzy, thundered after me, barking their heads off. We clambered into the back seat of my father's green Oldsmobile convertible. According to Sal, I had been named after the first springer spaniel, Mary, because my mother was so crazy about her. I had every reason to believe Sal was serious.

A moment later, my father and Little Louie got in too. His dove-grey fedora was still on his head. He liked the 1953 convertible because even with the roof up, it was the only automobile big enough to let him to drive with his hat on. Halfway down Whitefish Road, he stopped unexpectedly.

"Who lives here?" my aunt asked.

"Cap Lefroy. Sal says he's dying of lung cancer," I whispered as Morley got out of the car. My aunt scoffed and lit up a Sweet Cap to show me how little she cared about the disease. Together we watched Morley plod up the drive, Joe and Mairzy bouncing at his heels. I had dreamt about Cap's three-storey brick house the night before, and my dream depicted the same scene I was looking at from the back seat of the Oldsmobile: fat, puffed up snow clouds swarming around Cap's place. I had no idea what kind of menacing energies the clouds in my dream suggested, and I didn't want to guess. It was bad enough that a snowstorm was coming our way and we had gone out minus our winter coats and boots. Inside the car, the chilly March air was drifting up through the floorboards, making us shiver. There was no heater in the Oldsmobile, just the warmth from the engine.

At last Morley came back, bringing Cap, who opened the door to the back seat and peered in. "Our town is sure lucky to have Doc Bradford," he said, winking at Little Louie and myself. "He's the town saint, eh Mary?"

"I guess so," I said shyly.

"You guess so? Our country was built by men like your father! They don't make 'em like him anymore."

"That's enough guff, Cap. We're off to see the hockey killer," Morley said. Cap whistled, long and low, and we drove off, the uplifting strains of Pat Boone singing "April Love" blasting from the car radio.

4

THE PARKING LOT WAS ALREADY NOISY WITH CARS AND PEOPLE who had come to see the mad killer. Morley pulled up alongside a line of police cars and a van owned by the psychiatric hospital. Sprawled on the northeast hill above town, it was a secret world that refracted the town's rational mindset.

On the station platform, the final snow of the season had begun to fall. I could feel its icy dampness seep into my Oxford with its built-in heel. Now see here, Mouse, I told myself, Morley doesn't have on his galoshes and he expects you to ignore discomfort the same way he does. My father's hand was resting on my shoulder as if he knew I was getting cold and thought he should do something, but per usual he was distracted. His eyes kept turning to the wooded hill beyond the grain elevator, and the opening in the trees where the train would appear before its plunge to the station house.

By my elbow stood Ben Shulman who, like me, had dressed up to see the killers. Ben wore his new orange cowboy chaps and a gun belt with two six-guns that fired real caps. He also had on a baggy Toronto Maple Leafs hockey sweater that hung almost to his knees. Ben imagined the sweater made him look thin, but no sweater could disguise his soft, doughy-looking hands and chipmunk cheeks. His plump cheeks and hands were exactly like the cheeks and hands of his roly-poly father, Dr. Shulman, who bore the uneasy distinction of being the only Jewish man in our town, where everyone was either French-Canadian and Catholic or English-speaking and Protestant. To the right of Dr. Shulman stood John's mother, Mrs. Roy Pilkie, who wore an expensive-looking Persian lamb coat and matching pillbox hat, plus a pair of weird wrap-around sunglasses. Even though she was the mother of a killer, I guess she wanted to look nice for her son. As we stamped our feet to keep warm, she said, "My poor boy just has no luck. Does he, Doc Bradford?"

My father shook his head gravely, his eyes turning back again to the hill where John's train was expected to appear. On either side of Morley were Chief Doucette and the reporter Kelsey Farrow. Balancing on our tiptoes, Ben and I tried to read the small, spidery symbols scrawled across Kelsey's notepad, but neither Ben nor I understood shorthand, so we turned our attention back to my father.

"Is it cold enough for you, Joe?" Morley asked Chief Doucette.

"'Spozed to turn to sleet tonight," Chief Doucette replied.

"We're in for it then," Kelsey said without looking up from his notepad. In *The Chronicle*, Kelsey had reminded us that John Pilkie was a local boy who had played with the hockey team in Madoc's Landing as well as the Oshawa Colts before he went across the border to play defence for the Detroit Red Wings. According to Kelsey, John kept a photograph of the young Queen Elizabeth in his pocket for luck; he could rag the puck, which was another way of saying that no matter where he was on the rink, the puck stayed glued to the blade of his stick. His bodychecks, along with his hooks, trips, slashes, elbows, and punches made him a dangerous opponent, although off the ice he was known for holding the door open for his female fans. But there was no mention of my father in Kelsey's story and I wondered if Kelsey knew what Sal had told me that morning at breakfast. John Pilkie had been my father's patient.

According to Sal, my father had helped John Pilkie's father take out John's appendix when a November storm trapped the lightkeeper's family on their island in the middle of the Great Bay. Sal swore what happened at the Western Light was better than the Biblical tale of Abraham and Isaac; but she warned me not to breathe a word about it to anyone — especially not to Little Louie — because Morley disliked Sal discussing his patients with anyone.

Sal also said my father believed that a hockey concussion had turned John Pilkie violent, although nobody, including Sal, felt the same way.

FROM THE DIRECTION OF THE grain elevator came a low, hooting whistle. It was now snowing too hard to see the train, but all of us on the station platform could hear it coming down the hill. We heard the rasp of hissing steam as it pulled into the station. A conductor blew his whistle. Then there was the sound of a door opening, and John Pilkie stepped through a ghostly curtain of snow and stood before me. I recognized him from the newspaper photographs that Little Louie and I had seen that morning, but I was still surprised by how nice he looked. He had on a chocolate-brown fedora with an upturned brim, a striped chocolate-brown suit, and an unbuttoned raccoon coat that fell to the top of his fleece-lined galoshes. Three men along with the armed railway guard followed him as he trudged through the falling snow holding up a white Bristol board sign. In huge, block letters, it said: I AM INNOCENT. His companions were neatly dressed and clean-shaven, and they looked more concerned about getting out of the snow than escaping their jailer. I examined them in wonder. Did the boy in a toque really blast his mother to smithereens? The men were smiling and talking to the guard, as if their train ride was an ordinary Saturday outing.

More passengers came spilling out the coach doors, carrying their bags. The guard asked the crowd to step back so the prisoners could pose for Kelsey's camera. While they huddled together, a man in a hunting cap tried to snatch the sign out of John Pilkie's hand. "Go back where you came from, killer!" the man cried. A police officer quickly pushed the man off the platform, and the crowd shuffled closer for a better view. John Pilkie waited for the crowd to grow quiet; then he fished a harmonica out of his pocket and played a tune that Ben and I knew from school: "Hail, hail, the gang's all here. Never mind the weather. Here we are together. Sure we're glad that you're here too."

He pointed up at the snow drifting down from the heavens. And, like sheep, we looked up, too, expressions of awe and fear on our faces, although some people had started to laugh. One or two men clapped. John Pilkie took off his brown fedora and held it out as if he expected people to drop money in it. "Stand back! Let us pass!" The guard shouted and began herding his prisoners in our direction. Next to me, Morley stirred. My father rarely exerted himself, because he saved his energy for his patients; but, kicking the freshly fallen snow off his wingtips, Morley shuffled forward. "Hello, John!" Morley boomed.

Mid-stride, John Pilkie stopped. "Hullo, Doc Bradford!" he cried and shook my father's hand.

"This is my late wife's sister, Louisa," Morley said. "And my daughter, Mary."

"Why, you girls are shivering!" John Pilkie smiled at my aunt, who lowered her eyes and didn't smile back. "Would you like to share my coat?" He opened it so wide we could see its dappled silk lining.

"We're fine," Little Louie replied, her cheeks reddening.

"I can see that." He shook Little Louie's hand, then reached down and shook mine.

"John, it's been a while," Morley remarked, shushing Joe and Mairzy, who had started to growl.

"A coon's age," John Pilkie agreed, turning towards some noise in the parking lot. There were wild shouts and a gang of boys raced across the platform throwing snowballs at the prisoners, who ducked or covered their faces. It was Sam Mahoney and the Bug House kids. At school, I was known as a Bug House kid too, because we lived in "the doctor's house," which had stood on hospital property until one of its owners subdivided the lot. Sam let another snowball fly. John Pilkie stood his ground. What came next felt like a movie camera had tripped its switch to slow motion, so each second lasted a lifetime. Sam's snowball hit John on the side of his head and knocked off his hat. He didn't move. Two more snowballs smashed against his shoulder. He made a playful half-lunge in the air, while we held our breath and waited for him to demonstrate the murderous side of his character. A final snowball hit him in the middle of his chest, near his heart. Instead of knocking over the railway guard and running after the boys, he carefully brushed the snow off his raccoon coat.

"Aim low and you hit something, eh, Doc Bradford?" John Pilkie said.

My father grinned. "See you around, son."

As the crowd watched, Morley clapped the hockey killer on the back and then Morley lumbered off with Little Louie, our spaniels racing ahead, their ears flapping. The sight of my father sent the boys clattering down the station stairs and into the crowd by the Dock Lunch stand.

My fingers still tingling from his touch, I watched John Pilkie climb aboard the hospital's van, and I imagined his broad, dimpled face smiling at me through the window before the van disappeared into a cloud of whirling snow. Behind me came a series of sharp, crackling pops and the smell of burning cap-gun paper. Ben shoved his smoking six guns into their holsters. "Let me feel where he touched you, Mouse," he whispered. Giddy with pride, I extended my right hand and Ben's stubby fingers pressed my skinny ones in wonderment. Somewhere in the crowd my father was calling my name.

"Ben, I have to go." I yanked away my hand. Dropping my eyes so I couldn't see people staring, I trudged after Morley. I was used to people looking, although I didn't exactly limp. I walked with a slight roll, like a sailor, because my weight sank down onto my good foot, especially if I was tired. That day my roll was jerkier than usual because I was trying to step into Morley's footprints where the snow had been beaten down. He was too far ahead to notice, and that made me go faster although the space between his footprints felt a mile wide. Down by the last coach, my grandmother had spotted me. Big Louie waved excitedly, one hand on her hat to keep it from being blown off. "Mouse! Over here, Dearie!" I waved back and shuffled forward, the freezing wind whipping my hair into my eyes, my fingers turning to ice in my pockets.

5

MY MOTHER'S FAMILY WAS GOOD AT PRODUCING POWERFUL women and Big Louie was our second matriarch this side of the border. The first was my great-great aunt, Louisa Vidal, or Old Louie, as she was known inside our family, who, at the age of 74, followed my Yankee great-grandfather to southwestern Ontario to keep house for him. My grandmother Big Louie was my great-grandfather's daughter and, like my own father, my grandmother stood out in the crowd. It wasn't just her jolly patrician face, but her clothes, which she ordered from New York designers. That afternoon, she wore an orange sack coat with a collar of fox heads, and a matching orange hat spouting upside-down pigeon feathers. My grandmother's extravagance was a sore spot with Sal, who sewed her own outfits.

"Hello there, favourite grandchild!" Big Louie hugged me to her bosom and I took a grateful sniff of Ode to Joy. She applied her favourite perfume so lavishly I could smell it on her egg salad sandwiches. When nobody reacted, Big Louie poked my father in the ribs. "Get it, Morley? Mouse is my only grandchild!"

Morley smiled faintly.

"This is for your composition, Mouse," Big Louie said, thrusting a book into my hand. It was a beat-up leather history book of southwestern Ontario.

"Say 'thank you,' Mary," my father told me.

"Hold your horses. I haven't finished." My grandmother pointed to a bundle of papers sticking out of her purse. "I brought up dad's picture and some of his early letters for Mary to quote in her essay."

My grandmother bent towards me, exuding more Ode to Joy, and I took the small tintype she handed me. It was dated "Oil Springs, Ontario, 1864," and the clean-shaven young man standing by a wooden oil derrick was my Yankee ancestor.

"I wouldn't kick him out of bed, would you, Mouse?" Big Louie said, lighting up a Camel.

"Mom, what a thing to say!" Little Louie giggled like anything. I giggled, too.

"It's a nice photo, Big Louie," I mumbled. "Thank you from the bottom of my heart." I placed the tintype inside my grandmother's history of southwestern Ontario.

"By the way, I've invited the prisoners and their guards for tea," Morley said as we strolled across the parking lot. "The water main froze at the hospital."

"Did I hear you right, Morley?" Lifting up the veil on her hat, Big Louie puffed angrily on her cigarette.

"I told Dr. Shulman there would be hot drinks at our house."

Big Louie gave me a shocked look as she slipped into the front seat of Morley's convertible. Morley climbed in next to her and I slid into the backseat with Little Louie and our spaniels, keeping one eye peeled for the van and its cargo of killers. We had never entertained insane murderers before, although we were used to mental patients. In the forties, the hospital gave art classes to its patients in our home, and some of their weird oil paintings still hung in our upstairs hall. By "weird," I mean that none of the people in the paintings by the hospital's mental patients had eyes or mouths.

I should also point out that a slight stigma was attached to anyone associated with the Bug House; at school this shadow fell across me. It didn't help that Morley supported Dr. Shulman's liberal practices and made Sal and me hand out prizes at the hospital's embarrassing track and field contests.

In the years before Dr. Shulman, there had been a good relationship between the Bug House and the town. For instance, it had been common once for some of the harmless patients to shovel snow off the walks of homes near the hospital grounds. Dr. Shulman had put a stop to using patients as free labour, although Archie Beauchamp, who was the second cousin of Sal's father, still raked our leaves, and sometimes Sal sat down with Archie and had a cup of cocoa with him.

6

MORLEY'S OLDSMOBILE CONVERTIBLE BEGAN ITS CLIMB UP BUG House hill and we quickly left behind the town, whose mix of French and English neighbourhoods I'd noted in *M.B.'s Book of True Facts*.

Sal herself came from French Town, the overgrown tract of land behind Bug House hill. Its winding streets had been built on old Indian trails, and its roads and old log homes were hidden in the same stand of maple forest that shielded the psychiatric hospital from Madoc's Landing. Sal and her friends enjoyed gossiping about what went on there. In French Town, people could live the way they had a hundred years before and not be criticized for it. Old cars and furniture sat outside rotting, people ran booze cans in their houses, and bootleggers plied their trade. A call to Thompson's taxi, where Sal's father worked, would get you illegal beer or a bottle of cheap wine called "Zing." Madoc's Landing was dry in the fifties; in the wet towns nearby, liquor board salesmen kept a list of how much you drank, and refused to serve you if you went over the limit. So citizens up and down Brebeuf County went to French Town for their liquor.

We lived in the English section; its leafy streets were lined with red brick houses and bungalows with aluminum siding. The English section, with its neatly mown grass boulevards and maple trees, ended at the harbour near the Dollartown Arena, our most important public building, more venerable than our Protestant churches or the Catholic cathedral with its twin spires. Every winter the Madoc's Landing Muskrats played hockey under its dome roof, and every spring the Rats lost another season and broke my father's heart.

Morley coached the Rats. He loved hockey more than anything, like most of the men in Madoc's Landing — and some of the women, too. Hockey had been a family passion for the Bradfords, who lived ninety miles north of Madoc's Landing, near the French River, where Morley's relatives fished Georgian Bay and logged its trees. Their grim faces in old sepia-tinted photographs suggested they had a hard go of things, and hockey was how they entertained themselves. Hockey wasn't important to the Vidals, who lived in Petrolia, once the oil capital of North America. The town was still prosperous when my mother had been a girl, so families like the Vidals went to Atlantic City or California if they wanted a good time.

SOON THE HUMBLING WIDTH OF Brebeuf County stretched before us. To the north shone the navy mass of Georgian Bay and the slab of headland where Samuel Champlain performed the first Catholic mass in Ontario with his Huron guides, although I would be lying if I said it was easy to find the wooden cross that marks the spot.

Brebeuf County was named after Father Brébeuf, the seventeenth-century Jesuit priest tortured to death by the

Iroquois. According to *Hansen's Handbook of the Georgian Bay*, Brebeuf County had always been dangerous and was dangerous still, especially the Great Bay, whose plainspoken names describe what you see: One Tree Island, Strawberry Inlet, Pancake Rock, Hole-in-the-Wall, Turnaway Reef, Steamboat Channel, and, more ominously, Grave Island. Its lonely stretches are one of the worst places for lightning in North America. Canoes overturn in waves at the drop of a hat, and swimmers are sucked to their deaths by undertows; in the off-season, the ice-cold water will take your life in three minutes. Back then, I knew all these dangers and a few more besides. If you went sailing without a long-sleeved shirt, the sun could give you a third-degree burn. If you fell out of a motorboat making a turn, the boat would keep making smaller and smaller circles until the blades of the propeller shredded you to bits — unless you knew how to duck-dive, that is, and could hold your breath while the boat passed over you.

The landscape seemed to ask for physical giants like my father and the Jesuit martyrs; even Jesus with his long-suffering nature would fit right into Brebeuf County.

NO SOONER DID WE WALK in the front door than the phone rang. My father took it, cupping his hand over the mouthpiece. He had to go, he told us, setting the black Bell phone back in its cradle. A man had been knocked unconscious after he fell into the hull of a barge.

"Mary, ask Sal to serve the prisoners tea," Morley called as he rushed out the door. "You'll see, girls. Everything will be fine."

"Little Louie, you help Sal," my grandmother said, taking charge. "Mary, you stay in the kitchen and stack teacups."

"Do we have to, Mom?" Little Louie whined.

My grandmother stared her down. "You know the answer," Big Louie replied stiffly and went off to find Sal.

We quickly did what Big Louie said. It was a waste of time arguing with somebody who could make grown men on her oil rigs cry real tears of shame over disobeying her. After I finished helping, I cleared off a space for myself on our kitchen table, already crowded with plants and old recipes. Satisfied, I opened Big Louie's book to a chapter titled, "The Romance of Oil in Canada West." I was glad to see the author supported Big Louie's claim that North America's first commercial oil well was dug by friends of my great-grandfather in 1858 in Oil Springs, Ontario, one year before the Americans drilled theirs in Titus, Pennsylvania.

From outside came the noise of car doors slamming. Peeking around the kitchen door, I saw Dr. Shulman coming into our living room with the prisoners and the hospital guards, Jordie Coverdale and Sal's boyfriend, Sib Beaudry. The men took off their coats and loosened their ties. With their slicked-back hair and shaved faces, the prisoners resembled travelling salesmen. Nobody would guess they were insane killers, except for the fact that Sib Beaudry looked scared to death. His big hound dog eyes were trained on John Pilkie, and I wondered what the hockey killer would say if he knew that Sib had brought beaverboard to the train station along with hammer and nails in case John Pilkie broke the windows of the hospital van.

In the living room, Little Louie's yellow hair and heavy-lidded eyes were drawing smiles from the men. "What can I give you, gentlemen?" she asked in her high, girlish voice. "A little milk and sugar? Or do you prefer cream?" The prisoners blushed or grinned and took a teacup from her tray, while my aunt helped them to lumps of sugar.

John Pilkie took off his brown fedora and pushed his cowlick back from his high, rounded forehead. As he slipped off his raccoon coat, he started to cough. It was a low, hollow-wheezing sound like the noise of a rubber plunger going into a human chest.

"That's a nasty cold you've got," Little Louie said.

"Sorry ma'am. I'm just getting over one." He gave her his big, dimpled grin. "They don't heat the rooms where I live, eh?" Then he said something in a lowered voice. She smiled back a little reluctantly and hurried off with her tea tray. When he realized my aunt wasn't returning, he glanced around. I held my breath, waiting for him to knock down Sib Beaudry and make a break for it. But he stayed where he was, so I let my eyes follow his around our comfortable living room, and it was as if I, too, were seeing it for the first time: our two big bay windows along with the double parlours with the matching coloured tiles on their fireplaces; the plump chintz furniture whose print was slightly faded because my grandmother believed bright chintz was vulgar; our brand-new black-and-white Zenith television with a mahogany console; the soft red tongue of carpet unwinding down our front stairs; and the life-size oil painting of my mother, Alice. Hanging near my mother's portrait was a glass cabinet holding my father's hockey trophies.

John (I began thinking of him as John long before I called him John to his face) stared longest at my father's cabinet. Was he thinking about his days with the Rats? Or did he miss playing hockey? He must have sensed someone looking. Turning around, he caught my eye and winked. I stepped back into the kitchen, and sat down at our kitchen table. Breathing hard, I opened Big Louie's history book again and forced myself to read about the Indians using crude oil to seal their canoes. They didn't understand oil's potential and neither did Upper Canada's first Lieutenant Governor, Colonel John Graves Simcoe. He barely mentioned the oil seepages he saw in 1793 near Bothwell, Ontario, not far from my mother's hometown of Petrolia. It was up to Mrs. Simcoe to scribble in her husband's journal: "a spring of real petroleum was discovered in the marsh by its offensive smell." Nobody knew what to do with the oil seepages until a man named Charles Nelson Tripp used the crude oil to make asphalt. In 1857, Tripp sold seven boats of asphalt to the French government to pave Paris streets. "Seven boats of asphalt! How about that, Sal?" I asked as she swept by with a fresh pot of coffee.

"Mouse, I don't have time for your studentin'!" Sal pronounced "studentin'" the same way she said "touristin'," her word for what summer visitors did in Madoc's Landing. She didn't worry about dropping the "gs" from her "ing" verb endings, although Big Louie said it was the mark of an uneducated person. After Sal left, I scribbled "not bad for us Canucks" in my Scholastic notebook, and underlined "seven boats of asphalt" three times. I didn't hear the kitchen door swing open.

"Mouse, do you want to meet a killer?" Sal asked. When I looked up she was standing there with John and smiling as if she were introducing me to a movie star. John and I stared nervously at each other. Then he started coughing again, making that low hollow-wheezing sound. I waited, half-embarrassed for him. After he stopped, I nodded yes, and he smiled his big, dimpled smile and sat down in the chair opposite. Sal poured me a ginger ale and opened Cokes for herself and him. "A ciggy, John?" Sal offered him her package of Matinees.

"Makes me cough, Sal." He trained his big, dark eyes on me. Did I mention his eyes? They were slightly exophthalmic, the term for bug-eyed that I had found in one of Morley's medical textbooks. I'd added it to my list of words like "execrate," which sounded thrillingly like defecate, and "vainglorious," an adjective even the grown-ups misused, not realizing it meant boastful.

He turned to Sal, popping his fingers against his palms. "Mary saw my sign protesting my innocence. I bet you didn't know mental patients can't get their cases reviewed, eh?"

I shook my head, taking in his clean, shapely hands. The moons at the base of his cuticles were shiny with clear polish, as if he'd painted his nails like a woman.

"You and everybody else. But I aim to change that. Well, I guess we're acquainted now, aren't we?"

"In a manner of speaking, Mr. Pilkie."

"In a manner of speaking, Mr. Pilkie! What a fancy way to put it! You have manners, just like your old man."

Flattered, I tried not to let it show.

"Okey-dokey, Mary. I'll behave." He pointed at my history book. "What have you got there?"

"I'm writing a composition about my great-grandfather, who was an oilman in Petrolia."

He examined the tintype of Mac Vidal thoughtfully. "Now isn't that something? You look just like him. Something determined about the mouth." He popped his fingers again and added, "My great-granddaddy was in the oil business down there. So you and I have a connection to Petrolia. How do you like that?"

"Maybe your ancestor worked on my great-grandfather's rigs."

"Maybe." He sounded doubtful. "You aren't fooling me now, are you?"

"I'm telling the truth, Mr. Pilkie. Cross my heart and point to heaven, my great-grandfather's boat ran into an oil slick on the Great Lakes. The slick was caused by an oil gusher near Petrolia and he followed the oil to its source and struck it rich."

"That's quite a story," he replied.

I showed him the page from my grandmother's book that quoted the *Sarnia Observer Advertiser* from August 5, 1858. He whistled as he read it out: "'We lately heard of the discovery of a bituminous spring in the Township of Enniskillen ... that will continue an almost inexhaustible supply of wealth, yielding at the lowest ... not less than one thousand dollars per day of clear profit ...' Imagine, Sal! A thousand bucks a day!" he said.

"That was in the old days," Sal replied. "They don't make a dime now."

"Sal's right. My grandmother says the price of oil hasn't gone up in years," I added.

He asked how my great-grandfather stored his oil, and I showed him a picture of the clay storage tanks like the ones my ancestor used. I skated over the mechanics of "puddling" the tank walls because I considered myself more like Morley, without a practical bone in my body.

"Did you know your father saved my life when I was a kid?" he asked after I finished. "I got an appendix attack at the Western Light. It was blowing up a storm so we couldn't leave the island."

I looked at Sal. I wasn't supposed to know about Morley helping John's father take out John's appendix.

"Or do you want me to tell you another story?"

"Well, we sure don't want to hear about your wife and baby girl," Sal said.

John's face closed up. He drummed his fingers angrily on the kitchen table, his dark angel's eyes glowing.

"Please tell me about you and my father, Mr. Pilkie."

"Call me John," he replied, his eyes softening.

"Okay, Mr. Pilkie."

He snorted. "We Pilkies are dogans, eh?" He lifted a gold chain out of his shirt and wiggled its tiny gold cross. I made admiring noises and he tucked away his gold chain and said: "Well, Mary, before Doc Bradford, we only went to Catholic doctors. But when my granddaddy put his fingers too close to the sawmill blade our Catholic doctor wouldn't come. It was January, and snowing hard. So the sawmill manager phoned Doc Bradford. Your daddy didn't care about us being dogans or cat-likers, as you Protestants call us, and he didn't care about the weather, either. If you ask Doc Bradford to come, he comes lickety-split. Everybody knows that. Doc Bradford is our hero, eh? And two hours later your daddy arrived in his sleigh at my grand-daddy's sawmill. He sewed two of my granddaddy's fingers back on and closed up the hole on the little one because the saw had chewed it to bits."

He bent back his baby finger, and I imagined I was looking at his grandfather's four-fingered hand.

"And then Doc Bradford went back out into the storm," Sal said. "Can you imagine anything so crazy? He drove the horse and sleigh across the frozen bay."

"He was just doing his job, Sal."

"You hush up, John," Sal interjected. "You don't know this part and I do. I know the nurse who was working in Doc Bradford's office back then. Doc Bradford lost his bearings."

"I do so know this part. Her daddy put down his doggy and let it find the way home."

"That's what Doc Bradford did," Sal said. "He had a fox terrier by the name of Tipper, and the little dog picked its way through the ice and led your father back. 'Course, once Doc Bradford got to the mainland, he knew where he was."

"But Mary wants to know how her daddy took out my appendix. Look girls, here's the damage." He lifted up his shirt and Sal and I gaped at the laddered scar that vanished under his belt.

"John, for the love of money." Sal slapped his arm and he tucked his shirt back under his belt. "I guess I need one of these to make me remember, eh?" He grinned at me and reached for Sal's cigarettes. "Well, here goes, Mary."

"Entertaining the ladies, Pilkie?"

We all jumped. Sib Beaudry stood in the doorway.

"Sal, you keep this. Your boyfriend here says I have to go." He threw over Sal's unlit cigarette and Sal caught it with a flirtatious yelp. For a moment, Sal looked almost pretty and it came to me that Sal was still a young woman even though she was ten years older than Little Louie, who was twenty.

"That's enough palavering, you two." Sib gave Sal a dirty look.

"Wait a sec, Sib, will you?" John leaned close, and I smelled something tangy, like shoe leather mixed with lemon juice. "Mary, a smart girl like you needs a desk of your own."

"Get moving, Pilkie," Sib snarled. "Now."

"Oh, cool your jets, eh Frenchy?" The next thing I knew John was kissing my hand and then he kissed Sal's. Sal giggled. I blushed. Sib's face turned red. "Don't take any wooden nickels, Mary," he called as he sauntered out of the kitchen.

"So what do you think?" Sal asked after they'd gone. "You met the mad killer, eh?"

"He doesn't look like a killer. He's not mean enough. Do you know what he said when the Bug House boys threw snowballs at him?"

"You tell me."

"He said, 'Aim low and you hit something.' Why would he say that?"

"He was making a joke, Mouse Bradford. John thinks highly of himself. I should know. He's my cousin. And he's slicker than a gravy sandwich."

"That's a fine way to talk about a cousin."

"Well, he's my third by marriage, so it doesn't count. Besides, you have to know what people are made of. It don't matter if you like 'em." Sal smirked as if she'd won another argument about me seeing the world through rose-coloured glasses. Big Louie said I was too trusting. Sal always saw the worst in people. I guess together we had the world covered.

"BY THE WAY," SAL SAID, as she began stacking dishes. "Next time I introduce you to somebody, don't wear that hat. You look like a darn fool with it on." My cheeks burning, I tossed my Lone Ranger hat onto the table. At that moment, Little Louie came in with a tray of coffee cups. We went to the window and watched the prisoners climb into the hospital van. The teenage boy got in first; the other men filed on next, while Sib and Jordie

Coverdale stood talking to John. In his dapper raccoon coat and chocolate-brown Fedora, he looked every inch Gentleman Jack, and I thought uneasily of the way he had glanced around our living room. Maybe he thought we didn't deserve our home. Or maybe he didn't mind, because Morley's family came from the wrong side of the tracks like the Pilkies so he was just damn glad that somebody like my father had made a success of things. While Little Louie and I watched, he grabbed Sib's cigarette out of his mouth and flung it into the air. He laughed as the burning tip of the cigarette plummeted downwards. Jordie laughed, too. Turning our way, John spotted Little Louie and me by the window. He waved. I didn't move a muscle. Then he waved again, so I waved back. Beside me, Little Louie made a soft, astonished noise in her throat as he leapt up into the bus, taking the steps three at a time.

7

I WAS TOO SHY TO TELL JOHN HOW MUCH I IDENTIFIED WITH Mac Vidal, who had been born an orphan in Vergennes, Vermont, and was brought up by relatives in a canal boat on Lake Champlain. Before he struck oil and found his long-lost father, my great-grandfather had a pretty hard time of things, which made me feel that he would understand my situation. Not just with Hindrance, but with Morley. It was my intention to borrow hope from Old Mac's success.

The oil boom had started before my great-grandfather arrived in Oil Springs. By the late 1850s, settlers realized that money could be made from oil seeping out of the gum beds in Enniskillen swamp. They drilled for oil to make kerosene, which provided good reading light. Before then, everyone used candles except for the rich, who could afford whale oil. But after a Canadian geologist, Abraham Gesner, found a way to refine kerosene from oil, people began using kerosene lamps, which burned at the rate of a quarter cent an hour. Soon men from all over the eastern United States and Canada came to Enniskillen County hoping to strike it rich.

My great-grandfather was one of those men, although he didn't start out looking for oil. As I'd told John, Mac Vidal stumbled by accident onto the boom in Southwestern Ontario. In 1862, he had come north looking for his father and he was crewing on a lumber scow on Lake St. Clair when an oil gusher blew on the Canadian side. The oil poured down the streams and rivers faster than the men could store it. Old Mac forgot about his father and followed the oil to its source in Enniskillen County, where he began drilling for oil himself. He was helped by his aunt, Old Louie, who brought along her meagre life savings, which came in handy when Mac Vidal owed $291 to another oilman. Old Louie auctioned off her things, including the mahogany cabinet that her Huguenot ancestors had brought over from England, and my great-grandfather paid off his debt and went back to drilling. When his oil gusher came in, he bought back Old Louie's things and they moved from their shanty in Oil Springs to the mansion he built in Petrolia.

After the mansion was finished, he called it The Great House and brought his father to live with old Louie and himself.

In my composition, I had been trying to describe the extraordinary details of old Mac's early life. Little Louie was encouraging me — or pretending to, that is. I couldn't help thinking my aunt wished she were back writing newspaper stories instead of researching our family history. She considered Big Louie's enthusiasm for our past "a bourgeois embarrassment," and she was fond of reminding my grandmother that Leon Trotsky said North American workers would rise up one day, and families like the Vidals, who considered themselves members of the educated upper class, would become social democrats like my aunt and her friends.

THE MORNING AFTER JOHN PILKIE came for tea, I overheard my aunt and grandmother arguing in the guest bedroom. I crept across the hall and peeked through the crack between the wall and the door. My aunt was in bed in her pyjamas, peering at a letter through a small magnifying glass. Newspaper pages lay scattered on the floor along with three apple cores, an empty box of Tampax, and a half-full package of Sweet Caps.

"Look at this mess, Little Louie. When will you grow up?" Big Louie picked up the apple cores and dumped them into a wastebasket, and then she started in on the newspapers. I waited for her to pick up the empty box of Tampax, but my grandmother ignored it, maybe because it shocked her. Sal hid her boxes of sanitary napkins in the towel cupboard and she would have died of shame if anyone found them.

"Mom, take it easy. I have to help Mouse with Old Mac's letters, remember?" Little Louie waved her cigarette at the bundle of papers on the bed. My grandmother said in a softer tone: "Well, I'm glad to hear that, Louisa. It's time you stopped thinking about yourself. Mary needs you."

"Mom, Mary seems pretty grown-up to me."

"Nonsense. She's under the influence of that woman."

"You mean the next Mrs. Morley Bradford?

"He'll never marry Sal. She's his ex-nurse," my grandmother said.

"I wouldn't be so sure. You didn't send me up here to look after Mary and you know it. You want to keep me from seeing Max. Mom, that girl tricked him. She told him she was pregnant when she wasn't."

"Well, she's married to him now, isn't she, Louisa?"

"It's not Max's fault. She lied to him."

"Dearie, we've been over this a hundred times and I'm as sorry as you are about the situation. But you'll have to move on. You need somebody solid, who can give you a comfortable life."

"I don't want somebody like that. They're boring," Little Louie shouted.

"Lower your voice, dear. Little pitchers have big ears." Big Louie started for the door. "I have to go now and see about lunch." I flattened myself against the wall. Out of the corner of my eye, I watched her saunter down the hall, her silk kimono floating behind her like a kite tail. When the coast was clear, I stared again through the crack in the door; this time, a faint, flowery smell tickled my nose. "I thought I heard you outside," Little Louie whispered on the other side. "Look, don't pay any attention to what Mom and I said. It was just girl talk. Do you want to read old Mac's letters?"

"Yes," I whispered back. There was no point explaining that Morley was too busy for a romance with Sal. Or asking my aunt about Max Falkowski and his shotgun wedding. I'd heard Sal call a girlfriend's baby "premature" when it was born seven months after the wedding ceremony, but what Little Louie said about Max's wife was something new: women pretending to be pregnant so men would marry them. It was unspeakable business, so for once, I tactfully avoided a dangerous subject, and accepted the letter my aunt handed me. It had been sent to Old Louie, my great-great aunt, and there was no doubt about its author. You could tell it was my great-grandfather by his bred-in-the-bone optimism. It tainted our family history with myth, a propensity (and yes, I knew I was using the word properly), a propensity I was guilty of myself. For instance, when he was an old man, my great-grandfather claimed it had been a beautiful, hot June afternoon when his ship floundered in the oil slick. This was one of Old Mac's exaggerations; in 1862, June on the Upper Lakes had been sunless and cold. He also claimed that the oil danced with iridescent lights. Crude oil is dark green as it spurts from the ground and it only sparkles if the oil is thinly spread, but according to the letters he wrote as a young man, that afternoon the oil lay as thick on the water as black mud.

8

June 30, 1862,
Oil Springs, Canada West

Dear Aunt Louisa:

Thank you for giving me the letter Father sent Mother in
which he stated that she was to forward her letters to him
via Fort Gratiot, Michigan. I believe circumstances beyond
Father's control were the reason he failed to contact us after
Mother died in childbirth. I hope Father won't hold it against
me that I was baptized a Vidal and not a Davenport.

Will you believe me if I say I have profited from seeing the
waters of Lethe first hand? It happened after we left Detroit.
The evening before, the lake was clear of oil; but, the next
morning, it was overcast and cold and the frost had froze
off the tails of cows on the American side. Soon the reason
for the gloom became apparent. A half hour out of port, our
scow ran into an oil slick. It covered the surface of the lake for
miles with a black and vile-smelling pitch.

The smell of rotten eggs was overpowering. I could hardly breathe in the stench. My eyes burned and all of us in the crew cried like whipped spaniels. In no time the smelly pitch coated the hull of our ship from bow to stern; it is no exaggeration to say we resembled a bark from the underworld.

The oil was from geysers in a hamlet called Oil Springs and it stopped shipping on the Upper Lakes. A single spark from a ship's boiler room would have set the oily waters ablaze. So we were obliged to head for Mitchell's Bay on the Canadian shore along with all of the Mackinaw fishing fleet.

After the lakes cleared, we ran into oil again in the marshlands below Wallaceburg, where the filthy stuff had finished off most creatures. The tall grasses along the riverbanks were flattened by oil, and we saw helpless sandpipers and crows flopping in the ooze. Strange to think this place is called "The Venice of America." In the marsh, we used pike poles to kill off the rattlesnakes, which crawled on board to escape the oil. A tug came and towed us up river, and that is when my fortunes changed. I hope you will not think poorly of me for jumping ship in Wilkesport, a real boomtown, very rough-and-ready. I felt compelled to see what had unleashed such a catastrophe.

So I followed an Indian trail along Black Creek and found myself standing on a vast floodplain when I came out of the oak forest. Not a single tree had been left standing. Tall, three-legged structures covered the plain, which resounded with the click-click of metal drills. I counted 200 oil derricks. Possibly there are a great many more. On the plain, men were making bungholes in barrels and others were engaged in filling them. Still others waded through puddles of oil to stack

a wagon with the barrels. On a ridge, men stood stirring huge
smoking kettles.

I was looking at the aftermath of the Bradley gusher,
which had coated our ship with oil. From the mouth of the
Bradley Well, where oil bubbles up in every direction, there is
a perpendicular tube some sixteen feet high and four inches
in diameter from which the oil is conducted into six or seven
large storage tanks. A great deal of oil spills over and is
lost. A stopcock has been inserted into the top of the tube to
prevent waste but even so it overflows. Imagine, if you can!
When it blew, this well produced 5,000 barrels of oil
a day.

Alas, I had no cash to lease a rig so I am back at canalling
again, dragging a stone boat stacked with oil barrels fifteen
miles through the swamp to the Wyoming railroad station.
In answer to your question, I am too busy to find Father,
although I have heard that a man with Father's name was
living at Maxwell, a Utopian Community on Lake Huron,
near Port Sarnia. When I strike oil, I will build a big, warm
house in Petrolia and bring Father home. No relative of mine,
be he named "Vidal" or "Davenport" shall find himself in
need of food and shelter as long as I live.

> *I remain your faithful nephew,*
> *Mac*

I finished the letter as Sal called us for lunch.

"It's sad, isn't it?" Little Louie said, tucking the letters away.
"The way Old Mac wanted to find his father?"

"Well, he found his father and struck it rich."

"Oh, is that what you think?" Little Louie asked.

"Big Louie told me Old Mac had his cake and ate it too. She says he crawled out of the sea mud and discovered gold in the muck he sprang from."

"Mom should have been a poet." Little Louie started to laugh. "She has a way of putting things."

DOWNSTAIRS, SAL HAD SET OUT a platter of egg salad sandwiches and brightly red, green, and yellow Jell-O desserts, which quivered in their bowls when we sat down.

"I hear you told Mary that Old Mac found his father," Little Louie said.

"Yes, he did; and that's enough out of you, Dearie. Father had a bad start in life, but he turned things around for himself. He was a great hero, a man for his time."

"Spare us the sermon, Mom," Little Louie said, rolling her eyes at me. I smiled timidly back. I hated getting caught between them.

"Old Mac's letters are historical relics. You'll see, Louisa," my grandmother retorted. "One day, they'll be enshrined in a museum."

Beside me, my aunt drew a noisy breath, and the three of us concentrated on finishing our Jell-O. It was true that Big Louie believed in continuity the way other people worshipped God, even though none of the Vidals had taken church seriously since my great-grandfather. My grandmother was fond of telling us that the tiny sea creatures in ancient Lake Michigan were the missing link in our family history. The story of the primeval fish was a Biblical parable as far as she was concerned.

According to my grandmother, over six hundred million years ago, when the planet was just four billion years old, these poor martyred sea creatures died for the Vidals and their tiny carcasses dropped to the bottom of the ancient lake. Two hundred million years later, the shellfish were crushed by Beekmantown limestone pressing down on the sea floor. And fifty thousand years later, the glaciers dumped clay sediments that pushed our shellfish deeper into the earth, turning them into the black gold that gave Old Mac his fortune.

Every time Big Louie told us this story, my aunt almost died laughing. Died laughing was one of the things that grown-ups said if they were having fun. Sometimes they said, "I laughed my head off." But when kids like me said somebody laughed his head off, it usually meant he was laughing at our expense. And that was how my aunt laughed at my grandmother's stories.

"Do Old Mac's letters mention the Pilkies?" I asked.

"Now why would they do that?" my grandmother asked.

"John Pilkie has relatives in Petrolia."

"I wouldn't take his connection to Petrolia seriously if I were you," Big Louie replied. "Put that man out of your head, Mary."

But I didn't put him out of my head. Not then, or later. I imagined the thrill of showing him my great-grandfather's letters. It amazed me that he and I had ancestors who drilled for oil in the same unlikely place, although I knew it wouldn't be right to let somebody like him see our family papers.

After lunch, I found myself having one of my useless conversations with Hindrance. Per usual, I tried not to listen, because Hindrance sounded like Sal blowing hot air.

A Sobering Conversation with Hindrance

Hindrance: John Pilkie is mean and cruel, Mouse, and you better watch out.

Me: What if he didn't mean to hurt his wife?

Hindrance: He wanted her out of the way and he didn't really like you either.

Me: He does so, Hindrance.

Hindrance: Who would like you? You're short and skinny, and you walk like a duck.

Me: That's not fair. Besides Mr. Pilkie asked me about my great-grandfather.

Hindrance: Listen to you! You're all puffed up because somebody asked you about your stupid composition. Well, sucks like you get fooled sooner than you can say Jack Robinson. So you better watch out or you'll get murdered too. See you later, alligator.

MAYBE HINDRANCE HAD A POINT. I felt flattered because a murderer listened to me talk about my school composition. What on earth was I thinking? I didn't want him to know I was interested in him — although I was. Wasn't everybody?

9

MADOC'S LANDING ABSORBED THE KILLERS LIKE WATER IN A PAIL absorbed a stone. But we didn't see John Pilkie or the other prisoners on the hospital grounds during the two weeks before Easter. For one thing, they couldn't wander around the hospital grounds like the harmless patients. Then Sal heard that John might go to the Anglican Church on Easter Sunday with his mother, who was a pot-licker (or Protestant) like us. In our kitchen, John had used the word "dogan" to describe himself. It meant Irish Catholic and I'd been surprised because "dogan" was usually said by a pot-licker with the word "bloody" or "damn" in front of it.

Now none of that mattered. Mrs. Pilkie had asked Dr. Shulman to let John worship with the Anglicans so John, along with the hospital guards, was coming to our church for Easter Sunday. Light-headed with excitement, I put on my new felt skirt and starched blouse plus my white ankle socks. For the first time in months, it was a mild spring day so I could go outside without my long woolen stockings.

WE DROVE TO CHURCH IN my mother's old Ford station wagon. Morley was off on a call. Going to the eleven o'clock service wasn't something required of the men in my family. As I struggled out of the backseat, my grandmother reached for my hand, and I politely shook my head. I didn't want the Bug House kids calling me a suck who clung to her grandmother's skirts. Luckily, the Bug House kids were still in Sunday School. So, one step at a time, I humped Hindrance up the stairs and into the church. As I took my seat in our pew, I spotted John standing near the vestry with two of the other prisoners. He carried his full-length raccoon coat over his arm and he had on the smart-looking striped chocolate-brown suit he had worn at the train station. Sib Beaudry and two other hospital guards stood nearby in the hospital uniform: a serge suit and bowtie that made them resemble the friendly baker in the Wonder Bread advertisement. The prisoners took off their hats and shrugged off their jackets. Then they sat down, clearing their throats and bowing their heads. The guards sat down, too. Mrs. Pilkie sat six rows behind them and something about the stiff way she held herself suggested she thought that everyone was watching her son. But neither the women, in their white gloves and Easter bonnets, nor their hatless men were looking at the killers. The same pride that lay behind our town's attitude to the hospital kept them from gawking (i.e., mental patients were part of the landscape, like our drinking water, said to be as pure as an Arctic glacier, and the Great Bay that brought tourists up from the city).

Fixing my eyes on John's ducktail, I tried not to fidget. Up on the altar, Reverend Attridge strolled towards us in his purple Easter surplice. Hitching up the legs of his ballooning trousers, he stepped into the pulpit. "Why is Jesus a hero for our times?"

Rev. Attridge cried. "Because Jesus put others before himself and he didn't expect praise for his actions. We should all follow his example and serve others." Rev. Attridge smiled down at the prisoners. "Now I want you to cast your minds over your own heroes. Perhaps for you it's Gordie Howe of the Detroit Red Wings? Or Frank Mahovlich of the Toronto Maple Leafs?"

Men and women chuckled in the pews. Even the hospital guards were grinning. John had his back to me so I couldn't see his reaction, but I wondered if he felt as surprised as I did. Nobody in my experience had compared Jesus to a hockey player. Then it came to me that Rev. Attridge had designed his sermon so John would appreciate it. He knew that John had played for the NHL so John was bound to be even more interested in hockey heroes than the people in Madoc's Landing. My own heroes included the most famous hockey star of all, Rocket Richard of the Montreal Canadiens, although I didn't bother mentioning how I felt about the Rocket because the English-speaking people in Madoc's Landing were fans of players like Tim Horton from the Toronto Maple Leafs.

My other heroes were Brébeuf, the Jesuit martyr who wore a necklace of red-hot axe heads. Then came my great-grandfather, who discovered oil and found his lost father, and finally, Morley, who put the needs of his patients before himself.

"I won't criticize you for being a fan of Gordie Howe, although I prefer Frank Mahovlich myself," Rev. Attridge cried in his electrifying voice. "Mahovlich stays out of the penalty box, for one thing."

The congregation laughed uproariously; everyone, that is, except Big Louie, who sat snoring softly between Little Louie and me while Rev. Attridge harped on his theme: "It's fine to admire hockey players. They give themselves to a great sport. But their contribution isn't as important as the contribution Jesus made. Why is Jesus so important? Because Jesus came to this earth so we would learn to give ourselves humbly to the task of helping others."

Beside me, Big Louie mumbled in a sleep-thick voice: "Oh, bugger off."

"Mom, you're in church," my aunt whispered. My grandmother jerked wide awake. Mortified, she looked around to see if anybody had heard, while my aunt and I giggled helplessly behind our gloved hands. Our attention seemed to waver for only a few minutes, but by the time we composed ourselves again, Rev. Attridge had come to the end of his sermon. "Blessed is he that considereth the poor," he said, quoting from Psalm Forty-One. Then he added: "And blessed are those that provideth for the sick and needy. The Lord shall deliver them in times of trouble." The congregation murmured, "Amen," and Rev. Attridge stepped down from the pulpit.

In his pew at the front of the church, John jumped to his feet. There were gasps and cries as he turned to face us. "I would like to invite the congregation to help these poor men sitting here." He waved at the other two prisoners. "I'm asking you to consider the injustice of giving parole to hardened criminals and denying it to those of us who are recovering from mental illnesses. How many of you good Christians know we can't have our cases reviewed?"

The guard pulled John down, but not before he turned around and grinned at his mother. She smiled back, shrugging her shoulders, while men in the back pews started yelling for Rev. Attridge to throw John Pilkie out.

"Now, now, gentlemen. Sit down, please!" Rev. Attridge shouted. "Let us pray for the lambs of God who have the misfortune to be in institutional care."

Looking up at Rev. Attridge, John Pilkie cried in a deep, confident voice: "Receive the Lamb of God to dwell in England's green and pleasant bowers."

The men at the back of the church started yelling again, and then everybody was on his or her feet talking. I jumped up too, praying nobody would hurt John. From the front of the church, Rev. Attridge had to shout at people to sit down. Finally, everyone did. When the view cleared, I saw Sib Beaudry grab John by the collar and shove him roughly out the vestry door.

ON THE WAY OUT OF church, a shaken Rev. Attridge pumped our hands. "Happy Easter, ladies!" he said. "What did you think of the hockey killer comparing himself to the Lamb of God?"

"I don't think he meant any harm by it," Little Louie replied, lighting up a Sweet Cap. "He was quoting Blake."

"My daughter had some poems published in her high school year book," my grandmother said proudly. Her eyes took in Little Louie's big, pretty mouth and the messy blond bangs under my aunt's bright blue veil. I was struck by the possessive look on my grandmother's face. She acted as if she owned Little Louie the way Sal sometimes acted as if she owned me.

"Now isn't that something!" Rev. Attridge smiled at my aunt. "And how did you like my sermon?"

"It was original, I guess," Little Louie replied, blowing one of her large, jiggly smoke rings. I tried to bat it away before it floated into Rev. Attridge's eyes. Too late. He coughed, covering his mouth with his hand.

"I have a question," I asked.

"Mary, nothing about John Pilkie now," my grandmother said."What would your question be, Mary?" Rev. Attridge asked.

"Jesus wants us to sacrifice ourselves for others, but what if being good hurts other people?"

"Most people aren't harmed by that sort of sacrifice." Rev. Attridge winked at Big Louie as if they were sharing a joke. "They know that being good helps those around them so they accept it, Mary."

"Mary asks too many questions." Big Louie said. She, too, knew I was referring to my father whose work schedule worried my grandmother and me. According to Big Louie, who enjoyed telling our family stories, my father sacrificed himself to others because my dead grandmother Phyllis Bradford told him boys were full of urges so dark and terrible she couldn't utter their names. My dead grandmother had tested my father's willpower by placing a plate of cookies in front of him. If he grabbed a cookie before she said he could, she smacked his palms with a leather strap. My father reached his full height of six-foot-six at fifteen, and when he told my grandmother he wanted to be a doctor, she said, "Thank the Lord, because a brute like you could go around killing them." My father took his mother's feelings inside himself and he fought her views every day of his life by shuffling with a sad, patient air towards whoever needed him. That was Big Louie's opinion, anyway.

"Would you like to come in for a glass of sherry?" Rev. Attridge asked, nodding towards the refectory.

"No, thank you." My grandmother gripped my arm. "Dr. Bradford will be coming home soon from the hospital. Goodbye, Reverend Attridge." I followed my aunt and grandmother over to our Ford station wagon, keeping my eye out for John. All around us, churchgoers were talking in high, excited voices. It struck me that John was going to change our town. Of course, I didn't know how right I would be. My premonition sprung from my childish love of the dark excitement that goes with somebody like John Pilkie who breaks the rules. They are living large, as people say now. I wasn't making a mountain out of a molehill, as Sal often told me. I was recognizing that mountains exist, and if we go up them and down the other side, we are never the same again.

10

SAL WAS WAITING FOR ME WITH THE TRICYCLE THAT MORLEY
had ordered from a New York department store. Its two back
wheels were larger than the single front wheel, and it was
chain-driven, so the rider was obliged to pedal in a downward
motion. As soon as we climbed out of the station wagon, she
wheeled it towards us, tossing her thick hair and fixing me with
her round Irish eyes. "Sal, you know how I feel about that thing,"
my grandmother said and looked over at Little Louie for help.
My aunt frowned. "Mom thinks too much exercise is bad for
Mary," Little Louie replied.

Sal ignored them. She pulled two long linen scarves out of
her pocket and waved them authoritatively as if only she, the
ex-nurse, knew what was good for me. I glanced apprehensively
at the bike and then down our long, sloping driveway. The
snow had melted from the asphalt, although the breeze from
the Bay still felt wintry. "Mary, you promised Doc Bradford," Sal
said in her sternest shaming voice, and when I went over and
stood beside Sal, Big Louie didn't protest. She muttered while
Sal helped me take off my Boston brace and tied my feet to

the pedals using a method from one of Morley's medical text-books: start with ascending turns at the upper end of the scarf and descending turns at the lower end and then tie both ends with a square knot. When she was done, Sal let out a holler because Morley's green convertible was coming along Whitefish Road. He had put down the top, and the wind was blowing his iron-grey hair back from his handsome head. "Doc Bradford! Watch Mary!" Sal yelled and gave me a hefty push. Usually, she let me start down the incline myself, but Sal was showing off for Morley. She pushed too hard.

My legs started going round faster and faster. My feet were tied to the pedals. I couldn't stop if I tried. Out on the road, Morley waved from behind the windshield of his car. I didn't dare wave myself. My legs were already aching, and it took all my strength to hold onto the handlebars. Halfway down the incline, the bike began to wobble. Closing my eyes, I whispered, "One for the mouse, one for the crow, one to rot, one to grow." It's what Old Man Beaudry chanted as he threw his corn seeds. I only said it when I was scared, because Sal claimed it worked for the Beaudry corn. When I opened my eyes again, Morley was getting out of the car with our springer spaniels. "Stop pedalling, Mary!" he yelled as Joe and Mairzy charged my bike. As if I had a choice. I turned the handlebars to avoid the spaniels, but the bike's front wheel lifted up on a ridge where the driveway met the sidewalk. My feet came free of Sal's scarves and I fell so hard the icy pavement scraped my knees. My aunt and my grand-mother rushed over while Sal stood back, gawking. Pushing away the spaniels, Morley crouched down to examine my legs. "Nothing broken." He pulled down my skirt. "It's not that it doesn't hurt, Mary. It's that you don't mind if it hurts. Pretend you're tossing the pain away." He reached towards his own knee and made a fumbling gesture as if he was tossing something into the air. "Like this. You'll see. The pain will stop."

"Morley, for heaven's sake," my grandmother exclaimed.

"Mary needs to exercise." Morley stood up slowly. "She could be in an iron lung like hundreds of other polio victims."

The phone rang in our kitchen. "Morley, that'll be for you," Sal said. Morley yawned and trudged up the driveway, Joe and Mairzy rushing after him.

"Are you all right, Mary?" My aunt gently touched my face and against my will stupid tears rolled down my cheeks.

"Do you understand me, Sal?" my grandmother said. "Mary is not to ride that bike again."

"If that's the way you want it."

"That is the way I want it." My grandmother handed me one of her perfumed hankies to dry my eyes. Then she and my aunt took my hands and together they helped me into the house for our Easter lunch of baked ham with pineapple rings and sweet potatoes.

II

THE FOLLOWING SUNDAY, THE DOORBELL RANG WHILE WE SAT at the table reading. My aunt had her nose in *The Face of War* by Martha Gellhorn while Big Louie was deep into the latest James Bond novel, *From Russia with Love*. I was only a quarter of the way through *The Secret Garden* by Frances Hodgson Burnett. I was taking my time because I didn't want my book to end. Morley was hiding behind the sports section of *The New York Times*. Morley and I always read at the dinner table and sometimes we didn't put down our books when Sal brought in our food.

The doorbell rang again. Morley didn't look up from his paper. Big Louie swaggered off to the front hall. We heard the front door open and my grandmother say in a false polite tone, after a minute of mumbling, "It's kind of you to have done this, Mr. Pilkie." Little Louie and I stared wide-eyed at each other.

"I made it in the workshop. Mary needs it, eh?" John Pilkie's husky voice said. "Will you give my regards to Doc Bradford?"

"Yes, of course," Big Louie answered. "By the way, I didn't know that you'd been released from the hospital."

"Oh, I'm still there. Jordie here is taking me to the Catholic mass tonight. The drunkard's mass, eh? I guess I ruined my chances with the Anglicans."

My grandmother didn't laugh. "Fine, then." She shut the door loudly. I rushed to the living room window and watched him sashay down our sidewalk in his striped brown suit and fedora. Jordie Coverdale walked beside him, his hips bumping John's. The two men were shackled together by a leash hanging from Jordie's belt. What must that be like, I wondered, to be guarded so closely? Out by the sidewalk, Jordie untied his prisoner and the two men climbed into the hospital van. This time he didn't wave. I didn't, either, because I heard Little Louie behind me. "He scares the daylights out of me," she whispered. "Does he scare you?" I nodded before Little Louie could suspect I thought otherwise.

In the front hall, my grandmother bellowed for Morley. My father dragged himself out of his chair, and Little Louie and I followed him into the front hall, where my grandmother stood next to a small pine desk. When she saw us, she threw up her hands. "John Pilkie left this for Mouse. My granddaughter can't accept a gift from a convict. He'll have to take it back."

"If you say so, Louisa." Morley glanced at the desk, a flicker of interest in his eyes.

Then from the kitchen Sal called Morley. "They want you at the hospital, Doc Bradford."

"Go ahead and eat. Don't wait for me, girls," Morley called as he walked out the door.

While my aunt and Big Louie watched apprehensively, I read the note from John that had been scotch-taped to a box placed on the top of the desk. The words were written in curly, spiraling letters on blue-grey hospital notepaper. *Happy Easter, Mary, from your friend, John.* Inside the box, a large chocolate Easter egg sat on a nest of shredded purple fibers. I bit into the egg, smacking my lips over its creamy yellow filling. The faces of my aunt and grandmother softened.

"Why don't you let her keep the desk, Mom?" my aunt asked. "What's the harm in it?"

"My father accepts presents from his patients. So why can't I? Mr. Pilkie was one of his patients."

"Was he, Mary?" My grandmother acted surprised. "Well, you aren't a doctor. You're a doctor's child."

LATER THAT EVENING, JORDIE COVERDALE drove up alone in his truck. When my grandmother opened the front door, Jordie was standing there, a cigarette stuck behind each ear.

"I don't want my father to feel badly," I said stepping in front of Big Louie. "You see Morley was too busy to notice I needed a desk."

"Mary, what do you mean?" Big Louie asked.

"The sick need my father more than me. And he works every waking minute to cure them."

Jordie and my grandmother regarded me silently. They didn't understand that I was proud to be neglected by Morley. Other fathers were sissies who pushed their children on park swings or barbecued for their family. It was enough for me that Morley and I watched *Hockey Night in Canada* every Saturday evening. I liked to sit in the chair opposite his and stop Sal from disturbing him if he fell asleep before the game, the newspaper in his lap.

Looking up from the sidewalk, Jordie reassured my grand-mother. "Never mind about the desk. I'll tell John that Mary liked it and he won't feel so bad."

My grandmother held my hand and together we watched Jordie carry the furniture out to the truck like a circus strong-man. The next day my grandmother took the train back to Petrolia. Three weeks later a new study desk from Eaton's was delivered. My grandmother had ordered it. Nobody mentioned John's present again.

12

ONE FRIDAY AFTERNOON, AS WE SAT DRINKING NEILSON'S COCOA in the kitchen, Sal confided that John's mother had asked her to tea. It had something to do with a letter Mrs. Pilkie was writing my father; Sal didn't know the details. "The old bat must have her reasons," Sal said, her round eyes glowing like headlamps. "Want to come? It'll make it easier for me if you tag along."

She didn't have to ask twice. I was ready in five minutes, my hair combed, my face washed. Hand in hand, we walked down Whitefish Road. Mrs. Pilkie had been born French-Canadian, but she didn't live in French Town. According to Sal, Mrs. Pilkie's father had been a successful dentist who looked after English-speaking patients so Mrs. Pilkie felt speaking the French language was beneath her. I didn't get these complicated distinctions, although they mattered to Sal whose Irish mother had married Tubby Dault, a French-Canadian cab driver who worked for Thompson's Taxi, our town's most notorious bootlegger. Once I recited the poem, "The Wreck of the Julie Plante" to Sal: "On wan dark night of Lac St. Pierre, De win she blow, blow, blow, An' de crew de wood scow Julie Plante, got scart and run' run below —" Sal threw me out of the kitchen for making fun of her father's accent.

On our way to Mrs. Pilkie's home, we passed the hockey arena, and turned up a path behind the post office. We were on the outskirts of town now. At the top of an empty lot stood a two-storey clapboard house. The front windows were half-hidden behind over-grown spiraea bushes. The bouncy branches covered in white lacy flowers made me think of Big Louie, whose standards of taste ruled my mother's family. Spiraea bushes were vulgar, or "plebeian," my grandmother said. As Sal knocked on the front door, I noticed all the window shades had been drawn. Maybe Mrs. Pilkie didn't want to look out on the world or maybe she felt uneasy about the world looking in on her.

"Was John's bedroom up there?" I pointed at a second-storey window imagining John's boyish face staring down at us through the glass.

"John slept at the back of the house."

"Did you know him then?" I persisted.

"Yes. Now quit pestering me," Sal said as the front door opened. The mother of Mad Killer Pilkie stood before us wearing her funny-looking dark glasses. "Sal, dear, you've brought a child with you." Mrs. Pilkie bent over to shake my hand. Up close, she wasn't stylish like her son John. She wore a baggy floral blouse and a long skirt that reminded me of my dead mother's clothes in her old photographs.

"Georgie, I am babysitting the doctor's daughter."

"The doctor's daughter? Sal, you should have told me so I could wash my floors."

I blushed at the idea of anybody going to trouble on my account.

"Mary doesn't care about your floors," Sal said, pushing me forward.

"Well, come in, both of you." Mrs. Pilkie ushered us into a room crowded with sofas and armchairs in plastic slipcovers, and I thought of Big Louie again who would consider the see-through plastic covers in poor taste, along with the shiny white Woolworth Department store blinds. But my grandmother's la-de-dah views wouldn't help me with the mother of the hockey killer.

She noticed where I was looking. "I can open them if you like. I'm afraid the light hurts my eyes."

"No, this is fine." Sal nodded at me. "Georgie has cataracts. She can't see well anymore."

"Sal, dear, I will be able to see perfectly well after my operation. But that's not for a while yet."

I took off my Lone Ranger hat, and we settled ourselves on a hard-looking sofa. The plastic cover stuck to my thighs. I looked around for signs that John had lived here, but the parlour was disappointingly average. The clean white walls were covered with framed photographs like the ones published in *The Chronicle* under captions such as, "First Snow on the Wye River" and "The Approaching Storm." On the mantel, a cut-glass vase of purple pansies sat next to a porcelain figure of a shepherd and his sheep. The vase of pansies was the only thing my grandmother would admire. "You wanted to see me, Georgie?" Sal smiled.

"Yes, Sal, dear. I'm asking Mary's father to get us a review of John's case."

Mrs. Pilkie didn't drop her "ing" endings or talk in a nasal twang like Sal and Sib, and I remembered what Sal had told me about John's paternal grandfather. So that was the reason John could talk slangy Madoc's Landing talk, or sound as educated as a man like my father. John's mother must have told him not to drop his "ings" the way Big Louie told me, and that meant he could adjust his speaking style to suit any situation.

"You think there's a chance of John getting out of the Bug House?" Sal asked.

"Of course I do. That fire was a terrible accident. You know John idolized his wife and child."

"Well, that's his story." Sal wiggled her eyebrows so I would know not to believe Mrs. Pilkie.

"I don't know why you're making that face, Sal. You used to be sweet on John once."

I had no idea that Sal had been sweet on John. Shocked, I turned towards Sal, who dropped her eyes. "Oh, go on with you. What do you want, Georgie?"

"Will you look at my letter to Dr. Bradford?"

"Guess I don't have a choice." Sal frowned.

"Good. And now if you will excuse me, I'll get our tea."

"No questions, Mouse!" Sal hissed as soon as Mrs. Pilkie left the room. So I sat meekly until Mrs. Pilkie came back, carrying a silver tray stacked with teacups. She set the tray down on a piano stool and began to pour, placing a lacy paper napkin under each cup in case the tea slopped over into the saucer. Sal watched, sucking her teeth. After Mrs. Pilkie handed Sal a cup, she asked me if I would like to go outside and play.

"Let Mary stay here, Georgie. She can help you with the spelling."

"If you say so, Sal." Mrs. Pilkie fetched the letter from a side table. "Dear Dr. Bradford," she began, lifting the letter up under a standing lamp so she could see it better. "I am taking pen in hand because a review of John's case is long overdue ..." Mrs. Pilkie put the letter down. "It is no use. My eyes aren't good today. Can you read it, Sal?"

"Let Mary do that, Georgie. I'll think better if I hear it read out loud."

Reluctantly, Mrs. Pilkie handed me the letter, and I started in:

As you know, my son is real soft-hearted. He is clever with his hands and he never could stand to see a living thing suffer. When we lived in town, John built houses for the kittens the tourists left behind. He filled their houses with straw so the cats sat warm and pretty all winter. John kept some rats as pets. But I digrress.

I paused at the misspelled word, "digrcss." Sal waved her cigarette irritably, and I read on:

When John scored the winning goal against the Rangers in the Stanley Cup playoffs, the sports columnist Mr. Miltie Burke said that my boy played with 'the mad glare of Rockct Richard.' But John was a real gentleman off the ice. Not like those crooks he worked for. I well remember you telling that manager of the Detroit Red Wings to pay for John's medical care and I am counting on you to speak up again for my boy when the time comes. John has never been the same after his hockey injury. If he was in his right mind that fire would not have happened.

Yours sincerely, Mrs. Roy Pilkie

I gave the letter back to Mrs. Pilkie, amazed by how involved my father had been in their lives.

"John is a good boy. He doesn't have a mean bone in his body, does he, Sal?"

"Oh, John has a good side, Georgie." Sal scowled at the ceiling, her lips compressed in a firm, hard line, and I couldn't help thinking of Morley's mother who shamed Morley for being big and full of energy. Did Mrs. Pilkie know what being a good boy meant? Maybe she didn't read the news reports about her son rough-housing the other players.

While I sat wondering what to say, Mrs. Pilkie retrieved a photo album from the coffee table. "John put this book together himself," Mrs. Pilkie said. "See? He's written his name here. Isn't that cute?" I leaned over for a better look. The words *Self with Smokey and Blue* had been written in white ink beneath a photo of a skinny, dark-haired boy petting a pair of kittens.

On the opposite page, the same skinny dark-haired boy stood with a tall, heavy-set man wearing a fedora. The boy was holding a hockey trophy. I took a breath.

"Your daddy always liked John." A long sigh escaped Mrs. Pilkie and she turned quickly to a photo of the same skinny boy holding a hockey stick and a man with a pockmarked face. A dusting of snow coated their jackets. "Some days at the Light, Jim took a hammer to my coat to get off the ice."

"Was it like that the November Mr. Pilkie took John's appendix out?" I asked.

"Well, yes, it was. Poor Jim. His hands were shaking in fear that night."

"Shaking from too much whisky, you mean," Sal said.

Mrs. Pilkie gave Sal a dirty look and flipped to a snap of a skinny teenage boy whose ribs showed above his plaid bathing trunks. A round-eyed girl sat beside him wearing a one-piece

suit with a flowered skirt. "Why, Sal. Here you are at the Light."
Tapping the girl's head, Mrs. Pilkie said, "My husband was in
Davy Jones's locker when Sal came to visit. Sal had a real crush
on John. Wouldn't do anything unless John did it first. Isn't that
right, Sal? You were so hurt when he broke your engagement."

"No thanks to you, Georgie," Sal snapped.

"Sal was engaged to John?" I asked wonderingly.

"You bet she was, but Sal didn't want to leave Madoc's Landing, and John wanted her to move to Detroit."

Sighing noisily, Sal lit up a fresh cigarette, and it came back
to me how Sal had flirted with John the day she brought him
into our kitchen, and how angry Sib had been over it. Now it all
made sense, and I prayed Sal wouldn't pick a fight so I could hear
more. As if she read my mind, Mrs. Pilkie flipped to a newspaper
photo of a younger Sal and John sitting at a nightclub table. He
held up a scrap of burning paper and Sal was laughing in a half-
frightened, half-admiring way. The caption read: "Gentleman
Jack Pilkie Burns a $100 Bill to Impress Girl Friend."

"You had some good times with John, didn't you, Sal? Too bad
he picked somebody else."

"Too bad for her, you mean," Sal replied.

"Now Sal, you know I don't like that kind of talk." Mrs. Pilkie
came to a page with empty photograph tabs. Before I could ask
about the missing photographs, she closed her album with a purposeful snap. "Do you think Doc Bradford will like my letter, Sal?"

Sal shrugged as she butted out her cigarette.

"May I make a suggestion?" I said. "You have used 'was' when
the verb should be 'were.' And you shouldn't say 'real soft-
hearted.' Modifiers are the leeches that infect the pond of
prose."

"Pardon, Mary?"

"That's what William Strunk says in *The Elements of Style*. And John didn't score the winning goal for the Red Wings. He made an assist in the third period and his assist helped them score the winning goal." When I looked over, Sal was grinning broadly.

"Yes, of course," Mrs. Pilkie said in a small voice.

"You should send your letter to Dr. Shulman too," I added, sorry I had picked on Mrs. Pilkie's grammar. "He has new ideas about the treatment of mental patients. My father says so."

"Does he really? Now bless you. That's the best news I've heard all day."

Sal sprang out of her chair. "Georgie, thanks for the tea. 'Course, you don't have a hope of helping a bad apple like John." Sal pulled me out of the sofa and pushed me towards the door. We said goodbye to Mrs. Pilkie, Sal steering me purposefully out into the spring night.

"The old fool." Sal glanced back at Mrs. Pilkie's house. "Once those nutcases are locked up, they should stay put."

"Mrs. Pilkie said you were sweet on John. Don't you care about his feelings?"

"As if he cares about mine." Sal stopped me under a streetlight. "I don't want any more questions, Lady Jane. Some things are better left dead-and-buried. Do you understand?"

I said "yes" and we walked the rest of the way in silence. All the way home I wracked my brains wondering how I could get Sal to talk. As we walked into our front hall, I burst out, "If John was a bad apple why did you like him?"

"Didn't I tell you: No more questions?" Sal said and rushed upstairs. There was no hope of getting a cup of cocoa now.

13

IN WARM WEATHER, WHEN WE DIDN'T TAKE THE BUS HOME from school, Ben and I used a shortcut through the grounds of the Bug House. We didn't tell anyone about it because the shortcut took us past Maple Ridge, where the criminally insane patients were locked up, and we'd been warned not to go near it. But, now that John was there, I wondered how he liked his life behind its stone walls. Did he spend his days thinking about his dead wife and baby girl? Or maybe he was hatching plans for another escape so he could draw attention to his case.

After school, Ben and I liked to stand behind the wire fence and stare up at the prison's Tuscan arches and rooftop belvedere. Some days we called out John's name, begging him to talk to us. No answering call came from inside the prison. A weird silence hung about the place as if nobody lived there. And no guards appeared either. We were the children of hospital staff, so we were like no-see-em bugs as far as they were concerned. On other days, Ben and I would try to guess which window belonged to John. Ben thought they put him on the top floor, so he was out of the way, while I was sure he had the largest window on the first floor because he was a famous murderer.

According to Ben, John's cell window was too high for him to have a view. There was no way John could see the water, which ran between two long wooded headlands before it opened out into the Great Bay. Ben told me that John couldn't see anything except other prisoners doing their business. From Ben, I also knew John was watched by guards and not by the attendants who took care of the harmless patients. The prisoners in Maple Ridge were expected to do chores like the harmless patients: under supervision, they milked the hospital cows, pushed rollers over the clay tennis courts, and stitched up the leather covers on baseballs in the Ball Shop with waxy pink string. In the fall, they harvested squash and pumpkins. No matter what time of year it was, the men at Maple Ridge worked all day. John was a creature of routine, just like Morley, except that Morley didn't try to run away and John did.

A Word about Ben

I should point out that Ben wasn't interested in John because John was a famous killer. Ben admired John because he wanted to grow up and play for the Detroit Red Wings. Unfortunately, Dr. Shulman wanted Ben to become a psychiatrist, like him. He often complained to me about Ben's marks. "My son will never get into medicine with a B-plus average," Dr. Shulman said. "Can you help him get an A-plus, like you, Mary?"

I did what I could, although Ben was more interested in playing road hockey with the Bug House boys than doing his schoolwork. But he never stopped hoping they would take him on, even though Sam's gang said Ben was too fat and that he talked with a lisp like a girl. Sam was the worst. In school, he would poke Ben's arm with a steel-tipped ruler. Or he'd yank a handful of Ben's red curls at recess and hiss, "Eat my dust, you tub of lard!"

Inside the Bug House

One day in late May when a rhesus monkey, called Able, and a squirrel monkey, named Baker, rode off in the nose cone of a Cape Canaveral missile, Ben and I took our usual shortcut through the Bug House grounds. In no time, Ben was far ahead. Every so often he stopped and waited for me to catch my breath and then he ran off again. It was true that Ben was on the plump side, but he was light on his feet, the way some fat people are. I found it hard to keep up with him. Then, too, going downhill for me was harder than going up. I had to pick my way carefully, throwing my right hip to the side and lifting up Hindrance. "We can do it," I whispered and Hindrance hissed back, "Fingers crossed, Mouse." I tried not to think of what my grandmother would say. She was against me taking excursions of any kind, except when the weather was nice and then she made me go at a snail's pace so I wouldn't get exhausted.

I stopped to catch my breath near the hospital's vegetable garden where some patients were lumbering around like zombies with wooden hoes. It was a humid, overcast day in late June and I was panting hard, so at first I didn't see John. But there he was, on the far side of the vegetable patch. Sib Beaudry was supervising a work crew made up of patients. John was handing down sod in the back of the truck, while Sib yelled at them to work faster. John looked hot and tired in his neatly pressed hospital overalls, and I thought of his hands, with their nails as shiny and clean as a woman's, wrestling with the grassy lumps of dirt.

He didn't look my way, and I stole closer and hid behind a tree to watch. When his group took a work break, he jumped off the truck and started to play his harmonica. A few sad-sounding chords of "Red River Valley" floated over to me. Sib and the other patients stopped their work to listen. Some of the patients in the vegetable garden listened, too. I couldn't hear what Sib was saying, although Sib's lips were moving rapidly up and down. Suddenly, John said in a loud, scoffing voice, "If Sib Beaudry were Santa Claus, there wouldn't be a Christmas." Some of the patients laughed. Now all the patients were laughing. I giggled, too. "Hey, Pilkie! Ready to cool off?" Sib snatched John's harmonica and beckoned to a guard who tied John to a leather rope dangling from Sib's waist. Then the guard uncoiled a hose hanging off a shed and turned it on. The water bounced off John in all directions, splintering into miniature rainbows that glistened orange, yellow, red, and blue, then faded and glistened and faded again. John didn't flinch; he stared down the hose wearing the same calm, self-satisfied expression he wore at the train station, as if he was saying, *Do your worst. I can take it.* Or maybe that was wrong. Maybe the look on his face meant he believed he deserved to be treated badly. The thought made me shiver. Now the hose was turned on full force; it soaked the front of John's overalls, turning the fabric dark with moisture. He closed his eyes. He wasn't ducking or trying to turn away. Of course, he couldn't run anywhere, not when he was attached to Sib by the leather leash. But he could have tried to protect himself. The other patients went back to laying sod, afraid they were going to be sprayed too.

"Please fight back!" I whispered.

Now the guard lifted the hose to John's face. The spray of water hit John between the eyes, flattening his cowlick. Immediately, John's expression changed to a look so threatening it stopped my breath. Or was I seeing things? Now John was wearing his calm, self-satisfied expression again. "Had enough, Pilkie?" Sib asked. John looked at his feet and didn't answer. The guard pointed the hose at John's mouth until he doubled over spitting. When he recovered himself, Sib and the guard hooted.

"Tell us, Pilkie. Had enough yet?"

His lips opened. He must have been saying "yes," because the guard untied him and pushed him over to the truck. He wiped his face with the sleeve of his shirt and started handing down pieces of sod again. I felt ashamed of myself for spying on him, and it struck me that all of us — Ben and me and the Bug House boys — were guilty of a mindless indifference. How could we run around in freedom while John's life was worse than anyone imagined? Nobody except his jailors knew what happened to him. He could have been in China as far as the people in Madoc's Landing were concerned.

BEN RAN OUT OF THE maple bush, swooping his arms and singing, "Up in the air, Junior Birdmen." Sam Mahoney was right behind making finger goggles around his eyes. He waited while Ben ran over and whispered: "The Bug House boys want to show us something at the icehouse."

"I don't play with meanies," I whispered back.

"Please, Mary? Pretty please with sugar on it!"

"Pretty please sounds babyish. I don't play with babies either."

Ben's face crumpled.

"Okay," I said, knowing I would regret it.

BY ONE OF THE COTTAGES, where some of the harmless patients lived, Sam motioned for us to crouch down under a window. We did what he said and peered in at the patients. We couldn't see them very well because a cloud of cigarette smoke hid their shoulders and heads, but their legs were visible in workpants and these truncated appendages dangled from benches or stomped back and forth. As we stared, the men's hands disappeared up into the smoke, and then slowly descended through the air to rest again on their trousers. Some of their boots were so worn the owner's toenails poked out through the leather.

"Guess what," I whispered to Ben and Sam. "I just saw John Pilkie get soaked with a hose."

"You did not!" Sam sneered.

"I did so!" I retorted. "Sib Beaudry did it."

No sooner were the words out of our mouths than a pair of trousered knees bent outwards and two workboots clomped towards us. "Up in the air, Junior Birdmen! Up in the air, upside down!" Sam ran off whooping. Ben jogged after Sam while I lurched after Ben, carrying my satchel with my composition.

DOWN BY THE ICEHOUSE, SAM and Ben huddled with the Bug House boys. When he saw me, Sam tapped the shoulder of a boy standing on an overturned milk carton. The boy jumped down. "If you want to see, you have to pay twenty-five cents," Sam said in a low, quiet voice. Ben handed over a quarter. With Ben's help, I got one leg on the carton and then I pulled up Hindrance while the boys talked in whispers behind my back. Inside, Sal's cousin, Archie Beauchamp, was marching up and down between blocks of straw-covered ice singing, "Old Macdonald Had a Farm." The goofy way he was swinging his arms in time to his song suggested he wanted to be funny. According to Sal, Archie was locked up for asking women to kiss his scalded face, but Ben told me that Archie was put away for starting a fire in a schoolhouse that burned off his own lips and ears. It struck me that John's face should be scarred too, considering.

"Old Archie whipped the Christly buggers, EE-EYE-EE-EYE-OH with an ouch ouch here and an ouch ouch there ..." Archie opened his mouth so wide I thought I could hear his teeth chattering.

"Sam, let Archie out," I cried. "He's freezing to death."

"Make her get down!" Sam shouted. "She forgot to whisper!"

One of the boys grabbed my shoulder and, because I was not as steady on my feet as I wanted to be, I pitched forward, dragging Hindrance like a dead weight. I hit the sandy earth, palms first and, when I rolled onto my back, the Bug House boys stood over me, their eyes wide as if they were looking at a giant earth worm. At first I thought they were gawking at my underpants because my skirt was hitched up around my chest. I yanked down my dress but their eyes remained glued to something below my head. Then I understood. It was Hindrance. Nobody except my family, along with some nurses and doctors, had seen Hindrance up close. To be honest, Hindrance was pretty withered-looking. The outer muscles of my left thigh would get strong again, but my atrophied muscles never did. Those muscles were wasted, practically useless.

Oh, Hindrance, I'm sorry, I thought, gazing up at the sky. *I didn't mean for this to happen.* For once, Hindrance didn't answer.

"Pull down her pants," one of the boys shouted. "Let's see her hole!"

"Maybe cripples don't have holes," another boy said. He nudged Hindrance with his toe and a great wash of hopelessness passed through me. Ben couldn't take on Sam and the Bug House kids by himself, and we both knew it. When I looked up again, Sam had on my cowboy hat and he was limping around in front of me, his weight sinking down on his right leg the way my weight did when I had to lift up Hindrance. In his hand, he held my composition. A stab of anger brought me back to myself. "Sam, give that back!"

Sam told me to shut my mouth. In a squeaky imitation of a girl's voice, he read out its title: "'A Short History of My Great-Grandfather, an Oil Baron of Canada West.' Well, la-de-dah! Mary thinks well of herself, don't she?"

Before I could stop myself, out popped the curse words that Big Louie had used in church: "Bugger off —!"

"Take it back, Peg Leg."

"No. And I won't lend you my coloured pencils anymore either."

Alarm flashed across Sam's face. It strikes me now that Sam was remembering I was the girl who sat across the aisle from him in school; and, not only that, his partner in the square dancing class every Friday afternoon when he would steer me carefully across the floor so I didn't stumble. He would politely allemande left with me and dosey-doe, before leading me back to one of the blond plywood chairs set against the gymnasium wall. Throughout our awkward dance steps, I would feel slightly ashamed but proud. Sam was not without his charms. He liked to laugh and he wore his hair in a smoothly woven ducktail, like John Pilkie, although Sam had been wearing it that way before John came to town, so it was more likely he was copying Elvis Presley than anybody else.

"You're going to be really sorry now, Peg Leg!" Sam shrieked and tossed my composition up into the air. Ben and I watched helplessly as the wind picked up the pages and blew them into the harbour, where they bloated with water and sank.

"Mary is a looney," Sam cried. "And we know what happens to them. Don't we, gang?"

The shrieking boys knocked Ben down and crowded round me, sneering and giggling. They were so close I could hear the dirty things they were saying about me under their breath and smell their sour boy smells, the stink of sweat and dirty socks and embarrassing pee dribbles on their underwear. Then their snickers stopped. Sam held up something that glinted in the sunlight. My spirits sank: it was a hypodermic syringe, the type with a sharp point and transparent cartridge that let you see the fluid inside. Sam must have stolen it from the hospital infirmary. The sight of its glistening metal needle made me swoon with terror.

While we watched, Sam took off his sweater and twisted it into a rope, and it came to me that Sam intended to act out his own dumb version of the way hospital guards handled violent patients. Sal had described in detail how Sib and the other guards choked a troublesome patient with a towel until the patient couldn't breathe; then they injected him with a drug to calm him.

From behind, something woolly and soft fell like a lasso around my neck. The touch of Sam's sweater set me off. I screamed Blue Murder. And, as if from far off, I heard my own voice yelling so loud and high I sounded like a whistling kettle blowing hot, wet steam. The boys stared down at me in shock. They were too surprised to hear the new sound, down by the harbour, where a hospital truck was driving along the lower road. The rumble of its engine grew louder and the heads and shoulders of men in the back of the truck came into view. Suddenly, John's head emerged among the patients holding rakes and hoes. He waved, but I couldn't wave back because somebody had pinned my arms behind my back.

"You little bastards, I'll skin you alive and hang you out to dry!" John cried. In a single, sure-footed motion, he threw himself over the side of the truck and took great, leaping strides in my direction. He seemed to fly up off the ground as if a tornado was blowing him my way.

"It's the hockey killer!" Sam cried. "Let's vamoose!"

Sam's gang galloped away screaming. "That's right, scram!" John shook his fist, his black, pop-out eyes fierce. "And don't come back or you won't know what hit you!" He collected himself and, smiling his big dimpled smile, he placed his hands under my armpits and lifted me up.

"Mary, nobody's going to bother you now," he said, holding me upright until I stopped shaking. "I figure it was a Mexican standoff. Am I right?"

I gave him a wan smile. In *M.B.'s Book of True Facts* I'd noted that a Mexican standoff referred to bandits who ran away instead of staying to fight, but maybe John didn't know about that.

"Good for you. The world would be a bad place if it was run by little boys, eh?" He brushed the dirt off my dress. "Just a few grass stains. Nothing serious." He put my cowboy hat back on and picked up the first page of my composition, the only one that hadn't blown into the water. "Did you throw away Mary's homework, son?" he asked Ben.

"Mr. Pilkie, it was Sam Mahoney's gang." I pointed at the icehouse. "And they locked Archie Beauchamp in there."

John loped over and jiggled the icehouse lock. Down the road, the work truck stopped. Patients holding rakes and hoes hung over the sides watching while Jordie and Sib ran our way, angry looks on their faces. I stopped breathing. Was John going to get beat up again?

"What's going on, John?" Jordie called. Breathing hard, he and Sib pushed us aside.

"A man's freezing in there," John said. "Let's get him out, eh?"

Jordie climbed up on the milk carton to look. "Archie's in there all right," Jordie said. John jiggled the lock again, and Archie stumbled out, tears leaking from his strange flat eyes, staring out from the burned skin of their sockets. Ben and I watched him, our mouths open. It wasn't only Archie's sad, scarred face that hypnotized us. We had never seen a grown man cry before.

"Hey, Mary!" John tipped his chin towards the road. Go home, he was signalling. I nodded. Yet I couldn't move my feet.

"Quit your bawling, Archie," Sib said, sneering. "Act like a man."

"Hey, Archie. It's not your fault." John clapped Archie on the back. "Sib doesn't have the courage to pick on somebody his own size."

Sib grabbed John's neck in a wrestling hold and squeezed hard. "Take back what you said, you crazy bastard!"

"Want a ciggy, John boy?" Jordie stuck a lit cigarette in John's mouth and John puffed on it nonchalantly, staring out at the harbour as if he was somewhere pleasant and nice. Sib's elbow was still squeezing John's neck. The droll effect of a man smoking, while he was being half-strangled to death, made everybody laugh. Sib dropped his arms, muttering, and Jordie offered him a cigarette, too. Soon they were all puffing away on their smokes as if they didn't have a care in the world.

When John realized Ben and I were watching, he smiled sheepishly and tossed down his cigarette. Throwing up his arms, he flung himself into a cartwheel. Now his legs flew up, and for a breathless second, his torso froze into a giant V shape. Then his legs tilted dangerously forward and he started walking on his hands. The sight hit me in the stomach. The manly grace of him. His shapely, dark head. His shiny cowlick. Then, worse luck, I could feel my cheeks burning. Gravity had pulled the cuffs of John's baggy workpants up his legs, exposing the dark hairs growing on the muscles of his calves. And now without warning, the feeling in my stomach moved down there, which is how Sal described the most womanly part of us, as if she was referring to Australia and its position vis-à-vis the rest of the world. I averted my eyes hoping he wouldn't notice.

The work crew in the truck cheered when John flipped right side up again. "Don't let the turkeys get you down, Mary," he cried as he hopped into the back. Jordie and Sib pushed Archie into the front seat and climbed in next to him. I kept my eyes on John until I lost sight of him among the other men holding rakes and hoes. I'd lost my composition and every part of me was aching, including my palms. But I walked home, closing my eyes and pretending I was taking the same graceful loping strides as John Pilkie.

Hindrance on Our Moral Nature

Hindrance: If I were you, I wouldn't take getting rescued by the hockey killer seriously, Mouse. People are either good or bad, and John Pilkie is bad.

Me: That's not true! People are good so their fathers will love them.

Hindrance: You may as well not have a father for all the time he gives you.

Me: You think so, Hindrance?

Hindrance: A girl without a father is like a town without streetlights. She can find her way but a lot of the time, she'll be groping in the dark.

A GIRL WITHOUT A FATHER is like a town without streetlights. I kept thinking about what Hindrance said and wondered if it was true of Morley and me. It wasn't like my father had died on me. He was home three times a day; we ate lunch and dinner together. But he wouldn't have time to rescue me from the Bug House boys. He had more serious problems than saving me from a bunch of creeps bent on humiliating whatever girl crossed their path.

Or was it that I didn't count in Morley's eyes? Don't be a nincompoop, I scolded myself. You have to take Morley's love on faith. One day, you'll spring from Morley's noggin like the Greek goddess Athena. She, too, had a strong, absent father and she rushed out of Zeus's forehead, fully armoured, ready to take on the world.

14

MY FATHER WAS ALWAYS TELLING ME TO PUT MYSELF IN THE other person's shoes. "There, but for the grace of God," he'd say if I complained about a problem like the Bug House boys. So I submit the following with a word to the wise, because Little Louie didn't understand I had sworn to Morley that I would try to see things through the other person's eyes. Being fair involved looking at things backwards, sideways, and upside-down, so that you got to know the other person's point of view as well (or almost as well) as your own. Sometimes being fair meant you had to read letters that weren't addressed to you. After all, how else could a girl like me understand anything?

I found Little Louie's letter to the mysterious Max Falkowski a few days after John rescued me from the Bug House boys.

June 12, 1959

Dear Max:

In your last letter, you asked me to tell you about Madoc's Landing, and said you'd like to come up for a visit. Please don't. It would get me in hot water with Mom, who thinks you and I are out-of-touch. And besides, I don't want to see you. I got over being mad when you found out that Charlotte had lied about being pregnant. I even felt sorry about it and admired your gentlemanly instinct to give the child a name. And I also meant it when I said I would wait while you got a divorce. But then yesterday, Willie phoned and told me that Charlotte is expecting. Two months gone, according to my brother. This is the worst news I have heard for ages! First, you let yourself get trapped into something you didn't want because you couldn't control yourself. And then you seal the deal by making sure she really is pregnant. Why are you so hapless, Max?

If it's any comfort, you've ruined my life too. Mom is always reminding me that this hick town is full of nice old Victorian homes left over from its days as a lumber capital. As if I care about old houses. I'm stuck in a backwater where all the locals care about is hockey. I doubt if anybody has read a book here in years, let alone heard of something like socialized medicine. At least my sister's house is nice enough, with fireplaces downstairs and new mattresses from Simpsons. I can feel Alice's presence in its rooms, despite the fact she has been dead for a while. And I have my crippled niece, Mary for a friend. She is a self-sufficient little character who limps around in a white cowboy hat. Her father is one of those men who gives everything to his community and neglects his family while the housekeeper, Sal, is downright unfriendly. Mom says what Mary needs is a stepmother to look out for her interests. Can you guess what Mom is thinking? Rots-a-ruck, Mom! Dr. Bradford is way too old for me.

That's all I have to say. Don't you dare come up, Max.
Please stop mailing me your books and magazine articles.
What we had is over. I thought you understood when I
explained why I wouldn't go all the way with you. If the
choice were between a hamburger and a lobster dinner, I
would rather wait until I can eat lobster every night.

Love, Louisa

Poor Little Louie. Max's wife pretended to be pregnant so she could trick him into marrying her and now the sneaky creature really was pregnant, and there was nothing my aunt could do about it. It was too unfair for words. And how terrible to want someone you couldn't have, although the world was full of such cases, like Sal admiring Morley, and getting the bully Sib Beaudry instead, and me longing for Morley's attention when sick people needed it more. Why couldn't we get what we wanted, like my great-grandfather, Old Mac? Now that was another confounding question. Were we designed to want too much? And, if we got what we wanted, why didn't it come in the right amount? Why couldn't the world hand out what we sought in exact measurements like the ingredients Sal used for baking my fave — angel food cake?

But there was something worse in my aunt's letter. The word "crippled." Physical flaws were common then, so people were more inured to the sight of kids like me with limps or facial deformities. Today, these problems are mostly fixed by surgery, or physiotherapy, but nobody expected them to be cured when I was twelve. You could even argue that such flaws were less deplored because people were used to seeing others with them.

And I, too, expected to hear people talk frankly about my leg in a way that nobody would now.

But it was hurtful to think that my aunt would call me crippled. It made me feel like a tragic character in somebody else's family. And she'd never criticized Morley to my face for neglecting me. She was always careful to point out that my father had treated more serious polio cases than mine. I put the letter carefully back on Little Louie's desk, and tried not to think about Sal saying snoopers are always sorry they snooped.

15

ON THE FIRST DAY OF THE SUMMER HOLIDAYS, I ROSE AT SIX, and pulled out the first page of my composition about my great-grandfather. At the bottom of this page, I stenciled in the words: MORE TO COME. I stuck the page into an envelope and stencilled, *Dr. Morley Bradford: Personal.* I underlined *Personal* three times. Satisfied, I put on my Lone Ranger hat and headed for Morley's office, carrying the envelope.

Morley's office was at the far end of the hall, in the storage room with its shelves stacked with old shoes, tennis rackets, and leather-bound copies of *Boy's Own Annual* magazine. I wasn't allowed in it, on account of his ship-to-shore radio. Morley kept the radio on day and night in case a freighter called about bringing in a sick crewmember.

At the door of the storage room, I heard its familiar crackles of static and a voice said: "Can anyone hear me? Over." I knew the sound would bring my father running so, as quickly as I could, I squeezed myself in behind my father's winter coat hanging from the window in a plastic cleaner's bag. Sure enough, Morley walked in a moment later. He sat down at his desk and put on his ship-to-shore earphones. His fingers, twice the length of mine, fiddled with the dials. Dr. Shulman's voice immediately filled the room.

"Are you there? Over." When the static died away, my father said: "I'm here, Rob. Over."

"I'm on my boat." Dr. Shulman's voice broke up. "Pilkie has escaped. Over."

"When?" Morley asked. "Over."

"Last night. Over."

"The poor bugger."

"Damn it, Morley, speak up, over."

"I said Pilkie wants attention for his case. Was anyone hurt? Over."

"No. We found Sib Beaudry tied to a block of ice. Over."

"A block of ice? Over."

"Sib had some ice sent up to cool his soft drinks. He claims Pilkie pulled a knife on him. But we think Pilkie bluffed his way out with a piece of flatware. Over." I grinned at the thought of Sib tied to a block of ice, but the sound of dog claws scratching the floor brought me up short. Joe began to bark while Mairzy, who couldn't see very well, circled my father's coat, sniffing my bare feet.

"Rob, I have to go," my father said. "I'll run over today and calm everyone down."

"Thanks, Morley. Over and out."

My father shut off the radio and stood up. "Is that you in there?"

I stepped out of my hiding place holding out my envelope. "I have the composition ..."

"You mean you have a composition," Morley replied.

"Well, I only have the first page of it."

"Give it to me when you finish then," he said.

"I promise. Will John get caught?"

"Hard to say. Listen, Mary. Don't mention Pilkie's knife to Sal or your aunt. Do you understand?"

"I promise."

"Thatta girl." He walked out, cuffing the side of my cheek with the back of his hand. Joe and Mairzy scrambled after him. Downstairs, in the kitchen, the radio announcer was talking about the hockey killer's "elopement," the old-fashioned word the hospital used to describe a patient's escape. The announcer repeated the story of Sib tied to a block of ice. "I guess Pilkie thought his jailor needed cooling off," he chortled. "Well folks, better bolt your doors tonight. We're not safe in our beds. The hockey killer is on the loose again!"

My aunt exclaimed: "Not safe in our beds! Sal, will you go and stay on the Beaudry farm?"

"I'll be safe here," Sal said. "John won't tangle with Doc Bradford."

I couldn't hear my aunt's answer and then someone, likely Sal, turned off the radio. I looked out the window, expecting to see people running screaming out of their homes. But there was no one on the street except the postman. And when I listened for the siren at the hospital, which sounded if a criminal escaped, the only noise was the rustling of the maples outside the storage room window.

TWO HOURS LATER, MY AUNT and I said goodbye to Morley on the back steps.

"Will you come to Petrolia tomorrow?" I asked my father.

He had on his Other Worldly Stare (i.e., the raised eyebrows that expressed surprise and bewilderment). Sal claimed Morley looked like that when somebody was dying and he was trying to figure out how to save his patient's life.

"I'll have to see, Mary."

"Will you phone me in Petrolia?"

He nodded, but I knew he would forget. Per usual, Morley often forgot what I asked him. Per usual, Morley was Morley. It didn't matter. I was on my holidays and John was roaming scot-free in the hills of Brebeuf County.

"Morley, do you think we will get through the road block?" my aunt asked.

"Chief Doucette will let you through. Just don't pick up any hitchhikers. It might be Pilkie in disguise."

"That's not funny," my aunt said as she slipped into the front seat of our Ford station wagon. She put *The Face of War* by Martha Gellhorn on the floor near her feet and rolled down the window. Her purse, bulging with Old Mac's letters, rested against her hip.

"Goodbye, Morley," my aunt called.

"Drive safely," my father answered. He looked sad, standing on the back steps by himself. I felt sad, too. We were abandoning Morley, although the truth was he wouldn't put his work aside and come with us the way I wanted.

"Morley doesn't want us to go," I told my aunt.

She laughed. "Mary, other children don't call their parents by their first names! Do you know that?" She stuck her head out the car window without waiting for my answer. "Shall I tell Mom that you'll join us in a day or two?" my aunt called.

Morley, do what she says. Please come.

My father regarded us impassively.

"Of course, you never took any interest in Alice's family," my aunt said under her breath. Morley frowned as if he had heard Little Louie. Or was he frowning at Sal, who had come out onto the back porch, a look of expectation on her face? "Never mind. I'll tell Big Louie you were busy," my aunt said. She tossed her yellow hair and rolled up the window, shutting out Morley and Sal. We were off and I kept turning around to wave at my father who didn't move from his position on the back steps. When we were all the way down Whitefish Road, he raised his hand and waved back. Then he put his hand on Sal's shoulder and they went inside.

MY AUNT AND I RAN into the roadblock set up to catch John by the south entrance to the Ontario Psychiatric Hospital. Little Louie rolled down her window and smiled at Chief Doucette, who stood by his squad car talking to drivers going in and out of the gates. He strolled over and peeked in, slinging his arm above the car door. "Going for a spin, Miss?"

My aunt drummed her fingers on the steering wheel. "I'm Mary Bradford's aunt and I'm taking my niece to see her grand-mother in Petrolia."

"Pretty gals like you and Mary should be safe from Pilkie down there." He winked at my aunt. She sighed. Men like Chief Doucette got on her nerves.

"I hope so," she said. "Do you have any idea where Pilkie is?"

"We heard a rumour he's hiding in a barn near Lafontaine." Chief Doucette waved towards the leafy hill on the other side of the harbour. "Or he could still be on the grounds. You never know with him."

"That's what I don't like," my aunt replied.

"He's crazy like a fox, eh?" Chief Doucette tapped the hood of our station wagon, dismissing us. My aunt drove off, hands gripping the wheel.

THE ROAD OUT OF BREBEUF County was an unpaved, meandering cow path. A local reeve had designated it a highway in the hopes of encouraging tourists. In the summer, dust from the gravel floated up through the floorboards and engines overheated if the temperature rose above seventy-two degrees Fahrenheit. It was already baking hot in the station wagon, even though my aunt had rolled down all the windows. On the car radio the announcer was talking about Ingemar Johansson who had floored heavyweight champion Floyd Patterson in the third round.

Suddenly, John's name popped up. The announcer said John had told one of the patients at the psychiatric hospital that he was going south to Windsor, where he used to live. My aunt gasped. Windsor is close to Petrolia. When the announcer mentioned the murder of his wife and child, my aunt switched the radio off.

"What if he's going to Petrolia instead of Windsor?"

"Don't talk like that, huh? Do you want me to jump out of my skin?"

"I don't think he'd hurt us."

"That's what you think. Why don't you listen to some music and let me concentrate on driving?"

My aunt turned the radio on. She flipped the dial past the station playing a crooner ballad by Johnny Mathis and turned to CHUM, which was spinning Elvis Presley's top ten hit, "A Fool Such as I." Then she turned up the volume as loud as it could go and we sang along.

PART TWO

PRODIGALS

16

OUR CAR STARTED TO OVERHEAT JUST SOUTH OF WYOMING, Ontario, where not quite a hundred years before, my great-grandfather had dragged oil barrels to its railway station through the Great Swamp of Enniskillen. Our clothes were gritty with dust, and the breeze blowing through our car window no longer cooled us.

My aunt drove up to one of the houses and went inside to call Uncle Willie. Thirty minutes later, Big Louie's ancient Packard came bumping down the dirt road, throwing up dust. Its purple chassis was the same shade as the eggplants Big Louie grew in her vegetable garden. It had a double row of white-walled tires and fenders painted a shiny black. Uncle Willie sat in the passenger seat next to a stranger wearing Maurice's chauffeur uniform. "Hello, Louisa," the stranger called out the window. His face was smooth and almost feature-less, except for his horn-rimmed spectacles and full, oversized lips. Leaping out of the Packard, he took off his chauffeur's cap and bowed towards my aunt. The blond finger waves surging back from his forehead didn't move. After her hair had been freshly set in a permanent wave, Big Louie's hair showed the same stiff quality.

My aunt shrunk down into her seat, and I took a hard look at the man who was making her nervous. Morley's size made women feel safe, but the stranger's soft blond looks suggested women should take care of him. Bit by bit, my aunt recovered her composure and slid out of the front seat, shielding her chest with her leather purse. Its strap caught on the door handle; its clasp popped open and Old Mac's letters fell out, along with three tubes of Revlon lipstick. In a soft, musical voice, the stranger began to sing, "Beautiful dreamer, awake unto me, Starlight and dewdrops are waiting for thee." My aunt lowered her eyes, the blush on her cheeks deepening. Before she could bend down, the stranger grabbed the lipsticks and my great-grandfather's letters and one by one he handed them back. "I didn't expect to see you today," she said. Avoiding my eyes, she crammed everything back into her purse.

"Well, I wanted to see you." The stranger hugged my aunt a few moments too long before she wiggled out of his arms. "Is this your charge?" he asked, turning to me. My aunt replied, "She's Alice's child, Mary. She had polio six years ago."

"I see. Does Mary take after her father?"

My aunt said, "yes." The stranger said, "Mary, I'm not really the chauffeur, you know. I'm Max."

"You're Max?" I exclaimed.

"Yes, Mary. Max is my friend," my aunt said quickly. "Has Big Louie let Maurice go?"

"No, he's back at the Great House." Uncle Willie grinned. "Mother won't cut back on her spending — you know that." Uncle Willie waved at the Packard. "It cost a bundle to rebuild this baby. But she wanted the works for her celebration of Vidal Oil."

"Oh, stop boring us with your money problems," Max said. "Your family can just sell another oil well."

"Max thinks he's smart because he's head of his union local now," Uncle Willie said.

My aunt replied, "Well, I guess that helps with the family bills."

Max looked hurt. Uncle Willie said quickly: "Come on, pal. Let's call the garage." The two men went inside the farmhouse. When they came back, we climbed into the Packard and Uncle Willie opened its trunk and pulled out a Zoom-8 movie camera, like the ones I saw on television. "It will be like old times, Little Louie. You and Max together! Snuggle up to him now," my uncle called. My aunt jerked her head away, frowning, and Uncle Willie pointed his camera at Max as he started up the Packard. We drove slowly down the farmhouse lane, Uncle Willie running alongside, filming us. Max stopped and Uncle Willie climbed in the backseat. He swatted Max's head. "Get on with it, Jeeves!" Max put his foot to the floor and drove flat out down the country road. As the Packard sailed over a bump, Uncle Willie and I rose off the seat.

Uncle Willie yelled, "Bull's-eye, Jeeves!"

My aunt said anxiously, "Willie, this is far too fast for an old wreck like the Packard." A second bump lifted us off our seats again and our heads just missed the ceiling. I screamed and Uncle Willie batted Max's head again.

"Slow down, old boy! You're scaring the horses."

"Rightie-o, Your Highness!" Max straightened his chauffeur's cap. "Do you wish to film the main drag?"

"By Jove, that's a capital idea!" Uncle Willie exclaimed.

Max turned down the main street of Petrolia and Uncle Willie leapt out, aiming his camera at an old farmer on the sidewalk. "Look sharp!" Uncle Willie shouted. "That's right! The Vidals are coming!" The farmer shook his head and walked away. Uncle Willie told my aunt and me to smile for posterity, so we grinned and waved while the Packard glided past stores with canvas awnings and brick walls decorated with ads for Sweet Cap cigarettes. Next to Madoc's Landing, Petrolia felt like the centre of the civilized world, although rowdies motored to its bars on Saturday night, shouting and fighting, breaking windows, and the air was always heavy with a sulfur smell from the oil wells. That day, with the heat, the smell was worse. I was relieved when Uncle Willie got back in and the car sped up so the breeze came through our windows again. "See that house, Mary?" Uncle Willie said, aiming his Kodak movie camera. "It belonged to your great-grandfather's friend, Van Tuys. And that big mansion was owned by the late Charles Pilkie. 'Course, the Pilkies have moved away. Not one of them left here now."

I sat up when I heard the Pilkie name.

"Is the family any relation to the hockey player who killed his wife?" Max asked.

"He's a cousin," Uncle Willie replied. "The Pilkies were ashamed of him. How would you like a cold-blooded murderer for a relative?"

"I know Gentleman Jack Pilkie," I said. "I think he's nice."

"Mary has struck up a friendship with the hockey killer," my aunt said.

"Have you, Mary?" Uncle Willie turned his eyes to me, his

voice taking on a serious tone. "You're not going to get in trouble with the law now, are you, Mary?"

"I hope not," I said, and Uncle Willie laughed. "All right, Jeeves," he cried. "On to the ancestral seat!" Max flapped his hand out the car window and the Packard laboured through a pair of iron gates and up a small gulley past a meadow where sheep were grazing. The pump jacks bobbed up and down like giant birds pecking the earth. Next to the pump jacks stood one of the wooden oil derricks my great-grandfather had used and an old field house. The car motored slowly through a stand of oaks and passed under a cloth banner that said: VIDAL OIL — THE LONGEST OIL SERVING COMPANY IN THE WORLD! A moment later, the Packard's engine hiccupped twice and we came to a rolling stop in front of the Great House, which Old Mac had built in 1890 for my great-grandmother, who died after giving birth late in life to my grandmother, Big Louie. The sheep grazing on the grassy slope down to Bear Creek stopped to look at us; and, for a moment, I sat there staring, trying to take it all in. Not far from Big Louie's home, my great-grandfather had sailed upstream on his lumber scow, looking for the gushers that lay at the headwaters of the local creeks. What would he think if he could travel through time and meet us? Would he be shocked that Big Louie said he found gold in the muck he came from?

Big Louie and her housekeeper, Willa, sat fanning themselves on the front porch, while Maurice, the real chauffeur, weeded the lawn.

"Out of gas, kids?" Big Louie laughed.

Clutching my notebook with the first and only page of my composition, I wriggled off the seat, and walked over to my grandmother, hoping Max wouldn't see me limping.

"Is this what I think it is, favourite grandchild?" Big Louie asked when I held up the notebook.

"Yes, but it's not done yet."

"Why not, Dearie?"

"The Bug House boys threw it away. I saved the first page, though."

My grandmother's face fell. But she was no longer looking at me. She was watching Max approach with Uncle Willie. My aunt was coming our way too, walking behind the two men, her head down.

"Hello, Max," Big Louie said in an unfriendly tone. Max bowed, sweeping his arm in front of him the way he had for my aunt.

"You don't mind, do you Mother?" Uncle Willie said. "Max had some business in town today."

"And that's why he wore Maurice's uniform, I suppose," my grandmother said sarcastically. "Really, Max, you have the nerve of a canal horse."

"It was just for a laugh," Max replied nervously while Uncle Willie's camera whirred in our ears.

"That's right, Mother. Nobody likes a laugh more than you. Now curtsy, why don't you? You too, Mary," Uncle Willie shouted. "And pick us a few flowers."

Big Louie stiffened disdainfully and tapped my shoulder. We curtsied together, and sauntered through the pergola, admiring the climbing roses threaded through the trellis. Then we strolled on to her cutting garden. Big Louie handed me a pair of scissors. "Mouse, you know how I do my flowers, don't you?"

Of course I knew. I was to give her the flowers one by one and she'd arrange them in her hand exactly as she wanted them to look in her vase. All year round, the artistry of Big Louie's bouquets dominated the Great House: sprays of moose berries in October; in November, pots of cyclamen; December, paper whites in iron bowls filled with plum pudding stones from Lake Huron; forced forsythia branches in February; and on it went until the daffodils. In every season, my grandmother placed only small *boule* vases on the dining table so the guests could see each other's faces. Big Louie pointed at a Jerusalem lily. "See the huge bee crawling inside? Women are like these lilies and men are the bees who want to get their honey." I was aware my grandmother was acting in a forced and exaggerated manner.

"Mom, what are you telling Mary?" my aunt asked. "I hate it when you talk about me behind my back."

"You've got the wrong idea, Dearie. I was telling Mary that you're in your prime like these lilies and plenty of bees want your honey. If you give them half a chance."

Little Louie eyed her feet, frowning.

"Stop blathering, Mother," Uncle Willie called from the other side of the pergola. "Put your arms around Mary and Little Louie. Pretend I'm not here. Act natural. That shouldn't be hard for you."

Big Louie snorted. "Isn't Willie clever, Mary? He's going to be a great director one day, aren't you, Willie?"

"Yes, of course, old girl," Uncle Willie said. "If you'll pay my way to film school in California. Now back to the house for some shots with Willa."

The three of us walked slowly across the lawn, trying to look relaxed for the camera. The whirring noise stopped. "Oh, dang it," Uncle Willie called. "I've run out of film."

"You must be hungry, Mary. Willa has your dinner ready." My grandmother planted my hand inside Willa's papery fist. Holding my breath in anticipation, I followed Willa into the Great House. When the tall wooden door swung open, I took off my Lone Ranger hat and stared down the hall; the dark wainscoting had been made from the oaks on Old Mac's property. To the left was the music room where Big Louie practised on the grand piano and Uncle Willie used to take boxing lessons from a retired American champion and, before that, his singing classes with one of Big Louie's friends. Uncle Willie started hobbies the way Willa planted seeds for my grandmother's vegetables; when he grew tired of his latest craze, his hobbies sickened and died like Willa's beans if she forgot to water them.

In front of me rose the grand staircase with its hand-carved banisters and family portraits. Five people could walk abreast up the staircase to the ballroom where orchestras from New York played on New Year's Eve. If the guests didn't feel like walking, they could take Big Louie's elevator to the third floor. She installed it after Old Mac died, because she knew he would never have tolerated such extravagance. Smiling to myself, I walked over to look at the painting of Old Mac in his quilted dressing gown. He never wore anything but that dressing gown after he was banished to the third floor where Willa looked after him. My grandmother claimed he used to shout at them to turn down the gramophone and they didn't consider a party any good unless Old Mac threatened to call the police.

On the walls by the staircase were more interesting pictures. Framed photographs of bearded men tromping down on the log treadles of old oil wells, which was how they pumped oil then, and more photographs of the same men, clean-shaven and wearing pith helmets, drilling for oil in Borneo as well as photographs of Petrolia when its office buildings were made of wood. There were also black-and-white photographs of burned-down buildings after the big fire in Petrolia in 1867, along with pictures of the Imperial Oil Company Refinery when it was just a shack on the main street. There were photographs of Big Louie with her husband, Reginald Barrett, the notorious rumrunner and father of her children. Reginald Barrett kept bathtub gin in the Vidals' unused oil wells, where the police couldn't find it. Nobody could prove he was breaking the law, although he was shot dead in a speakeasy on the St. Clair River. My grandmother suspected a temperance reformer had done it. In their wedding portrait, he and Big Louie stood on the lawn of the Great House in the middle of a long line of smiling men in dark suits and women dressed in flapper skirts. My grandmother, the woman with the thin arched eyebrows and laughing mouth, was pointing at a sign hanging from a striped awning on the verandah: THE NEW MR. AND MRS. OF OILY MANOR.

There were photographs of my mother, Alice, and Little Louie as girls, but I didn't look at any of those. I turned instead to my fave, the large oil painting of my great-grandfather's lumber scow sailing out of the oil slick on Lake St. Clair. The name of the painting was *Black Ship* and the boat's hull was coloured a dark, oily black. Unfortunately, the stubby-looking boat was not a real lumber schooner, but a canal boat like the kind my great-grandfather sailed when he was a young man. It had a fat round stern and small bowsprit because the artist had painted a cannaller by mistake. Big Louie said the mistake didn't matter. The painting was allegorical. My great-grandfather wanted to depict himself heading into sunnier climes.

"Do you think it's inspiring, Willa?"

"It's just a picture," Willa said. She had set up a card table for me on the back verandah overlooking the oil wells. I loved to watch the pump jacks bob up and down, and to hear the creak of the wooden jerker rods that snaked across the meadow to the field house where a giant spider wheel supplied the power to pump the oil out of the ground. The jerker rods creaked, rain or shine, and the noise was so constant that no one heard it; or smelled the stink of crude oil coming from Bear Creek. If a visitor complained, Big Louie said, "I can't smell anything but money."

After I finished Willa's pork chops and scalloped potatoes, Willa sent me upstairs to bed. I crept into the sewing room to pay my respects to the dressmaker dummy, which had been cast in papier maché from Big Louie's body when she was forty-five. It was standing next to Big Louie's Vibro Slim machine with its leather belt that fit around your waist and shook you senseless. The dummy's stout contours asserted Big Louie's voluptuous proportions, but its headless torso, not to mention its missing legs, hinted that it had suffered a tragic dismembering. Looking at the huge, shiny breasts and rounded stomach, I imagined the dummy flying on invisible legs through the rooms of the Great House before stopping to open my door and whisper: *Big Louie is the ruler here. If you don't do what she says, she will banish you from her world of pleasure.*

I wished good night to the dummy and, trying to contain my excitement, I hurried to my bedroom where I removed the grille from a heating vent in the floor. The chatter of the adults drifted up to me. "Oh, go on with you, Willie." Big Louie laughed. "Get me another goddamn gin!" The tinkle of someone playing the piano floated upwards, too, and the high, silvery timbre of my grandmother's voice lingering on the verse: "Oh, my darling Clementine. You are lost and gone forever, dreadful sorry, Clementine ..." Uncle Willie made fake sobbing sounds as if he was part of the melodramatic chorus. My aunt and Big Louie laughed. I couldn't hear Max, my aunt's friend. I went to the window. Outside Maurice was polishing the antique Packard, his shirtsleeves rolled up. He had waited until the cool of the evening to do the hardest work. Overhead, the moon was almost full, and huge oaks by the Great House were throwing spidery shadows across the lawn. The shadows made me think of John, and I wondered if he was somewhere out there in the darkness, heading for the American border. The thought gave me a thrill. To protect him, I whispered my favourite nursery verse: "How many miles to Babylon? Three score and ten. Can I get there by candlelight? Aye, and back again. If your feet are nimble and light, you'll get there by candlelight." Well, John's feet were nimble all right. Smiling to myself, I went back to the vent. Downstairs, they had stopped singing and my grandmother said: "I hear that Pilkie man escaped again."

"Yes, he did," my aunt replied. "And he's headed our way."

"Oh kids, I hope not," Big Louie said. "The radio said he's going to Windsor."

"I read about him tying a guard to a block of ice," Uncle Willie said. "And threatening to kill him, too."

"With a kitchen knife," my aunt replied. "Sib told Sal about it this morning. The local people are terrified."

"The late edition of one of the Toronto papers has printed a letter from him. He wants a review of his case," Uncle Willie exclaimed.

"Don't talk nonsense," my grandmother said.

"Not so fast, Mom. Let me read you his letter." On the floor below, Uncle Willie cleared his throat: "'Escaped Killer Pilkie Demands Justice for Mental Patients.' That's the headline. Here's what Pilkie wrote: 'Dear editor: I am writing your newspaper to ask if a parole board will review my case. I have been in asylums for almost thirteen years after I received two concussions while playing hockey. Today I no longer suffer the effects of the blows that affected my judgment and caused me to harm my wife and child. Cold-blooded criminals get their cases reviewed by a parole board but I have no hope of release. Once a person is sent to an asylum, we stay until we die. Sincerely yours, John Pilkie, former defence man for the Detroit Red Wings.'"

"You mean his injury caused the murder?" Big Louie asked. "That's a good one."

"Lots of people get concussions and they don't murder their family," Uncle Willie replied. "But look, mother. You're in the paper too." He read out an announcement about several prominent Petrolia families bringing out their old cars for my grandmother's celebration of Vidal Oil. Among the cars was the 1929 Packard belonging to the Vidals.

"It says your Packard cost $28,000 when it was ordered from Detroit," Uncle Willie said.

"I wish they hadn't mentioned how much it cost," my grandmother said. "I don't want somebody like Pilkie driving off with my Packard."

Pressing my mouth against the heating vent grille, I shouted: "He won't steal your car. It doesn't run properly."

"You're right there, Dearie!" Big Louie shouted back, laughing.

"Well, if Pilkie shows up, you can talk him out of it. Will you do that for me?" She didn't wait for me to say yes. "Now go back to bed and close those big ears of yours."

Their voices faded. A few minutes later, someone came up the stairs. I slipped back into bed and pulled up the covers. The door squeaked open. "Are you still awake, Mary?" my aunt whispered. For a moment, I considered telling her John's knife was blunt. But I knew better. I kept my eyes closed and faked sleep.

17

THERE WAS ANOTHER STORY ABOUT JOHN IN THE MORNING PAPER. It described Dr. Shulman's liberal policies towards the mentally ill in Madoc's Landing and explained how the town council objected to Dr. Shulman removing the bars from the rooms of the harmless patients. On the front page, they'd reprinted an old photograph of Dr. Shulman from *The Chronicle*, which showed Ben's father standing beside a twenty-foot-high pile of steel bars, the ones taken down on his orders. According to the Toronto newspaper, Dr. Shulman claimed that the bars and locks were still on the cells of the killers in Maple Ridge, so there was no reason to blame his policies for John's escape.

The newspaper also ran a picture of John in his Red Wings uniform. He looked young, like a boy I might pass on the street playing road hockey. His hair stood up in an oily pompadour and his big eyes were dark and shiny under his brows. The photo caption read: "The hockey killer once bragged that he will spring himself from any jail that dares to hold him." I was so startled by the sight of John and Dr. Shulman appearing together on the front page of a Toronto newspaper that I almost didn't notice the story about Able, the rhesus monkey, who died from an infected electrode scientists had placed in his chest. At least Able made it back to terra firma. At least he didn't die alone in space like Laika, the Soviet dog.

I took the newspaper story to Uncle Willie in his private quarters above the old carriage shed. Uncle Willie had on the smoking jacket my great-grandfather wore in his portrait. Willa had taken it in so it would fit him.

"Your highness, I've been expecting you. Willa left some extra breakfast for you." He waved at a tray stacked with rusty brown pieces of toast and glass jars of creamy-looking butter and marmalade. "Homemade, Mary," he said. "Try some. Nobody makes jam better than Willa."

I applied myself wolfishly to the rest of Uncle Willie's breakfast, stuffing down the toast. My uncle climbed out of bed and joined me. Willa had made bran muffins, too, and Uncle Willie smeared one with double helpings of jam and butter and gulped it down.

"There's more about John Pilkie in the morning paper," I began. "Did you see it?"

"I saw it," he said. "Mary, let's forget about the hockey killer for a moment. Do you think Little Louie is mad at me for bringing Max yesterday?"

"I don't think so. She was only pretending to be mad, because she didn't know what else to do."

Uncle Willie threw back his head and laughed like anything.

"Is Max your friend, too?"

"Yes. Max and I used to play hooky from school together. Then Max started studying so he could go to university. Not me. I'm hopeless, you know. I can't work under the direction of other people."

"Why not?" I asked.

"Has anyone said you ask too many questions?"

"Yes, lots of times. What were John Pilkie's relatives like? Were they nice?"

"You don't quit, do you, kid? The Pilkies were God-fearing, hardworking people, like most of us old families in southern Ontario. Self-righteous, too, and opinionated. We think we know best. It's a terrible feeling."

"I suppose it is," I said.

"But never mind the Pilkies, Mary. I want to show you my new project." Uncle Willie fished out a typed-up manuscript from a box under his bed. "Here's my film script. I'm sending it with my application to a college in the United States." He sat on his bed and watched while I read its opening paragraph:

HARD OILING WITH THE VIDALS:
A FAMILY HISTORY

Scene One: Reginald Barrett and Big Louie (Vidal) Barrett on the ocean liner, The Princess Mary:

Voice Over: How did a Yankee canal boy named Mac Vidal become as rich as Midas? What role did he play in developing the oilfields of Enniskillen, which supplied ninety per cent of Canada's oil at the turn of the twentieth century? Let us start at the end of the saga, with his descendants, the modern prodigals.

Scene One: Two figures walk down the deck of an ocean liner while "Claire de Lune" plays on the soundtrack.

The male figure tips his hat to the camera. Now the female figure, wearing an evening gown and long gloves, throws her diamond bracelet into the sea. The man claps and both walk triumphantly towards the camera until they block out the lens. These are the prodigals, the carefree children of the pioneers who spend money like water. From shirtsleeves to shirtsleeves in three generations, as the saying goes.

"Big Louie won't like you saying she spends money like water."

"The old girl has a sense of humour," Uncle Willie replied. "That's the best thing about her. Besides, she'll look like royalty when I'm finished."

I wasn't so sure, although Big Louie didn't need Uncle Willie's movie camera to playact. "Can I ask you something else, Uncle Willie?"

"Well, okay," he said. "Shoot."

"Did your friend Max break Little Louie's heart?"

"I bet Mother told you that. But yes, it's a mess all right. He's married to someone else now."

"Will Max leave his wife for Little Louie?"

"Who knows? Little Louie is no pushover." Uncle Willie frowned. "It's the damnedest thing. If you tell my sister not to jump off a cliff, she'll do it. She's a real chip off the old block."

"You mean Old Mac?"

"No, I mean Big Louie. Those two women are a force of nature. You will be one day, too." When Uncle Willie saw my surprise, he squeezed my hand and we stared out the window at my grandmother's garden, where the morning breeze was making the big, white globes of the mopheads bob up and down beside their kissing cousins, the pink skullcap hydrangeas. What Uncle Willie said made me hopeful, even though I was not yellow-haired and big-boned like the women in my mother's family. I was short and thin and so undeveloped for my age that people thought I was younger than I was. To make matters worse, my hair was the same boring brown shade as Morley's dead mother, Mrs. Phyllis Bradford. I looked like my nickname, Mouse, and there wasn't a thing I could do about it.

WILLA THOUGHT I WAS IN bed asleep, but instead I stood in my pyjamas on the upstairs balcony pretending to be my great-grandfather spying on one of Big Louie's parties. From this vantage point, it was easy to see why Old Mac felt neglected. Like me, he was left out of family celebrations. I was too young, and he was too old. By the time he died, he was coming up to his third year of triple digits.

Across the lawn, the evening sun shimmered hot and low through the oaks, catching the guests in splashes of golden light. Big Louie stood on the front step handing out corsages made of the small onions, radishes, and parsley that Willa and I had put together from instructions in the *Matinee Party Guide*. My grandmother's voice floated up above the noise of her guests laughing about their silly corsages. She was telling them the radishes were specially shipped from Detroit, and her guests pretended to ooh and ah as they enjoyed my grandmother's joke. When the band played "I've Got a Lovely Bunch of Coconuts" my grandmother took Uncle Willie's arm and headed over to the tennis court, where people were dancing. I couldn't help admiring how the sun lit up the dark blue sequins on

Big Louie's dress. It also caught on Uncle Willie's wristwatch and the hood ornaments of the cars: a 1922 Chevrolet Coupe and a 1927 Cadillac. The Vidal Packard was parked in a special place by the carriage shed, and the sunshine glowing on its hood and white walled tires showed off Maurice's handiwork. I imagined Queen Elizabeth swanning around in the car with President Eisenhower and Mamie as photographers crowded them, flash bulbs popping.

Behind the old cars rose the oil derrick and field house and still more exhibits from the early days of oil that had been moved to the lawn for my grandmother's party. There was a tall oil wagon with high wooden wheels as well as several giant steam kettles used by my great-grandfather to refine crude oil. Only their spouts could be seen. The rest of the kettles were hidden by the stand of cedar trees near the carriage shed. Then I caught a movement by the cedars. My mouth fell open. John Pilkie was coming round the corner of the carriage shed, wearing his chocolate brown fedora. His face was hidden under the brim of his hat. I couldn't be absolutely sure it was him, but he walked with the same swagger, toes out, shoulders high. He had on tall rubber boots, which looked strange in the heat. He jiggled the handle of the Packard's door, hunching his shoulders as if he didn't want anybody to see what he was doing. The door opened and he leaned across the seat, looking for something. Suddenly, I knew what it was. He was looking for the key so he could drive off with the Packard. I considered yelling for my grandmother but she wasn't anywhere to be seen. *Remember your promise*, Hindrance whispered. *If it's Pilkie, you have to talk him out of stealing her car.*

Without worrying about what Willa would say, I took Big Louie's elevator down to the first floor and tramped as fast as

I could through my grandmother's petunia beds. It was still humid and my leg brace felt heavy and hot against my pyjama leg. Soon I was almost at the carriage shed, where the intruder stood brushing lint off his trousers. He glanced up and saw me. Before I could say hello, he disappeared into the cedars.

Unfortunately, the darkness was thickening in the oak woods and I could no longer see the ant holes with the sandy moustache rings around their burrows. Should I get Uncle Willie? But what if the man was John? I took a few more steps and somebody coughed, a hollow wheezing expunging of air. John had coughed the same way in our kitchen on Whitefish Road.

"Is that you, Mr. Pilkie?" I called. "If it's you, I won't tell. Cross my heart and point to heaven." Overhead, a nighthawk screeched as it landed on a cedar, making the branches quiver. Or was the stranger making the cedar shake? I took a gulp of air and cried, "You have to get away from here as fast as you can! Promise?" The coughing started again. It went on and on and ended in a long, bronchial whistling. I knew what my father would say — "Too many cigarettes."

Nearby, the oil exhibits looked bigger and creepy in the evening shadows, and the fusty smell of Big Louie's petunias pushed over to me from the garden. Summoning up my nerve, I yelled, "I am truly sorry Sib Beaudry was mean to you but you have to go — now!" Why didn't he answer? Was he mad at me for drawing attention to him? There was a new rustling sound and the cedars started shaking again. Now I understood. John was angry and he was going to strangle me with his bare hands. Putting my weight on my good leg, I humped myself off, listening for the tromp-tromp of his footsteps. "Hurry, Hindrance," I whispered. "Don't let him catch us." The rustling sound grew louder. Behind me, a male voice said my name with a question mark behind it. I whirled around. Maurice was smiling down at me.

"John Pilkie is stealing the Packard!" I cried.

Maurice smiled. "Willa's looking for you," he said.

I narrowed my eyes trying to decide what to do, and Hindrance whispered cunningly: *Mouse Bradford, only you can save the day.* Mollified, I limped over to warn Big Louie's guests.

18

AT FIRST, NOBODY NOTICED ME. THE DANCERS FLEW ROUND AND round the tennis court to the "Beer Barrel Polka." How could I tell anyone about John stealing the Packard when they sped by me so fast? A dejected-looking Max stood at the bar with a red-haired woman who had linked her arm tightly with his. As soon as Max saw me watching them, he turned away, embarrassed. I looked around for Little Louie, but she had disappeared. Later, I found out she had hid in her bedroom for most of the party to avoid meeting Max's wife. While I stood wondering what to do, my grandmother emerged from a group of guests. "You got out of bed, Mary." Her eyes lit on my pyjamas. "Is something wrong?"

"Yes, something is terribly wrong," I replied, struggling to keep my voice steady. "John Pilkie is stealing your car."

Big Louie did a double take. "Where, Dearie? Where is he?"

"He's by the carriage shed. Hurry."

Big Louie took my hand and shouted, "Everyone stay where they are! There's an intruder on the grounds!" Frightened whispers rippled through the crowd. "Is it the hockey killer? A voice asked. "It's Mad Killer Pilkie! I saw him on the driveway," somebody answered. A woman cried: "I want to go home!" "Nobody's going anywhere until we find out where he is," Big Louie announced in a firm, calm voice. She told Uncle Willie and Maurice to search the grounds, while Big Louie stared down anyone who tried to leave.

A few minutes later, Uncle Willie and Maurice came towards us with a man in a brown fedora and rubber boots. "Mary, is this who you saw?" Uncle Willie asked. I nodded, and a look of relief passed across my grandmother's face. "Donald is Maurice's brother," my grandmother said. She turned to her guests. "False alarm!" she cried. "Strike up the band." Then she noticed my mortified face. "No harm done, Dearie," she whispered, squeezing my hand. "But it's time for bed."

MY GRANDMOTHER TUCKED THE SHEETS around my shoulders, her face pink from the effort of climbing the stairs. "Tell me why you thought it was Pilkie," she asked in an interested voice.

"It sounded like him. His cough, I mean."

"You thought it was Pilkie because you heard a man cough?"

"He had on a brown fedora and John wears one too ..."

"You call him John, do you? Well, it wasn't him, was it? It was Donald relieving himself in the bushes. He said you were talking a lot of nonsense about John Pilkie before you ran off."

My mouth went dry. "I ... I told him to run away."

My grandmother sank down on the bed beside me, her eyes soft. "Forbidden fruit tastes sweet, doesn't it? But look here. I can't cope with Little Louie and you falling for the wrong men. All right, Dearie?" She stood up, yawning, and stretched, the lamplight glowing on the ripeness of her heavy breasts, her calves still shapely below the hem of her dress.

"I was wrong about John," I burst out. "He would never steal your car. And he's kind too. He rescued me from the Bug House boys."

"Ssssh. Not another peep out of you. Now go to sleep." She left, and I lay there mulling over what Big Louie said. She compared my interest in John to Little Louie's feelings for Max. The thought shocked me. The idea of S-E-X with anyone felt embarrassing, like the bloody wads Sal wrapped with toilet paper and hid in the garbage. Sal called having her period coarse names like "the curse" or "going on the rag." Yet the napkins were behind Little Louie and Sal's appeal. Women had some secret thing men needed, and this gory affair made men want to love and protect them. Would John Pilkie want me if I started having periods, too?

When I was sure Big Louie was gone, I stole a sanitary napkin from a box under her bathroom sink and stuffed the bulky napkin into a pair of underpants, fastening its ends with a belt I had found in the box. Then I walked around the bedroom closing my eyes and willing my body to spill over with blood so I could be a capital W-O-M-A-N instead of a N-O-N–B-L-E-E-D-E-R (i.e., N.B.). But how would the blood come out? Like the drip-drip-drip of a leaky tap? Or would it pour forth like the flood waters in Genesis chapter six, verse seventeen, drenching everything with Biblical slime? Or would it go glug-glug-glug like honey from an upside down jar? I walked around concentrating, but after an hour and forty-five minutes of hard thinking, nothing happened. So I shredded the napkin, pulling off the spidery layer of gauze to see what was underneath and all I found was a lump of soft material that looked like cotton batten or Kleenex.

AT BREAKFAST THE NEXT MORNING, Big Louie didn't scold me. "My guests will talk about the party for years," my grandmother said. "Anyway, I was the one who joked about Pilkie stealing my car. I should never have said that in front of the child."

Uncle Willie laughed. "Mary's imagination ran away with her."

"*Quelle surprise*, huh?" Little Louie winked at me and I dropped my eyes so I couldn't see them smiling their heads off.

"Mouse, I don't want to hear that man's name again!" my grandmother said. "Do you understand?"

"I guess so." I kept my eyes lowered. My grandmother could make me promise not to talk about John but she couldn't stop me from hearing about him. There'd been several Pilkie sightings. When Big Louie wasn't around, Uncle Willie read the newspaper stories out to Little Louie and me at meal times. One day he was spotted in Detroit — the next, in Dearborn, Michigan. Uncle Willie said if he were Pilkie, he would escape to the American side, where he'd support himself folding clothes in a Port Huron laundromat. I doubted Uncle Willie would be any good at folding clothes, but I didn't argue because it was a relief to know that John was still at large.

19

ON AUGUST 7, THE POLICE CAPTURED JOHN AT MITCHELL'S BAY, the fishing village where my great-grandfather anchored after his schooner ran into the oil slick. August 7 was also the day the United States launched Explorer 6 from Cape Canaveral; the story about John was on page two, so fortunately, there were plenty of photos of John and Mitchell's Bay, which was so small you could count the houses: twelve along with three fishing lodges and a motel sign that read, BASS FISHING AND DUCK HUNTING. The black-and-white photographs showed the beach where he was apprehended. Beyond lay the reedy sand-bar where Pilkie went into the water when he tried to escape the cops.

Of course, it wasn't just the Petrolia paper that ran a story on him. *The Detroit Free Press* also covered his capture. John was acquiring the kind of fame that drove reporters to stay up all night composing sentences that inflamed the imaginations of readers like me. *The Detroit Free Press* described him wading out into the lake to avoid the police. When he realized he was trapped, the newspaper reported that he raised his arms like an

Old Testament prophet and the crowd on the shore applauded. I could see the scene as clearly as if I had been there myself: The shallow lake, dead calm and hot as bathwater. The sun roasting everyone's faces, while he wades farther and farther from the crowds on the shore, the water no higher than his waist.

On the shore, the policemen wait, their hands on their holsters.

He dives into the lake. For a few minutes, there isn't a ripple. Then a head breaks the surface, and he stands up, water streaming down his face and chest. He raises his arms in surrender and a woman screams, "Hi, Gentleman Jack!" He blows her a kiss and walks back to shore as if he's wading through molasses, wearing the same smile he gave me when he rescued me from the Bug House boys.

In my imagination, he looked triumphant, but when I stared at the newspaper photograph that showed him leaving the beach, his head down, he appeared discouraged, as if he expected them to lock him up and throw away the key. I thought of his words that afternoon by the icehouse: "Don't let the turkeys get you down." Did he have any hope of getting his case reviewed? The *Detroit Free Press* said that he intended to keep pleading his cause from inside the asylum, and that made me feel a little better.

ON THE LAST NIGHT OF our holiday, my aunt was talking in low tones to Max in the parlour below my bedroom. Per usual, I listened through the heating vent. At first I couldn't understand a word, because Max was playing the piano while they talked. His voice drifted up to me, singing the song my aunt liked: "List while I woo thee with soft melody. Gone are the cares of life's busy throng. Beautiful dreamer, wake unto me!" He sang the chorus two more times. He didn't use the same fake melodramatic voice that Uncle Willie did when he sang "Clementine." He sounded serious and sad; Little Louie didn't laugh. I put my eye to the iron grille of the vent and saw the orange light from my grandmother's Tiffany lamps shining on their blond heads. How natural my aunt and Max looked together. With their bright hair and tall, athletic bodies, they could have been brother and sister and something else, although I had no idea what that something else was. Now the piano stopped. Max tilted up Little Louie's chin and kissed her while his other hand disappeared inside her blouse. I imagined it roving like a fox snake across my aunt's bare skin. (To be honest, I didn't know if Little Louie went around without a brassiere, but my grandmother never wore them or underpants either because Big Louie was a freedom-loving flapper.)

"Don't touch me like that," my aunt said and jerked away.

He groaned. "You know how I feel about you."

"Then why are you with her?"

"Louie, I can't walk out on her when she's pregnant. It's not right."

"Your child's not going to thank you for staying in a bad situation. Not when he grows up. Your child will think you were unfair to yourself."

"I'm aware of that. But what else can I do? Please try to understand my situation, darling."

Little Louie raised her voice. "I don't want to understand. And I won't, either. You got yourself into this situation. Now get yourself out of it!"

Down the hall, a door opened. Heavy footsteps followed.

Leaning over the banister, my grandmother shouted, "Who's making that racket? I'm trying to sleep. Did you hear me, Little Louie?"

"I heard you," my aunt called.

Satisfied, my grandmother disappeared down the hall, the floorboards shivering under her weight. A moment later, the front door closed and my aunt began slowly coming up the stairs. I peeked through the crack in the door and caught a glimpse of her face. She looked as lonely as a person could look and frightened, too.

The next morning, my aunt and I kissed Big Louie goodbye and the two of us set off for home in our station wagon, my aunt's face glum. She drove chewing Wrigley's gum and didn't offer a stick to me. Finally, I asked for a piece. "Why didn't you speak up sooner?" my aunt asked. "Too much pride, huh?" She smiled slightly when I nodded and gave me a stick of Wrigley's. Then she didn't say another word for hours. I figured that she was worrying about Max and all the dumb things that made up her life back in Madoc's Landing.

PART THREE

RETURN TO THE NORTH

20

WE WERE BACK IN BREBEUF COUNTY. THE WIND FROM THE GREAT Bay blew its fresh damp smell in our faces as my aunt and I stood at the top of the headland facing Madoc's Landing. She said she wanted to put off our return for as long as she could, and I knew better than to pester her with questions.

Across the huge inlet, our town looked no bigger than a lone seed in a giant watermelon. You'd never know that people could live in the tiny houses lining the shore, or that somebody like me belonged to one of them. I imagined that I could see our house near the trees on Bug House hill, and that my father was there waiting for us, his calls done for the day. Maybe he, too, like my aunt and me, was looking at the horizon where the pale limestone tower of the Western Light lay in a hopeless muddle of shoals, twelve miles out in the open, as the open water was called. It made me happy to think about my father again and, before I knew it, I was telling my aunt about the generations of Bradford families who ran a fishing station near the lighthouse and brought the whitefish and lake trout over to Owen Sound, most of them never learning to swim. I wanted to cheer her up and make her love the Bay the way Morley and Ben and I loved it, and maybe the way John Pilkie loved it, too. For me, it was a deep-down feeling of lastingness that had to do with the water and the rocks. The Bay was closer than the stars, I explained, but every bit as remote and mysterious. It had the oldest exposed rocks in the world and its deep waters kept us cool in the humid summers of Brebeuf County. "The Great Refrigerator," as Morley called it. It was so much deeper and colder than the shallows of Lake St. Clair where John had been captured. Little Louie listened quietly, but when I told her that the Bay reached a depth of 540 feet near the entrance to Lake Huron, she shuddered. "Mary, deep water scares the heck out of me." She spoke in the sad, frustrated tone she had used with Max the night before. Then she climbed back in our car.

Stung, I got in too. If Morley or John were with me, they could have shown my aunt why the Bay was wonderful. They both grew up beside it, although you would be hard-pressed to find two more different men. They swam in its same cool depths, and felt the freshening of the same westerly winds. Morley and John were children of water, while my aunt came from a typical southwestern Ontario landscape with mile after mile of flat, furrowed fields. Like Morley and John, I was a child of water; I wondered if my aunt would ever be able to understand us.

I WOKE UP AS THE station wagon turned into our driveway, the broad shape of our house rising up out of the darkness. The yellow light from its windows spilled across the large lawn and illuminated the back of a man standing at our side door. The door faced the backyard, not the street, and there was something odd about him waiting at an entrance we didn't use. Morley's patients rarely came to our home after hours. When the man saw us, he pulled his fedora down to hide his face and ran off.

"He was one of Chief Doucette's officers," I whispered.

"Ssssh, not now," my aunt said. Squaring her shoulders, she walked up the kitchen steps, a suitcase in each hand.

I trailed after her, glad for the dark. I'd spent over seven hours in the car and Hindrance felt so stiff I had to drag my leg in a dumb half-limp-half-shuffle.

When he heard us, Morley rushed into the kitchen. "Make yourself a cup of cocoa, girls," he said before he hurried back into the living room. "I'm not ready for you."

Little Louie put down our suitcases, scowling, and lit a cigarette, while I peeked around the swing door. In the living room, Morley was sticking a needle into the arm of a man with a rolled-up sleeve. The man watched my father do it with a wondering, childlike expression. Then the man rolled down his sleeve and hurried out the side door. I ducked back into the kitchen.

"I left a message with Sal that we were coming home today," my aunt said as Morley came in.

Morley shook his head. "I didn't get it."

"What kind of shots were you giving the men?" I asked.

"Penicillin," Morley said. "The drug cures all sorts of diseases."

"And what disease do these men have?" my aunt said.

Morley hesitated. "It's not for young ears. And there's something else. I don't want you to speak of this to anyone."

My aunt's face registered shock. "All right, Dr. Bradford." Without another word, she took me upstairs to bed.

When my aunt went into her bedroom, I crept to the top of the back stairs and listened as somebody else came in by the side door. Perhaps it was the police officer who had been waiting outside, but I couldn't get a good look at the man's face. The patient didn't talk about what was wrong with him, and my father was careful not to mention it. The conversation was about the hockey season starting up in the fall, and I overheard my father say the Rats would do better this year. The Rats had lost the season before, but like all the hockey fans in Madoc's Landing, Morley was always hopeful the next year would be better.

Downstairs, the man said, "Pilkie pulled a knife on the guard."

"Pilkie wouldn't hurt anyone intentionally, son. The knife was blunt," my father replied.

Their voices faded away, and I hurried to my bedroom window in time to see a figure disappearing down the lane by our maple trees.

At breakfast Sal told Little Louie and me that the men had the love disease. "They get a shot every four hours. For thirty-six hours, eh? Or their noses will fall off."

"The love disease hurts you?" I asked.

Sal snickered. "You're too little, Lady Jane. When you get the curse, you'll find out soon enough."

I drew back as if Sal had struck me, and my aunt said quickly: "I realize Dr. Bradford means well. But I don't think this sort of thing is a good influence on Mary."

"Well, it's typical of Doc Bradford," Sal snapped. "He's the only doctor in town who'll get up in the night to give it to them."

"I guess Dr. Bradford can do no wrong," Little Louie said coldly. Then she went back to eating her soft-boiled egg. Sal started doing the dishes, making a lot of noise. I thought about telling them that one of Chief Doucette's officers had received a shot of penicillin from Morley. But I nixed the idea in case Little Louie told Sal about me imagining I saw John hiding in the cedars near the Great House. I didn't want Sal saying my imagination was running away with me again, although it usually did.

THE NEXT MORNING AT BREAKFAST, Morley announced that we were going on a picnic to the Western Light with Sib and Sal.

"It's time you took a look at paradise, Louisa," Morley said. "There's nothing else like it."

"If you say so," Little Louie replied anxiously. My father didn't know that my aunt was afraid of water.

As for me, I had a hard time hiding my excitement. While I ate my cereal, I copied information about the lighthouse from *Hansen's Handbook to Georgian Bay* into *M.B's Book of True Facts*. "Our pioneer world was technically advanced," I told my aunt. "As early as 1857 the Western Light had a state-of-the-art Fresnel lens, shipped from Paris, France."

She looked up from her newspaper. "Stop pulling my leg, huh? Brebeuf County was never that sophisticated."

"It was, too." I gave Little Louie my haughtiest smile and she laughed. I didn't care. If the Ontario Psychiatric Hospital reflected the world of Madoc's Landing back to itself, the Western Light was the town's true north — a sign of constancy in times that kept changing. I felt glad that John was associated with something so mystical and beautiful.

21

THE DUST FLEW UP THE CAR WINDOWS AS WE SPED PAST FRENCH-
Canadian farms and their small roadside shrines sheltering tiny
Virgin Marys. Their sleepy faces and heavy-lidded eyes reminded
me of my aunt, except that Little Louie would be reading a
book, not holding Baby Jesus. Soon we left behind the stands
of reforested pine and dwarf apple trees growing wild, and the
highway dwindled to a sandy ridge of backcountry overgrown
with Shasta Daisies. In the distance, the shiny aluminum roofs
of French-Canadian barns mirrored back the cloudless sky. The
last barn belonged to the Beaudrys, whose red brick farmhouse
overlooked the Bay. When he wasn't working at the Bug House,
Sib grew corn along with Christmas trees in its sandy soil. In
the winter, he drove his scoot across the ice delivering supplies
to the reserve on the Île au Géant, and on weekends, Sal cooked
for Sib and his father, Old Man Beaudry.

The front door opened and Sal came out carrying a picnic
basket. "Well, look who you meet when you don't have your
gun." She climbed into the back seat beside me. Our car careened
bumpily down the old logging road to the ferry dock. My father

parked near Towanda Lodge, where its caretaker, Old Man Beaudry, lived. Unable to restrain myself, I shouted, "Hooray! We're going to see John Pilkie's old home!"

"Did he really live in such a godforsaken place?" Little Louie asked.

"Yes," Morley replied. "But it's a beautiful spot, Louisa. Wait 'til you see it."

"And you helped Mr. Pilkie operate on John's appendix," I pointed out.

"Who told you that story, Mary?" Morley said.

"I guess I did." Sal nodded. "I didn't mean any harm, Doc Bradford. Maybe you could tell us how you did it, eh?" Morley scowled as if he was going to chew Sal out, and then he thought better of it. "I'll tell you about it later. Out at the light."

"You knew the murderer?" Little Louie asked. "Was he always violent?"

"I knew John when he was a little boy. Some of us think he was punch-drunk after he was hit on the head."

Little Louie looked skeptical while I listened, rapt, wondering if I should pinch myself. Morley had confirmed it — John didn't mean to throw the match that started the fire.

"Looks like some people are waiting to see you," Sal told my father. On the porch of Towanda Lodge, six pregnant women sat in rocking chairs waiting for Morley, who was known in Brebeuf County for predicting when a baby would arrive. He was like a dowser, Sal said. He knew to the day and sometimes the hour when the baby was going to come. The women stood up as my father approached, their stomachs hidden under layers of clothing even though it was summer and hot.

"I'll just be a few minutes," Morley called apologetically. He hurried inside, and the women went in after, their faces wearing the expression I often saw on the faces of my father's patients. The adjective "adoring" comes to mind.

ABOVE OUR HEADS, THE LIMESTONE tower rose up between two high, lichen-covered granite humps while around us, in every direction, stretched the calm waters of the Bay. The gears on Sib's inboard began to grind, and there was a gurgling noise as Sib reversed into the harbour. When he turned off the motor, we heard nothing except the sound of waves washing against rocks. Who would guess that John had grown up in such a lonely place? Only to kill his wife and child? Of course, he wasn't a true killer. Morley as much as said so.

Under the hot August sun, the five of us climbed out of the launch. My father clamped his hand on my neck, gripping me hard. I was aware of him breathing slow and deep, as if he was more exhausted than he was letting on. Chances are the heat was getting to him, since we no longer had the breeze from the motorboat to cool us. Or maybe my father's mind was still back with the pregnant women at Towanda Lodge. I had no way of knowing what was going on in his head. We followed Sal and my aunt across the scorching rocks. Underfoot, the granite felt dense as iron, and the rocks were slippery with lichen the colour of light green spearmint gum. Sal kept sneaking glances at my aunt, who had on a sundress and high wedge heels. Little Louie was having a hard time keeping her balance.

"What did you wear heels for?" Sal asked. "Only cijits walk on the rocks on those things."

"What's a cijit?" my aunt asked.

"City idiot," Sal said. My father chuckled. Sal threw him a mollified glance and my aunt flushed. At that moment, Sib appeared on the rocks below, holding a pair of sunglasses and calling my aunt's name. Surprised, Little Louie whirled around and the strap of her sundress fell off her shoulder, exposing half her breast. Sib put his fingers between his teeth and whistled, and my aunt quickly pushed the strap back up, her cheeks darkening in a self-conscious blush, as if it was she, and not him, who had done something wrong. I was struck by how unsure of herself she seemed. She quickly took the dark glasses from Sib and hurried after Sal while Morley and I followed along behind. Suddenly, nothing felt the same.

It occurs to me now that the atmosphere was charged with sexual tension. Everything had changed because my aunt's strap had fallen down in the bright, fierce light of the August sun. In that instant the grown-ups felt free of the mainland, where life unfolded in respectable rituals, and I wondered if my aunt and Sal realized that walking ahead gave my father and Sib the chance to admire their backsides. You couldn't see much of my aunt's bottom in her pretty sundress, but Sal's heart-shaped rump was evident in her worn jeans. The sight of the two women, so different from each other, made me thoughtful. My fair-haired aunt, with her powerful, loping strides was more beautiful; but there was something appealing about Sal, who was shorter and thicker, and the saucy way she looked about her, tossing her thick, dark hair. I admired their feminine curves, and my own body, with its straight angles, felt like a crude approximation of theirs. To be honest, I looked like a stick drawing of a girl. Paste on a narrow face with a lopsided smile and that would be me, Mouse Bradford. I suspected Morley saw me as a disappointment, too. If I were his age, he would never choose somebody like me as his wife.

THE PILKIES MUST HAVE PLANTED a garden, because on either side of the pathway wild irises and day lilies grew inside circles of whitewashed rocks. By the door of the old lighthouse stood two wizened apple trees, their stunted boughs hanging with baby green fruit. Sal and my aunt waited by the wooden ramp that led up to the house. "See that old thing?" Sal called, waving at a flagpole that lay flat on the ground. "John's father tied him up to it during a thunderstorm. I guess you could say he left John high and dry. Well, not so dry." Sal smiled knowingly and we all nodded. Sal had us in the grip of her storytelling powers now, and she was enjoying herself. "The waves were so big they sucked the water back, and John could see clear down to the bottom of the lake."

"Was John's father mean?" I asked.

"He was a no-good drunk, Mary," my father said, the bitter sound of his voice surprising me.

"That's right, eh? Roy Pilkie was soused when he drowned out here," Sal added. "His heavy boots pulled him down before anyone could save him. Say, Doc Bradford. Isn't that the coast guard?"

We turned and looked at a launch approaching the Western Light. When my father saw it, his mouth tightened and he looked worried.

"Guess we'd better see what they want, Sib," my father said. Sib nodded, and the two men started back down the rocks.

"Doc Bradford won't be long, Mouse," Sal said. To distract me, she pointed at a bright turquoise paddle that had been fashioned into a railing for the stairs up to the lighthouse. "Isn't that folksy? Jim Pilkie carved that paddle. Jim was good with his hands, I'll say that for him. He taught John to be good with his hands, too. That's why John knows how to rig up his escapes. Remember how he made a key out of a jam jar?"

"The jam jar key sounds like a yarn to me," my aunt replied without glancing at the railing. Sal's jaws worked angrily; but, instead of arguing, she pushed open the old door of the light-house, and we peered inside. Its windows were shuttered, except for a small pane of glass above the front door; the baking sun that filtered through its portal exposed a mudroom stacked with rubber wading boots and oil slickers. Stepping carefully around broken beer bottles, we entered the cool dark living room. Half-way across the creaking plank floor, Sal made us peek behind a canvas curtain at a pair of army cots. Old socks and shirts lay on the floor where they'd been tossed and the sheets on the cots had been chewed as if rats had been at them.

"This place needs a good going-over," Sal said. "I'm sure glad I don't have to clean it. See the clever way the shutters work, eh?" Sal pushed at some boards covering a window and the boards opened out, exposing sleeping bats that came to life and started climbing the glass with their tiny claws.

"Mary, over here!" my aunt called. "Look at these old photos." As my eyes adjusted to the dim light, I saw framed pictures of women in long summer dresses carrying parasols and men in rolled-up trousers holding up strings of fish. I thought of the photographs in the Great House, the oilmen at their rigs or outside their field houses, their faces dark with grease. Here was proof that the Western Light possessed a past, too.

I made my way over to a rotting sofa piled with faded orange life jackets and discarded fishing tackle. On a shelf above it were a Snakes-and-Ladders game and two old guidebooks that I'd never seen in Madoc's Landing stores: *All You Need to Know about Sports Fishing* and *How to Survive in the North*. I pulled down one of the guides and flipped through its foxed pages. It said that pioneers sometimes suffocated after bugs flew up their noses; but, more often, they died from cold. Its account of hypothermia caught my eye:

> If you fall into water sixty degrees or below, all efforts should be put into getting out as fast as possible or death will result. Symptoms include shivering, slurred speech, apathy, unsteadiness, skin blue-grey to the touch. Treatment: cover the victim's torso with hot cloths or place victim in hot bath, leaving out legs and arms to avoid After Drop, which occurs when the cold blood from the limbs is forced back into the torso, fatally lowering the body's temperature.

"Will you look at Lady Jane?" Sal laughed. "We're out at the Light and she sticks her nose in a book!"

I quickly put the book back and joined Sal and my aunt in the kitchen. "See that square?" Sal pointed at a faded outline on the oilcloth covering a shelf. "That's where the ship-to-shore used to sit."

"How do you know?" Little Louie asked.

"Mrs. Pilkie told me, that's how. Here's where Jim talked to Doc Bradford when John got his attack of appendix. And just look out there, eh? When the waves are high they hit the house." We looked down at the water lapping at the rocks. "And that's the table that John lay on. You can bet he was twitching." Sal laughed as our eyebrows flew up our foreheads. I closed my eyes, picturing a boy about to be cut open on the kitchen table and from an immense distance my father's voice booming instructions over the ship-to-shore radio ...

Sal shook my arm. "Got your head in the clouds again, Mouse? Better come along. There's more to see."

I followed Sal up the stairs, leaving my aunt to stare out the kitchen window. The Pilkies had lived in the old lighthouse as simply as some of the poorest families in Madoc's Landing, except that they were self-sufficient and proud of it. And besides, as Morley said, the Bay was paradise in the summer.

Upstairs, it was hotter and there were no hallways. One bedroom led to another as if the builder wanted to conserve space. There were no shutters on the windows; the August sun streamed through the ragged blinds. The room with the double bed was strewn with more dirty-looking clothes and newspapers. Sal said the room belonged to John's parents. There wasn't much furniture — just a chair and a few kerosene lamps with dusty glass mantles. As we walked into the second bedroom, Sal pointed at marks gouged in the wooden floor. "Their dog must have left these behind. Oh, oh." Sal glanced out the window, blowing out her cheeks. "I guess the coast guard needed Doc Bradford."

Down by the boathouse, Sib stood on the dock waving. My father waved back from the bow of the coast guard boat as it reversed slowly out the harbour. Sal put her hand on my shoulder and together we went back downstairs. "I guess we won't hear the story of John Pilkie's appendix today," I said sadly.

"Not this time, Lady Jane," Sal replied.

Yet Another Warning from Hindrance

Hindrance: Morley doesn't have time for a pipsqueak like you, Mouse.

Me: All fathers have time for their daughters, Hindrance.

Hindrance: Tell me another one. Now you think a concussion made John Pilkie crazy?

Me: Morley thinks it's possible and so do I.

Hindrance: Don't be a fool. A leopard doesn't change his spots.

Mouse: Well, I'm a fool then because I believe my father. He thinks there's a chance that John's concussion affected his judgment. Maybe it did.

Hindrance: Okay. I beg your pardon, I grant your grace. I hope the cat will scratch your face. Don't say I didn't warn you when the hockey killer carves you up like the Christmas turkey.

22

A MONTH LATER, AFTER I WAS BACK AT SCHOOL, I TOOK THE shortcut home. I heard the melancholy plink-plink of a harmonica drifting down from the maple trees. The harmonica was playing "Happy Trails to You." I was wearing my Lone Ranger cowboy hat. Startled, I gazed up into the clouds of yellow leaves; and, from somewhere in the branches, a man's voice called: "Howdy, cowgirl. Can't you see me?"

I craned my neck so far back my hat fell off. "Over here, eh?" When I looked in the direction of the voice, John Pilkie was grinning at me through the maple leaves. The frost had turned the trees a deep gold and the sunlight streaming through the yellow leaves seemed to be coming from him. The effect stopped my breath, and it struck me, staring up at him in the fall sunbeams, that human goodness was an emanation of light, and that Morley's light was so big and bright it washed over all us in Madoc's Landing. Like the sun, it shone on everybody, although it moved past me so fast it barely warmed my face. Of course, Morley's light had a long way to go. It had to stretch south to Lake Ontario and north up the wild shores of Georgian Bay. There were no limits to Morley's light except this physical limits of Morley himself. John's light, like the pool of sunshine by my feet, was only big enough to light up one or two people. But weren't most of us the same? We were kind to our family, and maybe a few others. Except that John had let his circle of light dwindle to almost nothing after he set his house ablaze.

"What are you doing up there?" I called.

Leaning over the branch, he pulled back his lips. Then he stuck his thumbs in his ears and waggled his tongue at me. "Guess I'm just being my crazy old self, eh?"

I froze. *Mouse Bradford,* Hindrance hissed, *You're alone in the woods with a cold-blooded murderer.*

Above me, he coughed his low, hollow cough. "Look, Mary, you're safe, eh? Sometimes I make bad jokes, okay?" When I dared to look at him again, his face was back to normal, and he pointed through the trees at a man standing by the hospital's maple sugar shack. Jordie Coverdale saw us looking. Raising his beer can at us, he disappeared inside.

"You remember Jordie? Well, Jordie treats me better than the other guards, so I play a tune or two to keep him happy. See if you know this one." He blew three times on his harmonica and exclaimed in a loud, shrill voice: "A fiery horse with the speed of light, a cloud of dust and a hearty 'Hi-yo, Silver!' It's the Lone Ranger! Hip-hip, Hooray!" There was an answering "hip-hip, hooray" from inside the sugar shack, and the sound of Jordie laughing. I couldn't help laughing myself. When I stopped, John said: "I guess you're wondering why I'm not in Maple Ridge. Well, this is our little secret. It doesn't hurt anybody if Jordie lets me get a little air. So listen, Mary. I want you to understand something. The day Peggy and my little girl left this world was the saddest day of my life." He cleared his throat. When he spoke again, his voice sounded husky, as if he'd been crying, although the light filtering through the yellow maple leaves made it hard to read his expression. "Nobody believes me, but honest to God, if I'd been in my right mind, I wouldn't have harmed a hair on Peggy's head. My hockey injury made it hard for me to think straight, eh? I'm better now and I'm asking them to review my case. Maybe your daddy will put in a good word for me. He's the only one who can talk sense into that fool running the Bug House."

"My father thinks your concussion made you punch-drunk."

"Well, your daddy's right. But that's enough of that. Take a look at this."

Something small and papery fluttered to the ground. "Pick it up, Mary. It won't bite." I wondered if he was toying with me, but I picked it up anyway. It was a photo of him gripping his stick and glaring at an unseen opponent. He wore his Detroit Red Wings sweater. "Gentleman Jack Pilkie" was written across the bottom of the picture in round, curling letters.

"The photo was taken seventeen years ago — when I was nineteen. My assist won us the Stanley Cup that year. Sometimes an assist is better than a goal. You can't score without teamwork, eh?"

It sounded like something Sal would say: that it was better to help out behind the scenes than assume the vainglorious — and I knew I was using the adjective properly — the vainglorious role of winner.

"Will you give Doc Bradford my photo and tell him I'll play for the Muskrats if he gets me a review of my case?"

I put the photo in my pocket, nodding.

"Are you going to come up here with me? Or should I come down to you?" he asked.

"You'd better stay in the tree, Mr. Pilkie."

"Okey-dokey. I'll do what you say." He held out an Oh Henry! chocolate bar. "Jordie gets these for me at the tuck shop. I like to give all my girls candy."

I took his chocolate bar without letting my fingers touch his hand.

"I bet your boyfriend wouldn't take candy from me."

"Ben's not my boyfriend."

"Is that his name? Well, you're braver than he is. Now I'm going to tell you the story of your daddy taking out my appendix. Where will I start? The Pilkies were nobodies, Mary. Your family is town royalty on account of Doc Bradford, but people didn't notice when we left in the spring for the Light or when we came back after freeze-up. And we didn't care, either. If winter came early, I played hockey on a patch of ice behind the breakwater. Daddy Pilkie would strap pillows to his knees and play goalie so I could practise my slapshots."

"Was it lonely at the Light?"

"My folks used to call our island 'Little Alcatraz' so that gives you the general idea."

"What did you eat?"

"If my daddy didn't catch any bass, we ate seagull eggs, tinned vegetables, and bacon. Mother Pilkie had to clean the bacon with vinegar to rid it of mould. But no more questions until I finish my story."

The Tale of John Pilkie's Appendix

"The night in question I was seven years old and feeling poorly. Daddy Pilkie said I couldn't go to bed. My daddy's assistant, Ralphie Bowman, was taking a weekend off and my daddy wanted me to take Ralphie's place. We still had the old coal-oil beacon, so every four hours we had to charge the engines and crank up the weights that turned the Light. Daddy Pilkie said the chores would make a man of me, but I was bound and determined to remain a boy.

"That Friday in November, I woke up in the middle of the night. The wind was howling, and the waves were pounding my bedroom wall. Pretty soon, the west wall and the windows were iced up solid. The force from the waves hitting the house pushed my bed across the floor so it hit the opposite wall. This always happened in a high wind. You can still see the tracks my bed carved in the floor."

"I saw the marks," I exclaimed. "Sal said the dog made them."

"Did she, now? Well, bless her heart. Sal's wrong. My bed made those marks and Mother Pilkie was forever painting them over. But imagine how scared we were. Aside from the coal beacon burning inside the lantern gallery, you couldn't see another light on the Bay. The government dock was taking a battering and the waves froze solid when they hit the wooden boards of our house. The sound was terrifying, eh? Like the noise of unset concrete hitting something solid. Ordinarily, a storm wouldn't bother my old man. He'd say, 'Let her rip. It can't hurt us now.'

"But that night he wasn't saying anything of the kind, because I was wailing like a banshee. I wouldn't stop no matter how much he swore at me. So Mother Pilkie made Daddy Pilkie call Doc

Bradford on the ship-to-shore radio. She knew something worse than the flu was going on. When my daddy tapped the right side of my belly button, I yelped, and Doc Bradford said it sounded like appendicitis. He told my daddy to bring me to town and my daddy told Doc Bradford there was no way he could bring me in, so Doc Bradford said that my daddy would have to operate on me at the Light. He promised to walk my daddy through it, step by step, and said everything would go like clockwork.

"My daddy started sharpening the butcher knife on Mother Pilkie's whetstone. I began to cry. I was just a little tyke, and I thought Daddy Pilkie meant to kill me. Mother Pilkie stroked my forehead and said she would take a teeny drop of Seagram's Rye, if I would too. Mother Pilkie didn't drink, so I knew this was serious and I drank so much whisky I was drunk as a skunk by the time Daddy Pilkie lay me down on the kitchen table. I can still see it — white Formica top with black trim, government-issue, that type of thing. I promised Doc Bradford I'd be brave, but when Daddy Pilkie yanked off my pyjama bottoms I shook all over. The next thing I knew my daddy stuffed a leather belt in my mouth and tried to tie me to the table. I broke free and ran outside. It was blowing so hard I nearly fell over. I had to hold on to the railing with one hand and my side with the other. Somehow I made it to the Light. Inside, I locked the door and started up the stairs to the gallery. I didn't get very far because my stomach hurt like the dickens. I sat in the dark, listening to the weights hit the wall as if some giant was smacking the light-house. I always hated the thudding sound, and that night the thud-thud-thud was so loud, I didn't hear Daddy Pilkie outside jigging the lock. But in walked my daddy waving a knife, and I passed out. Afterwards, Mother Pilkie said the kitchen floor looked like Daddy Pilkie had gutted a bass. Are you okay, Mary?"

"Yes," I said in a small voice. The idea of being cut open like a fish had me squeezing my legs together in case I wet my pants.

"I woke up to the noise of a plane. The coast guard decided to come when Doc Bradford told them I was only seven. I guess they felt sorry for me, being so young and sick way out there. By that time, the waves had shrunk to rollers, so Daddy Pilkie rowed me out to the seaplane. I don't remember flying to Madoc's Landing or Doc Bradford waiting for me on the town dock. His operation saved my life, because I was doing poorly again. But you know what? It wasn't my daddy who took out my appendix. Mother Pilkie did the job with her kitchen knife, because my daddy lost his nerve. Doc Bradford told Mother Pilkie it was up to her. You wouldn't think Doc Bradford could talk her into it, but he did. He said the appendix lies right next to the skin so it would be easy to cut it out.

"Afterwards, Mother Pilkie claimed that your daddy on the ship-to-shore radio was like the voice of God come to deliver us Pilkies from our troubles. So there! It was your daddy and Mother Pilkie who saved me. What do you think of that?"

"Big Louie says nobody gives women credit for things."

John didn't laugh. "Well, she's right. Look, thanks for listening. One of these days, you'll tell me how you got polio. Sharing our stories will make us friends for life. Oh-oh, do you see what I see?"

Jordie Coverdale came out of the sugar shack and pointed up the trail. John jumped down from the tree and loped off into the sugar bush without saying goodbye. It was what you do, if you're in a hurry; leave without saying goodbye. I expected it of Morley, but I didn't expect it of John — although he had no choice. Jordie motioned for me to go. Without another word, I hurried away down the trail, dragging Hindrance behind me.

23

I WALKED THE REST OF THE WAY HOME, THINKING HARD. MOUSE Bradford, you have just had a heart-to-heart with the hockey killer. Have you no common sense? But wasn't it the best story you ever heard? And doesn't it make you jealous to think of John getting Morley's attention for a whole night?

Walking in our front door, I took a giddy, self-important breath. I don't care what Hindrance says, I told myself. *John chose you to be his messenger.* I retrieved one of Morley's medical textbooks and looked up the definition of appendicitis. It was called a lumen, a worm-like growth at the opening of the large intestine. ("Lumen" is definitely a Morley word.) If it wasn't taken out lickety-split, an infected lumen could kill you. I hated thinking about worm-like growths in our bodies, waiting to hurt us, but if I had been at the Western Light instead of John, no one could have persuaded me to lie down on the table and let myself be cut open. I would have jumped out the window first.

FROM MORLEY'S DRESSER, I BORROWED a snapshot of my father as a college hockey player and compared it with the photo of

John standing by himself on a rink gripping his hockey stick. His smile was wide and reckless and his Red Wings sweater with the famous winged insignia appeared brand new, like his skates. His shiny black hair fell over his left eye, and he looked lonesome, and menacing. "I will score the next goal," he seemed to be saying, "And may the Lord help and protect you, if you stand in my way."

In his photo, Morley stood with his teammates. He wore a frayed shirt, because he gave his good wool sweater to Dr. Shulman, whose father was even poorer than Morley's dad, Duke Bradford. The photograph showed Morley in his prime, and my father did look young and brainy, with his kind, sad eyes, and his hair parted in the middle of his forehead, making two black wings. The young men standing with my father were dressed in different sweaters and pairs of padded shorts. Morley's university had no money for sports uniforms, so the players had to come up with their own outfits.

I put Morley's photograph back and stuck the photo that John gave me under my sweater.

I SAT DOWN BREATHLESSLY AT the place Sal had set for me, and smiled at Morley who was coming in for dinner. The late night edition of *The Telegram* with the stock listing on its pink pages was under his arm. Unfortunately, Morley wore his Other Worldly Stare (i.e., the lofted eyebrows that meant somebody was seriously ill). I felt terrible for him having a patient at death's door, but I was counting on John's photograph to get Morley's attention back on the living. Morley lowered himself into his chair, his eyes flicking over to the telephone that Sal had set down next to his placemat. Now my aunt breezed in carrying a volume of poetry by Edna St. Vincent Millay.

"I have something important to say," I announced.

"Go ahead, kid. Spill the beans," Little Louie said.

"I — I — saw — somebody my father knows —"

Morley yawned as if he hadn't heard me, and I found myself clinging to the arms of my chair. Slowly but surely, my body was growing lighter. Soon I would be as weightless as a cloud drifting across a mountain face. Then, per usual, the phone rang. My father picked up the receiver with his long-fingered surgeon's hands that could poke around in a boy's stomach without killing him. "Oh, it's black, is it? Have you been taking iron pills? No. It should be yellowish-brown and shaped like a banana. You'd better come and see me this week."

My aunt giggled and, for a second, I forgot John's photograph and giggled too. Morley put down the phone and trained his kind, sad eyes on Sal, striding in with our mashed potatoes. Mashed potatoes were Morley's favourite and mine, too, and this serving bore my aunt's signature: a pinch of paprika and fork marks that marched like ski tracks up the snowy peaks. Morley and I preferred my aunt's potatoes, because she whipped them with an electric beater and applied extra dollops of butter and cream. Sal beat them by hand with a big fork, using only a drop or two of milk.

"Dr. Bradford, Mary has something to tell us," my aunt said.

"Pardon, Louisa?"

"Tell us, Mary," my aunt commanded.

"I saw John Pilkie today. He was in the old sugar bush."

"That's enough, Lady Jane," Sal said, setting down the mashed potatoes.

"I'm not telling tales!" I took out the photo of John in his Detroit hockey sweater and showed it to Morley. "John told me to give you this. He says he'll play for your hockey team if you help him get a review of his case."

Morley grabbed the photo and brought it close to his face. "He wants to play hockey again, does he?" The snapshot had pressed a button inside my father, springing him to life.

"Shouldn't we call the police?" my aunt asked.

My father met my aunt's gaze. "Louisa, everything's going to be fine. Pilkie doesn't leave the grounds. He does chores with that Coverdale fellow, but the other prisoners have complained so Rob is putting an end to it."

"Dr. Shulman is pretty lenient, isn't he?" my aunt said. Morley nodded and began gulping down her potatoes. I waited for him to tell us how Dr. Shulman was going to stop John from doing what he wanted, but Morley kept bolting down his food, his eyes on his plate. The phone rang again and Morley picked it up. "Who is it this time?" my aunt asked. "Cap Lefroy," my father said. He stood up, tucking John's photo into his vest pocket.

"Thanks for the photo, Mary!" he called on his way out the door.

I couldn't believe my ears. My father was pleased with me. And there was something else. Morley coached the Madoc's Landing Muskrats, because he was too old to play hockey himself and John was smart enough to know just how much hockey mattered to a man like my father.

I Was Ten when I Found Out
How Much My Father Loved Hockey

I was ten when I found out how much Morley loved hockey. It was the first time Frank Mahovlich played with the Toronto Maple Leafs. The game started the way it usually did with Clarence Campbell addressing the crowd as "Ladies, Gentlemen, and Frenchmen," and nobody thought anything about how rude Campbell was being. Campbell was an English-speaking Canadian and the English had more power then, so they got away with prejudiced remarks. Then, too, our national game was how Canadians worked out our differences. Contrary to what you might think for such a peace-loving, northern people, winter is our passionate season. Hockey is where we show the aggressive side of our character, and everybody is crazy for the fast, wild male world of ice hockey, a world of blowing snow and stormy winter nights when cars go slip-sliding over icy roads to get to the game in time and men fight their guts out inside freezing arenas.

It didn't matter that there were Quebec players on the Toronto Maple Leaf team or English-speaking men playing for the Montreal Canadiens. In those days, there were only six NHL teams and each season we relived the Battle of the Plains of Abraham, which the French and English had fought in Quebec. You could see the thrill of battle on the shiny, hopeful faces of the fans and on the faces of the hockey players themselves.

On the Saturday night in question, Morley had gone to Toronto on business, and Sal and I were watching *Hockey Night in Canada*. We knew my father wouldn't be pleased when the Montreal Canadiens started to win. "It looks like we have an overexcited fan," the announcer bellowed as the camera zoomed in on a familiar figure climbing the wire fence behind the goalie's net. Sal and I gaped as the figure swung free off the fence and shook its fist at the referee. "My Lord!" Sal cried. "It's Doc Bradford!" The camera zoomed in, and my father jumped down and waded into a crowd of men in long, dark winter coats pushing and shoving each other. While we watched, my father squashed the hat of a man wearing a Canadiens scarf. "Well, I guess that Montreal fan got his," Sal muttered.

After the game, Sadie, the Bell operator, handled calls all night about my father taking down a Montreal Canadiens fan on national television. My father had been sitting beside a Montreal Canadiens fan, so the story goes, and every time the Canadiens scored a goal, the Canadiens fan had slapped Morley's back so hard Morley's fedora fell off. Morley told the man to stop, but the Canadiens fan kept up the backslapping until finally Morley flattened the man's hat. Morley wouldn't confirm or deny the story, although Sal had seen my father get into hockey fights before. She claimed the fights taxed his heart.

24

TWO DAYS AFTER I GAVE MORLEY THE PHOTOGRAPH OF JOHN
Pilkie, the upstairs phone rang. When I picked it up, Morley was
talking to Dr. Shulman on the other end. Unable to believe my
luck, I listened in, covering the receiver with my hand so they
couldn't hear my breathing.

"Sib will help me coach the Rats this year. He'll settle John
down."

"If John plays by the rules," Dr. Shulman said. "He's got a
temper, Morley. Last week he had the cell block banging their
dinner bowls."

"I can control John's temper," my father replied.

"I wouldn't be so sure, if I were you."

"John listens to me," my father said. "And it'll help your
cause if John wins games for the Rats."

"Well, maybe so."

"Give John's guard a gun and tell him to keep it out of sight,"
Morley said.

"Guns are against hospital policy," Dr. Shulman replied. "But
all right. Just this once. For hospital safety."

"Good," my father said. "By the way, the newspaper is sending my sister-in-law Louisa to write up the team. Kelsey Farrow is sick."

"They're sending a woman?"

Morley laughed. "Louisa is working part-time for the newspaper now. She'll be okay. She wrote some sports stories for *The London Free Press*."

"All right, Morley. See you at the Beaudry farm."

"You can count on it." The line went dead. My aunt hadn't told me she had gone back to newspaper reporting. Maybe she felt shy about it, but it was good news. Now she would have a chance to find out that John was nicer than she thought.

ON SATURDAY MORNING, BEN AND I and Little Louie climbed into the Oldsmobile convertible with my father. Ben and I wore shorts, while my aunt had on one of her old sweaters, jeans, and a pair of saddle shoes with frayed laces. With her tousled yellow hair and messy clothes, she didn't look like a real reporter. Humming to herself, she took out a notepad and began to scribble down what the Rats were going to do in the day ahead. Morley explained that the men would lift weights and scale the chicken-wire fence donated by the town reeve; they'd also shoot pucks at a board, trying to get it through small, puck-sized holes in the wood, and they'd broad jump, high jump, and jog down the lumber road that ran through the Beaudry woods. Little Louie wrote it all down.

Ben handed me a Red Wings hockey card. I took a gulp of air. On the hockey card, John was a dead ringer for the singer Ricky Nelson. Why didn't the resemblance strike me before? The very same shining cowlick. The very same full bottom lip and glistening eyes.

"Is this for me?"

"You have to play me for it," Ben whispered, putting the hockey card back in his banana box. He had traded his baseball glove for the old banana carton, which was exactly the right size for Ben's collection of hockey cards. He had 192 "Toppies," the name for the American cards, every one in full colour, plus 308 Canadian cards called "Parkies," which were only in black and white. Ben's most valuable card was Rocket Richard of the Montreal Canadiens who had scored his six hundredth goal the year before, and Gordie Howe of the Detroit Red Wings who had scored his four hundredth. Sal called Gordie Howe and the Rocket "dirty players" while hockey stars like Jean Beliveau of the Canadiens and Frank Mahovlich of the Leafs were known as "gentlemen." Ben and I didn't care about these distinctions. We only cared about finding out the number of each player's goals and assists.

AFTER HALF AN HOUR ON the county roads, we arrived at the Beaudry farm. Except for the gold and red maples on the Beaudry hill, it could have been a day in late August. The air was soft and warm. On the horizon, the Western Light poked out of the heat haze like a pale candle.

I introduced Little Louie to the players who were dressed in shorts or bathing trunks. They were local men, in their late twenties or thirties, and I knew most of them. She shook hands with Toby Walker, whose son went to school with Ben and me, and Kid McConkley, now the foreman at the lumber mill. Kid looked trim, but most of the men were overfed or just plain old. How could they play hockey? My aunt threw me a puzzled glance before Morley sent Ben and me off to fetch water buckets. Sal had set the picnic table with French's mustard, green relishes, hardboiled eggs, whole tomatoes, lettuce, cheese wedges, and slices of buttered Wonder bread. While Sal brought out a cooked ham, Morley laid out his instruments on a second table. There was a reflex hammer, syringes and prescription forms, plus several copies of *Time* magazine, which Morley used as splints in an emergency.

I staggered over with my bucket, hoping my father would notice how hard I was working. In his honour, I'd memorized new hockey facts. I knew, for instance, that the colours of the Leafs' uniforms — blue, white, and silver — were chosen to represent the blue of Canadian skies and the white of Canadian snow. I also knew that Johnny Bower, the Leaf goalie, made forty-five saves in 1958. Thinking about how I was going to impress my father made me feel hopeful.

OUT ON THE ROAD, THE hospital van turned down the lane of the farmhouse and headed for the front porch where Ben and I were sitting. Jordie Coverdale climbed out of the driver's seat and a man wearing a fringed leather jacket and jeans with a crease down the legs hopped out the passenger side. At first, I didn't recognize John out of his Bug House overalls, but he spotted me and sang out: "How-de-do, cowgirl!" Some of the men turned my way, looking surprised. Morley turned too, lifting his eyebrows. I felt a twinge of pride. John had said hello to me first.

"You can change in there, John!" Morley shouted, pointing at the barn. John hurried off, while Jordie unzipped a long duffle bag. There was a shotgun inside and two hockey sticks. He grinned at the sight of our bugged-out eyes. "It's a semi-automatic twelve-gauge," he said lifting out the shotgun. He checked its lock carefully. "Doc Shulman made me pack it on account of John. But John's playing hockey again so he's not going anywhere." Ben and I nodded gravely and Jordie withdrew the hockey sticks from the duffle bag and handed them over. They were smaller than the standard hockey stick, and made in the same style, with a long sloping wooden handle and a flat blade covered in sticky black masking tape.

"John carved these for you," Jordie said. "And here's a spare puck. John wanted you guys to have some fun." I didn't tell Jordie that I never played hockey on account of Hindrance.

LITTLE LOUIE JOINED BEN AND me just as John came out of the barn dressed in neatly pressed navy shorts, a white T-shirt, and high-top running shoes. The three of us were impressed by how young and cleaned-up he looked. He wasn't fat and bald, like Toby Walker. Per usual his pompadour was slicked back neatly, although a few black curls hung over his forehead. Maybe it was because he ate his Cheerios, but the other men's hair didn't stand up so straight and shiny.

As soon as he appeared, Kid McConkley stopped high-jumping and Toby Walker put down his dumbbells. They walked over to the other players and the group began chattering among themselves, throwing suspicious glances at John. "Can I have your attention, everybody?" My father strode into the middle of the barnyard with Dr. Shulman, their faces solemn and purposeful. John joined them, snapping his fingers so quietly you couldn't hear their joyful pop-pop. "As some of you know already, I've obtained special permission for John Pilkie to play with the Rats this season," my father said. "He's going to help us win the Pickering Cup. I hope you will welcome him. Rob?"

"I'd like to back up what Dr. Bradford said," Dr. Shulman remarked. "There is no security risk. A hospital guard will be with John at all times. I think you'll find John a congenial teammate. Would you like to say a few words, son?"

John stepped forward. "It's an honour to be back with the Rats, sir. It feels like coming home."

Next to me, Little Louie was making notes. Was she worried the men wouldn't accept him? Was John? He didn't show any sign of nerves. *Oh please*, I thought, *somebody say something.*

Somebody did. Staring at his feet, Toby Walker said in low, half-embarrassed voice, "I played with John in the old days. And I'll play with him now, too." There was scattered applause and the men started talking loudly now, their voices strained with excitement. Morley gave John a wide, approving smile. It struck me that Morley didn't smile like that at me, but I pushed away the depressing thought and followed Ben to the porch to drink lemonade. Sal had made several batches of it for the players who were back skipping rope, or running on the old lumber trail. By the barn, Toby Walker and Sib Beaudry were hanging from the chicken-wire fence like frightened cats. As Ben and I watched, they dropped back down shaking their heads. John scrambled up, hand over foot, easy as pie. In no time, he was straddling the top.

"I'm king of the castle, boys," John called to the men below, raising his arms above his head. "And Sib's the dirty rascal." Toby Walker laughed and poked Sib. "John's quite the card, eh Sib?" Sib grunted something back, his hound-dog eyes black and mean. I held my breath. Would he do something cruel in plain sight? No, for once, Sib had to stand there looking dumb, while John sat on top of the fence smiling back at Sib. And then, before you could say "Boo," John jumped down and ran at top speed towards the high jump. Or was he making a dash for it? If so, Jordie was too busy eating Sal's cheese to notice.

In the meadow, John cleared the high jump by a foot. "Nice work, Pilkie!" somebody yelled. John grinned and began to run with his big springy steps into the Christmas trees. A moment later, Jordie started jogging after him, a cigarette hanging out of his mouth. Someone whistled behind me, and when I turned around, Little Louie was standing there with her notebook.

"He's quite something, isn't he?" she said in a way that suggested she didn't expect an answer.

JOHN CAME BACK TWENTY MINUTES later, his chest heaving and his face red. One by one, the other men returned, looking even worse after their two-mile jog along the old lumber trail. They drank water or lemonade while Ben and I tossed Ben's hockey cards against the wall of the farmhouse. Our rules were simple. If one of my cards landed closer to the baseboard, then Ben had to forfeit his card. I won Ben's Rocket Richard card and a card of the Rocket's brother, the Pocket Rocket. Ben said we're going to play for the Detroit Red Wings card, which had John Pilkie on it. Ben placed the hockey card against the wall and went first. Maybe he wasn't trying hard, because he wanted me to win, but his toss was feeble. His card fell short. My new Frank Mahovlich card landed squarely on top of it.

"Look what I've got!" Waving my prize, I hobbled over to Morley's table where Little Louie was drinking pop with John and my father. I concentrated hard on making my sailor's roll as smooth as possible, and John and Little Louie grinned while Morley regarded me dolefully. It was obvious what Morley was thinking: As if Hindrance wasn't bad enough, I was too skinny by half, and I had bags under my eyes from reading under my bedcovers with a flashlight.

After John and Little Louie examined the card, my father looked at it, and I told myself — it's now or never. "Mr. Pilkie, did you know my father wanted to be a professional hockey player?"

"We don't have time for this, Mary," Morley said. "Now scat! Don't bother us again."

I waited for Little Louie to say something in my defence. Instead, she stared down at me through her dark glasses. John stared down at me too, his eyes soft and quizzical. I imagined myself shrinking until I was the size of a June beetle crushed under Morley's shoes. Or maybe I was a balloon drifting off above the Beaudry woods and Morley forgot to grab my string.

Steady on, Mouse, Hindrance whispered as I hobbled off. *Don't get all dramatic.* When I turned around again, John was nowhere to be seen and Morley was back behind his table listening to somebody's chest through his stethoscope. "Never mind your dad," Ben said. "Let's play road hockey."

25

BEN CAME BACK CARRYING OUR NEW STICKS AND TWO EATON'S catalogues he had borrowed from Sal. He strapped the catalogues to my shins with Sal's leather belts and tapped my homemade goalie pads authoritatively. "Okay, let me take a shot at you."

The blade of my hockey stick wasn't quite wide enough and Ben easily slammed the puck past my padded shins. Sometimes he lifted it as high as my head. I protested that hoisting the puck was illegal, and Ben said it wasn't. As we argued, John came out of the bushes, smoking. He winked when he saw my face.

"It's okay, Mary. I shouldn't have snuck up on you. But I wanted to see you play. Exercise is good for your leg, eh?"

"My grandmother says exercise will hurt me."

"No kidding. Why?"

"Because I get exhausted too fast. And then it takes me a long time to feel better."

"Well, fine. But I see it differently. You can do everything other kids do. It's just going to take you a little longer. You're an athlete, eh? You have to build up your endurance so you don't tire easily. Do you follow?"

"I guess so," I replied.

"Good. Now let Mary have a turn." He squatted down beside Ben, and I took off the straps and handed the catalogues over to John, who strapped them on Ben. Kicking the puck my way, he shouted, "Take a shot, Mary." I did what he said, but I fanned and missed the puck. He picked up the puck and tossed it back at me. "Again." I raised the stick and this time I connected. The puck made an oomph sound against Ben's shin, like somebody getting punched in the stomach. Ben fell down.

"Most girls have weak arms, eh? But you've got a wicked wrist shot. Let me feel those muscles of yours." Shyly, I held out my arm and he gently pinched the flesh under my cotton blouse. "Hmmn ... pretty strong, all right. Maybe Doc Bradford will make you a rink this winter."

"He's too busy."

John butted his cigarette in the sand. "Is that so? We'll see about that."

Over by the farmhouse, the men were getting into their cars and going home. "Hey, Pilkie! Let's go, eh?" Sib shouted in our direction. "Oh-oh. I gotta run or Frenchy will have my head." John made a throat slitting motion as he handed me back his old hockey card. "Thanks for showing it to me. I looked a darn sight better then. Right, son?" Ben grinned up at him. "Thanks for our sticks, Mr. Pilkie. Will you tell us about playing for the Red Wings?"

"Sure, one of these days. But it's John to you and Mary. Okay?" he asked.

Ben exclaimed, "Okay, Mr. Pilkie," but by then John was already climbing into the hospital truck.

I HID JOHN'S HOCKEY CARD under my pillow. Then I put on Ricky Nelson's 45 and listened to him sing "Poor Little Fool." And, even though nothing could come of my feelings, I imagined what it would feel like if I were Mrs. John Pilkie and lived in a rambling Victorian house with a widow's walk like Cap Lefroy's place, and John played hockey, not for the Rats, but a team like the Toronto Maple Leafs. Naturally, I would be in the stands every night cheering. He would kiss his picture of the Queen and then he would blow a kiss to me, his young wife. The crowds would look my way and, although they would be shocked by my age, they would clap and grin.

After the game, he and I would go upstairs and he would sing Ricky Nelson's song about giving away his heart. Then he'd take off his jeans with the press down the leg and look at me the way Joe, our spaniel, looks when he wants to lick the roast beef platter. Of course, he wouldn't take off all his clothes; he'd keep on the crisp white shirt that hangs over his Fruit of the Loom underwear, and his shirt collar would show his black chest hair. I'd know I had to respond, but what would I say? I didn't want to strip naked so he could see me close up, because I was like Elvis Presley on the *Ed Sullivan Show* — I couldn't be viewed below my waist. And it was impossible to imagine him pressing his lips against mine, or his hand roving across my breast, which was what happened when Max kissed Little Louie on the mouth in my grandmother's living room. (Of course, in my case, there was no breast to speak of. Not yet.)

26

LITTLE LOUIE TOOK OVER A WEEK TO WRITE UP HER STORY ON John Pilkie. She said she was out of practice and she wanted to get it right so *The Chronicle* would assign her more stories. I worried secretly. What would she say about John? Maybe she wasn't sure if she should praise or criticize him, although she knew that my father and Dr. Shulman were hoping the Rats would win the Pickering Cup because John was playing for the team. Naturally, Ben and I told Little Louie that we were all for John. I reminded her that Morley thought his concussion made John violent. Little Louie scribbled what I said down on her notepad. When I peeked at it, I caught the words "head injury" followed by a row of question marks. She asked me about the day I talked to John in the maple tree and if I thought Dr. Shulman was right to give John so much freedom. Of course Dr. Shulman was right, I said. Little Louie wrote down my answer, looking interested.

A FEW DAYS LATER, BEN burst in on me drinking hot chocolate in our kitchen on Whitefish Road. He had something important to show me. I knew by the look on Ben's face it had to do with John. We went upstairs to my bedroom, where Sal couldn't hear us, and Ben brought out a typewritten document that he found on his father's desk. Dr. Shulman was encouraging Ben to read psychiatry textbooks, which meant Ben spent more time in his father's office. That afternoon, Ben had stumbled across the file when he was reading one of his father's books. The date on the file was April 20, 1959. Inside it were several typewritten pages that described a conversation between Dr. Shulman and a patient called J.P. When I noticed the initials, I couldn't help grinning.

Met Ptn in my office yesterday in order to familiarize him with the hospital.

Ptn was incarcerated for murdering his wife and child. His files show he is prone to rages as well as minor depressive episodes. Ptn's agitation includes inability to sit still, pacing, popping his knuckles. Haven't seen a demonstration of his temper or pathological tics. Ptn well known for eloping from psychiatric institutions.

Ptn well defended and cleverly guards his innermost feelings. My training tells me to distrust someone like Ptn who is highly skilled at telling others what they want to hear. But Ptn is good-humoured and knowledgeable about woodworking. Ptn has been put to work making desks for school superintendents in local schools.

Today Ptn's primary concern was to get to a review of his case. Obliged to point out that under the provisions of the law, there is no regulation granting mental patients the right to a review. Encouraged him to discuss his feelings about his crime. Ptn claims assistant coach of the Detroit Red Wings witnessed hockey players becoming aggressive after they suffered concussions. Ptn noted that New England Journal of Medicine has written about dementia pugilsta (known as the punch-drunk syndrome) in connection with boxers. Asked Ptn why dementia pugilsta hadn't been discussed at his trial. Ptn claims his lawyer felt a head injury wouldn't hold up as an alibi, particularly since Ptn's symptoms of slurred speech and impaired movements had disappeared by the time of his trial; his lawyer felt Ptn would be unable to demonstrate the effects of the injury to the jury. Told him I concurred with his lawyer and reminded Ptn that my job is to offer therapy to improve his condition.

Since he has been with us, Ptn has incited other patients to protest their living conditions. Ptn's protests include clogging toilets and banging dinner bowls. Asked if he would try to escape from Maple Ridge, and Ptn promised to co-operate if I got a review of his case. Have included part of Ptn's old file from the Ontario Hospital Whitby dated shortly after Ptn suffered a concussion twelve years ago. The file notes what is likely the after-effect of the cerebral salt-wasting syndrome. Syndrome lasts for short time and results in low sodium counts and leads to agitation and irritation of Ptn: "The equilibrium or balance, so to speak, between his intellectual faculties and animal propensities, seems to have been destroyed by his cerebral hematoma. He is fitful and irreverent, indulging at times in the grossest profanity, which was not previously his custom. Manifesting but little deference for his fellows, impatient of restraint or advice when it conflicts with his desires, at times pertinaciously obstinate, yet capricious and vacillating, devising many plans of future operations, which are no sooner arranged than they are abandoned in turn for others appearing more feasible. A child in his intellectual capacity and manifestations, he has the animal passions of a strong man. Previous to his injury, although untrained in the schools, he possessed a well-balanced mind, and was looked upon by those who knew him as a shrewd, smart athlete, very energetic and persistent in executing all his plans. In this regard, his mind was so radically changed that his teammates said he was "no longer Pilkie."

WHEN LITTLE LOUIE CAME HOME from the newspaper office, Ben and I took her upstairs to my bedroom where Ben showed her the file. She read it once through, and then she read it again; something shifted in her expression. I couldn't put my finger on it, although it seemed she saw something she'd refused to look at before. I hoped it had to do with John.

"Where did you get this?" she asked.

"Ben found it on his father's desk."

Little Louie laughed. "Ben stole it, you mean."

"I'm going to put it back," Ben said stiffly.

"Yes, do that," Little Louie replied. "But why don't I talk to Dr. Shulman? And if he won't level with me, I'll pretend somebody at the hospital gave me John Pilkie's old file from the Whitby hospital. An informed source. That's what a person like that is called in my business. We don't need to give their names."

"You won't tell on me?" Ben asked.

"Reporters have to protect our sources, Ben. You have nothing to worry about."

Ben's eyes searched my face. I nodded. Then he nodded. Little Louie nodded, too. Something important had been decided among the three of us, and nothing more needed to be said.

27

LITTLE LOUIE'S STORY ON JOHN APPEARED ON THE FRONT PAGE
of the newspaper under the headline, "Local Boy Sprung from
Asylum to Play for Home Team." Her write-up drew an excited
reaction from the town, although I was disappointed because
there was nothing in it about John's head injury being behind
the murder of his wife. In the very last paragraph, my aunt said
that psychiatrists like Dr. Shulman thought head injuries could
sometimes lead to personality changes, but this paragraph was
buried inside the newspaper. I wondered how many people
would put two-and-two together if they bothered to read that
far.

Mostly John came off sounding dangerous, because her story
repeated in "lurid detail" (as Sal put it) the story of John's wife
and child dying in the flames. It said John threw the match "fully
aware" that his wife had spread kerosene on the floor to kill
cockroaches and it described the court testimony about John's
wife shrieking that John would pay for what he did.

The day after the story appeared, I quizzed Little Louie about
it while we drank our nighttime cups of hot cocoa. Little Louie

told me what had happened. The editor at *The Chronicle* refused to let her put the information from Dr. Shulman's file in her story. Little Louie wouldn't tell him how she got the information, since she didn't want Ben getting punished, and the editor said Little Louie's information was hearsay and that suggesting a connection between head injuries and violence could ruin his newspaper's credibility; besides, when she interviewed them, neither Morley nor Dr. Shulman could vouch definitively for the connection, so the editor had cut out the information and inserted in its place verbatim sentences from old newspaper stories about the death of John's wife and child.

"Newspaper editors make the rules, Mouse. It used to drive me crazy at the *Free Press*."

"You mean you didn't quit your old job on account of Max?"

Little Louie fixed me with her heavy-lidded eyes. "Let's not talk about him."

"Okay. Is his wife nice?"

She snorted. "No. Well, maybe. Anyway, I'm sorry about the story."

"I don't think the editor should have changed it."

"I don't, either. It makes John Pilkie look heartless. I hope he won't blame me."

I reassured her that John would understand, although I doubted if Dr. Shulman would like my aunt talking about how he ran the mental hospital. Our town was suspicious of his policies, and people like Sal believed the shrinks were as crazy as the N.C.'s (i.e., nut cases). So Little Louie wasn't doing Dr. Shulman any favours when she described his ideas. For instance, my aunt quoted him as saying that even psychopaths could be cured. She also said that Dr. Shulman used a new drug

called lithium on patients with depression, and a drug referred
to as DDT (Defence Disruption Therapy) to break through the
defences of the prisoners in Maple Ridge. According to my aunt,
John playing for the Rats would help reinforce Dr. Shulman's
theory that mental patients suffer from an illness that could be
cured.

Her news story was the start of my sympathy for Ben's father,
whose mind worked along parallel channels to mine, although
I wouldn't have put it exactly that way then. Like Sal, I, too,
was suspicious of anybody who went against the regular way
of doing things, and I had to examine their actions carefully
before I accepted their behaviour. For instance, I felt shocked to
think the mentally ill could be cured. The idea was new to me.
I had always considered them hopeless cases.

So it didn't surprise me when Little Louie said that
Dr. Shulman had to be careful about what he told people about
the hospital. Already his policies had created problems with the
town (i.e., our neighbours were against the harmless patients
being allowed to wander although these patients rarely came
into town, and when it happened, they asked to be taken back
to the hospital. Most of them had been there so long the place
felt like home). But our neighbours kept complaining and, even-
tually, Dr. Shulman had to put locks back on the rooms of the
harmless patients although the bars stayed off their windows.

Then there was something else, something more astonishing.
Ben had told me his father believed that mental patients should
have their cases reviewed, which is what John had been arguing
for since the day he arrived in town. Two things were stopping
it from happening. Number one, it hadn't been done before.
And number two, it cost money to set up a regulatory body to

review the cases of mental patients, and the government was cutting back their costs. It was bad enough, Ben said, when his father tried to squeeze out a few more pennies to improve the living conditions of the harmless patients whose nineteenth-century cottages lacked hot water. Dr. Shulman had made a habit of showing government deputies the decrepit wooden houses, hoping the men (and they were usually men) would give the hospital more funds. But Ben said the state of the cottages didn't worry the government people. They would say, "Maybe next year." And that would be that.

Still, there remained one more important thing about Little Louie's article — it got the town even more interested in the Rats. Pretty well everybody showed up to see what John could do the night of his first hockey game.

28

WE DROVE OVER TOGETHER TO DOLLARTOWN ARENA, WHICH Kelsey Farrow claimed was the largest ice surface between Toronto and Winnipeg. In order to withstand our winters, the concrete building had been designed to handle forty pounds of wind pressure and fifty pounds of snow per square foot. Nine tons of granulated cork went into its insulation and thirteen miles of pipes ran below the surface of its rink. The arena used seventeen tons of calcium chloride for the brine solution and fifteen-hundred pounds of liquid ammonia were added to make ice. As Kelsey Farrow liked to point out, our arena was one of the first to be built without pillars so the fans had an unobstructed view of the game.

We arrived forty minutes early; not early enough for Morley, who could hardly talk he was so wound up. He directed my aunt, Sal, and me to the bleachers behind the players' box before he left to talk to a referee. Chief Doucette, Kelsey Farrow, and Dr. Shulman were already there. Ben had saved a seat for me next to Kelsey, who was well enough again to write about the game.

"Guess you're too busy to do up your boots!" Sal stared in disgust at the rubber tongues flopping out of Kelsey's galoshes.

"Oh, yeah. Well, I'm excited about seeing Pilkie play," Kelsey said.

"John won't show up," Sal replied. "Just you wait and see."

"Sure he will!" Kelsey scowled. "He's got too much riding on this."

"John gets penalties, not goals," Sal interjected. "That man just loves roughhousing."

"That's B.S., Sal, and you know it," Kelsey replied. "A player who won't get physical is no use to his team."

I couldn't hear what Sal said back, because people had started screaming. The Rats were coming out of the dressing room in the new gold and white sweaters Morley had bought them. The sweaters were a version of the Maple Leafs' uniform, except that their primary colour was gold instead of blue. Gold for victory, as Morley put it.

"Look! There he is!" I waved his old Detroit Red Wings card at John who waved back. To my surprise, he came over, his skate guards clunking across the wooden arena floor. "I'm sorry about the story," Little Louie said, leaning out over the railing so he could hear. "They rewrote it at the office."

"What can you do, eh, Louisa?" He gave her his dimpled grin. "Glad you came. And you too, Mary!" He blew a kiss at us before turning his back and shaking out his shoulders. He was getting ready to play, and I could sense his excitement. Then Jordie opened the door in the boards, and John glided onto the ice. Near us, a man booed. "Get off the rink, you loony!" John gave the heckler a friendly smile and bowed at the organ player sitting near the scoreboard. A jazzy version of "For He's a Jolly Good

Fellow" started to echo through the stands. John skated once around the rink, lifting his stick in the kingly gesture of victory that he had made at the Beaudry farm. A few people clapped.

Soon both teams were skating round and round the rink, the ice ringing with the savage drawl and scrape of their blades. The crowd turned silent and worshipful. We were ready to see what John could do, and we watched with our mouths open, as he passed beneath us, leaning impossibly far forward, then impossibly far back, skimming the ice like a human swallow, his dark pompadour shining under the arena lights, his perfect stops and starts setting off fizzy rooster tails of spray. Grinning from ear to ear, Morley clapped enthusiastically. Jordie hung over the boards and clapped too. Half turning in our direction, John took a photograph out of his pocket and kissed it. "He's giving the Queen a smooch!" a fan shouted. As John put the photo back in his pocket, it came to me what Morley had done. John was free, freer than me and Ben, or my father and Dr. Shulman. Out on centre ice, waiting for the puck to drop, he could play hockey as if his life depended on it and nobody had the power to stop him.

I welled up as the organ player started on "God Save the Queen." The Muskrats stood at attention. Maybe John was wet-eyed too.

"Pilkie's going to win the game for us," I whispered to Little Louie.

"Let's hope so, Mouse." She mock-punched my shoulder.

"And another cow flew over the moon!" Sal scoffed. She didn't fool me. She pretended she wanted John to fail, but secretly she longed for him to prove her wrong. Except that Sal couldn't admit it to anybody, not even herself.

He Shoots, He Scores

The story of the Muskrats beating the Flyers was on the front page of *The Chronicle* under a banner headline. I didn't care what happened in the rest of the world. I didn't care if Charles van Doren told the House Committee in America that his answers on his TV quiz show were rigged. Or that Montreal player Jacques Plante had gone against the wishes of his coach Toe Blake and become the second NHL goalie to wear a face-mask. (The first goalie was Clint Benedict, but he only wore it once.) All that mattered was *The Chronicle* headline that said, "Rats defeat Flyers 4–1 — Thanks to local boy, John Pilkie."

Morley read Kelsey Farrow's report out loud to us, while Little Louie and I ate our soft-boiled eggs. Sal listened, too. "Off the ice for more than thirteen years, John Pilkie of Madoc's Landing led the Rats to victory last night in a display of stick handling that hasn't been seen here since Pilkie left town."

Our eyes never left Morley's face. We felt glad for my father, but he didn't notice. He'd gone to a place with no room for us.

Kelsey's article didn't mention John's crime until the last paragraph. "Dr. Bradford, Pilkie's physician, obtained special per-mission from the Ontario Psychiatric Hospital for the hockey killer to play for the home team. Thirteen years ago, Pilkie was incarcerated for starting a fire that killed his wife and child."

Looking over my father's shoulder, Sal said, "Here it is, Morley. Three penalties against John. Two for high sticking and one for slashing."

Morley smiled at me. "But John scored three goals, didn't he, Mary?"

I grinned like anything.

"So I guess there's no more to be said," my father summed up.

AFTER THE FIRST GAME AGAINST the Flyers, John scored the winning goals in three more games. *The Chronicle* ran news of the Muskrats' victories on the front page. Dr. Shulman and Morley were proud of John. I felt proud of him, too. I slept with his old hockey card under my pillow and brought it with me to each game. One afternoon, when school was over, I sent John my composition about my great-grandfather. I didn't tell Sal or Little Louie. I kept my fingers crossed they wouldn't find out. I had rewritten it since the Bug House boys threw it away and I was especially proud of the first page:

A Short History of My Great-Grandfather, an Oil Baron of Canada West by M.B. Bradford

Every July when I go to The Great House for my summer holidays, my grandmother explains how my great-grandfather crawled out of the sea mud and discovered black gold in the muck he sprang from. My family has different versions of my great-grandfather's story so I will start by listing their versions here.

My grandmother, Louisa Vidal Barrett believes that my great-grandfather is a hero like the Greek warrior Odysseus who never took no for an answer while my aunt Louisa Barrett says my great-grandfather owed his fortune to Aunt Louie Vidal.

In my Uncle Willie's version, my great-grandfather Mackenzie Vidal was one shrewd customer.

My father Morley Bradford has a different interpretation. He believes my great-grandfather was one of the misfits who made up the population of early Canada. Our land was crawling with losers, my father says: orphans from Paris slums, loyalists fleeing the American Revolution, remittance men from the old country, and my great-grandfather fitted right in. After all, Mackenzie Vidal was a draft dodger who wouldn't fight against slavery. He came to Canada West to avoid the Civil War and he was given a lucky break when he struck oil in Enniskillen Swamp, a wilderness of clay mud in southwestern Ontario.

There is also my great-grandfather's version. My great-grandfather said that if he hadn't grown up on the canals, he would have lacked the patience and the know-how to drill for oil. Canals were everything in those days. It was how you shipped barley, pig iron, ore, and timber from Canada to New York. In the 1840s, you could get a tow on the Lake Erie Canal all the way down to New Jersey and then back again up to Niagara Falls, your boat carrying grain for the Americans and returning with farm machinery for the farms of eastern Ontario. The railroads weren't built then and in the summer the dirt roads dried out like old cow poop. When the rains came in the fall, the roads turned as sloppy as a kid's mud pies so everyone used the canals. The nerve of a canal horse was a popular expression but nobody except my grandmother uses it now. She doesn't mean it as a compliment.

SAL HAD LEFT THE MORNING mail stacked up on the kitchen table. My name was written on one of the envelopes in letters that coiled across the paper like snakes with stuck-up tails and rounded eyes. In the left-hand corner, John's name had been written in the same spiralling hand and the two I's in "Pilkie" were drawn as faces with friendly, half-moon smiles — one face had a cowlick on top of its head, while the other was framed by dark streaks that looked like hanks of black hair. The second head had to be mine because my brown hair hung down in the same lank style, although I wished it wouldn't. Smiling to myself, I stuffed the letter in my Scholastic notebook and went upstairs to read it.

Dear Mary:

I was pleased as punch to get your composition! So we're buddies now, eh? I especially liked the line about your great-granddaddy crawling out of the sea mud. That sentence is good enough for Hemingway. I read it out to Jordie and he was so impressed I went around all day grinning. You have a capital F future as they like to say in this two-bit town. Doc Bradford must be proud of you.

I've told Jordie Coverdale to make you a rink this winter in case your daddy is too busy. Jordie has nothing better to do after supper. Learn to skate, and I'll show you how to play hockey. You don't have to be big and strong. You have to be smart and read the play so you know how to position your-self. Remember. You're an athlete.

> *Your special friend,*
> *John Pilkie*

Excited, I hid the letter at the back of my closet where Sal wouldn't find it. John wanted to teach me to play hockey and he called himself my "special friend." Special in what way, I wondered. Special because he was old and didn't have young friends like me, or special because he thought about me in a romantic way? But how could somebody like him have such feelings for a girl like myself (i.e., who would want to kiss some-body so crooked and awful looking)?

29

THE NEXT DAY, BEN ASKED ME TO HIS HOUSE FOR DINNER. IT was the first of many times I would go during the next few years, although I had to beg like anything before Sal gave in. As she said goodbye, she whispered in my ear that the spicy "kike" food would burn my tongue off, and then she warned me not to pester Dr. Shulman with questions about Pilkie. I told Sal I couldn't help being interested in John, and Sal laughed. To be honest, it didn't occur to me to talk to Dr. Shulman about his patients, but asking Ben's father about John struck me as a good idea.

Little Louie drove me over to the Shulmans' house, which stood at the end of the hospital property on a long, snowy drive lined with glass lanterns on tall white columns. I'd noted in my book of true facts that in the early years, when the prison was a reformatory, the Shulmans' house used to be a cigar factory. But the boys rebelled against the hard work of curing the tobacco and the cigar factory was closed. Naturally, I was interested in any place where delinquent boys made cigars.

Little Louie kissed me goodbye and waved at Ben's father who was holding open the front door for me. A man I didn't know stood just inside. Dr. Shulman said, "Mary, I'd like you to meet Dr. Torval. He works for the ministry in Toronto. Dr. Torval, this is my son's friend, Mary Bradford. Her father is a popular doctor in town."

Dr. Torval stared down at me through extra large black eyeglasses. "Are you going to be a doctor too?"

"Yuck! I can't stand blood!" The babyish words popped out before I could help it and the two men laughed. Ashamed of myself, I hurried into the front hall where I took off my winter coat and walked bug-eyed into the large living room to see where the boys had rolled cigars, although it was impossible to imagine anybody rolling a stogie here now. There was blond Danish furniture, big, padded sofas, and standing lamps made out of Quebec pine that didn't match the modern tables and chairs. Mrs. Shulman liked mostly everything new. Big Louie liked mostly everything old, although "old" in Madoc's Landing was a relative term that really meant "Victorian." I was pretty sure the delinquent boys wouldn't recognize the place.

THANKS TO DR. SHULMAN, ALL the harmless patients ate on linen tablecloths and used proper cutlery. Their meals were served by the harmless patients who worked in the hospital kitchen. Mrs. Shulman used one of the patients who worked in the kitchen as her helper. His name was Jimmy and he welcomed me, a white linen napkin folded across his arm. Trying not to stare, I shook Jimmy's harmless hand, and he led me into the Shulmans' dining room.

AT WHAT POINT SHOULD I stop pretending Jimmy was normal and scream if Jimmy did something weird? Not at any point, it turned out, because Jimmy was polite. It was the Shulmans' food that gave me problems, but not for the reason Sal predicted. Dr. Shulman dumped a second helping of brisket on my plate without asking, and he gave third helpings to himself and Ben. Dr. Torval and I had to pep up the bland slabs of overcooked beef with mustard. When Jimmy brought in some tasteless white cookies called Mandelbrot, Dr. Torval began to quiz Dr. Shulman about John playing hockey for the Rats.

"Aren't you taking a big chance, Rob?" Dr. Torval raised his eyebrows above his eyeglasses, whose frames split his long, rubbery face in half. "Pilkie could escape again."

"It was Mary's father's idea," Dr. Shulman replied. "He and I consider hockey part of Pilkie's therapy. So far it's going well. The Rats have been winning all their games."

"How convenient for you," Dr. Torval said dryly. "You're a hockey fan, I understand?"

"Yes, I am. So is Addie." Dr. Shulman smiled at his wife. "Don't worry, Henry. Pilkie will be well-guarded."

"Rob, you know how I feel about that terrible man," Mrs. Shulman said. "Guards won't stop somebody like him."

The image of John's calm, manly face being sprayed by the guard's hose rose before me. "I think John Pilkie's nice. He rescued me from the Bug House boys."

Silence fell. Nearby, Jimmy set down the plate of cookies.

"Are you making up a story, Mary?" Mrs. Shulman asked.

I shook my head. "Cross my heart and point to heaven," I answered, holding Mrs. Shulman's gaze for one, two, three seconds.

"It's true!" Ben said. "Pilkie scared them off."

"Do you know, son, a patient told me about that incident?" Dr. Shulman smiled slightly. "Didn't you, Jimmy?"

"I was in the work truck that day," Jimmy replied in a low, nervous voice. We all turned around to stare at him.

"Thank you, Jimmy, for telling us." Dr. Shulman nodded at Jimmy who smiled shyly before he disappeared into the kitchen.

Across the table, Ben caught my eye. "Mary and I are very interested in killers. We want to know what makes a person good, and what makes people bad."

"I didn't know a subject like that would be of interest to children," Dr. Torval said.

"All children want to know if they're good, Henry." Dr. Shulman chuckled. "I'm hoping this interest will lead my son to study psychiatry, but I fear he has his heart set on playing professional hockey."

For a moment nobody spoke. Dr. Torval looked askance at Ben, as if wondering how such a plump boy would make it onto an NHL team. Ben's face fell.

"I want to know if adults are good too," I said quickly. "I mean, as good as my father. Sal says my father would withstand the devil himself to help his patients."

Dr. Shulman and Dr. Torval laughed their heads off, and I could feel myself flush. After they composed themselves again, Dr. Torval turned towards me, his lips compressed in a thin line. "You're too young to understand. John Pilkie never learned the golden rule."

"Henry, did you know the Christian religion borrowed the golden rule from us?" Dr. Shulman asked. He spoke in the boring "Old-Man-So-and-So" tone he used for scoring a point. "Rabbi

Hillel said, 'That which is hateful to you, do not do to your neighbour.'"

"You phrase it in the negative," Dr. Torval remarked.

"Yes, but we came up with it first. One of our scholars, Maimonides, created a code of charitable acts. What Pilkie did for Mary is an example of number five. Giving charity without being asked."

Dr. Torval's eyes turned dark behind his spectacles, but Dr. Shulman didn't seem to notice.

"Henry, you may not know this yet, but I'm pushing the government to review cases like Pilkie's. Some of our patients have committed crimes that won't be repeated. So why should they be locked up for life?"

"Rob?" Mrs. Shulman shook her head warningly. Dr. Shulman's smile faded. In a false, jokey tone, he added, "So why can't our patients get their cases reviewed? After all, Henry, how many times can you kill your wife?"

"That's not funny, Rob," Mrs. Shulman replied. "Shouldn't the two of you be getting back to work?"

"You're absolutely right, Addie." Dr. Shulman stood up abruptly. "Ben, show Mary the list of the eight levels of giving. It's in the Mishneh Torah." He nodded at me. "I think she'll find it interesting."

Is Goodness the Same Thing as Keeping Your Bedroom Tidy?

In the Shulman library, Ben showed me the legal book that listed the eight levels of giving, which the scholar Maimonides had written into Jewish law. I copied them down on a sheet of foolscap. Later, alone in my bedroom, I scribbled in *M.B.'s Book of True Facts: Dr. Shulman said that John Pilkie performed a charitable act when he rescued me from the Bug House boys.* Then I added: *So maybe John is a little bit good. But goodness is confusing. My father puts the needs of his patients before himself, and he does it over and over again. Is my father good if he's looking after other people because his mother told him that a man his size could go around killing them? And are you good if you're only doing good deeds because it's expected of you? Aren't you fooling yourself? What if being good is a habit, like keeping your bedroom tidy?*

I copied out the eight levels of giving into *M.B.'s Book of True Facts*, going from the least good to the most good:

8. *When donations are given grudgingly.*
7. *When one gives less than he should, but does so cheerfully.*
6. *When one gives directly upon being asked.*
5. *When one gives directly without being asked. (I wrote John Pilkie's name in capital letters beside this number.)*
4. *When the recipient is aware of the donor's identity but the donor does not know the identity of the recipient.*
3. *When the donor is aware of the recipient's identity but the recipient is unaware of the source.*
2. *When the donor and recipient are unknown to each other.*
1. *When the donor gives a loan that stops the recipient from becoming poor.*

As I was finishing number one, Sal poked her head into my room. "What on earth are you doing, Mouse?"

"Writing down a Jewish law," I replied. "Dr. Shulman says the Jews thought up the golden rule before we did. This proves the Hebrew faith is older and smarter than the Christian religion."

"Listen, Lady Jane. I never said Jews aren't clever."

"Well, you didn't come right out and say it. But you called them 'kikes.'"

Sal's face turned red. "You won't tell your father that, eh?"

She looked nervous. I shook my head. Then she swore that she wasn't prejudiced. But I suspected her of prejudice all the same.

30

FIVE DAYS BEFORE CHRISTMAS, SAL AND I STOOD AT THE LIVING room window watching a snowstorm.

"It's going to be an icebox winter," Sal said morosely.

"What's an icebox winter?" Little Louie yelled from the kitchen where she was typing up a newspaper story.

"Everybody knows what an icebox winter is," Sal snapped. "It feels like you're locked up in a fridge."

I didn't see it like Sal. After all, there's nothing more reassuring than watching a blizzard from inside a warm house. For one thing, the falling snow is so soft and quiet you know it can't hurt you as it eddies this way and that in front of the glass or cascades from the branches of the cedars after the wind shakes the branches. The snow brings a bittersweet lonely feeling, too: that you are on your own in your winter life.

As I stood watching the snow, Sal and I listened for my father's Oldsmobile in the muffled sounds of cars passing on the road. The snowbanks had grown so high we couldn't see them go by. Not that there were many to see because who, except my father, would go out on such a wild night? He had promised to come home early to watch the Toronto Maple Leafs play the Montreal Canadiens on our black-and-white Zenith television. Now there was no sign of him. But somebody was coming down the road. The figure struggled through the drifts, its face hidden behind a scarf. The figure turned up our unshovelled driveway and started to wade through the snow to our back door. At the same moment, Morley drove up and parked his car on the street. The figure hailed my father climbing out of his Oldsmobile, and they stood outside talking, the ghostly snow swirling around their bundled up shapes.

"For the love of God," Sal cried flinging open the back door. "Get in out of the storm."

They hurried into our kitchen, stamping the snow off their galoshes while the spaniels barked wildly.

"Why, it's you, Mary," Mrs. Pilkie said, unwrapping the scarf from her face. "John has been telling me all about you."

"He has?"

"You bet. He says you're learning to skate this winter."

Pleased, I rushed over to tell my father about John promising to make me a hockey rink. I wanted to hear his response. But something stopped me. The something that always stopped Morley and me from having a real conversation.

Morley cuffed my cheek. "Are our boys winning, Mary?"

"The score is two nothing for the Canadiens," I replied, shaking my head sadly.

Morley smacked his newspaper against the kitchen table. "What's the matter with those bums?"

"You know what happens if you get excited, Doc Bradford," Sal said.

"Get excited?" Mrs. Pilkie laughed. "Who doesn't get excited when he watches the Leafs?"

"Doc Bradford gets more excited than most," Sal answered.

My father poured himself a cup of coffee, pretending not to hear. "So Georgie, are you ready for your insulin shot?" he asked.

Sal quickly ushered me out of the kitchen. A moment later, Mrs. Pilkie hurried into our living room, rolling down the sleeve of her blouse. My father followed, his tired, deep-set eyes seeking out the television.

"Doc Bradford, with you behind us, I guess John and I have nothing to fear." Mrs. Pilkie grinned at Sal and me. "Nobody will go against Doc Bradford, eh girls?"

"Oh, now, Georgie." Morley coughed self-consciously.

"I wouldn't count my chickens if I was you," Sal said.

Mrs. Pilkie ignored her. "Oh Lordie, you have a Zenith!" She plopped her weight into a stuffed armchair. "Mind if I watch?"

"Nobody's saying you can't." Sal turned up the volume on the TV. "Even if you are Doc Bradford's patient."

"Well, that's not all I am to Doc Bradford." Mrs. Pilkie removed her dark glasses and rubbed her strange, milky-looking eyes. She'd never be able to take out a boy's appendix now.

"What are you talking about?" Sal asked.

"Doc Bradford and I have been through a lot together. That's why he's getting my boy a review of his case. He said so outside."

Sal's mouth dropped open. It was true that Mrs. Pilkie had a special relationship with my father. Together they had done a miraculous thing: they had removed a small boy's appendix far away from the safety of a modern hospital, my father coaching Mrs. Pilkie through every step of the operation. But I wonder now about Mrs. Pilkie telling Sal that my father had vowed to help her. Did Morley really promise to get a review of John's case? Sal and I couldn't hear what they were saying to each other out on the driveway. Maybe my father made a vague promise about seeing what he could do for John and that was enough for Mrs. Pilkie to place hopes on Morley too large for anyone to fulfill.

In any case, Morley didn't contradict Mrs. Pilkie. Maybe he hadn't heard her boasting about his help. He sat stiff and white-faced on the sofa, his eyes on the television. The same mood of religious awe we felt at the Dollartown Arena was sweeping up my father in its grip. Sal and I felt it, too, as we sat down, turning our faces towards the screen. We were taking part in something more holy and serious than our daily lives in Madoc's Landing. On the ice, Leafs player Tim Horton had just knocked down Jean Beliveau of the Canadiens. "That Horton, eh?" Mrs. Pilkie said.

"Beliveau started it," my father growled.

"No, Horton did," Sal retorted, coming in with coffee and a plate of the butter tarts she had baked that morning. It was the only baking she did well, and the tarts were Morley's favourite.

"Oh, they're all roughnecks!" Mrs. Pilkie held up her cup for Sal's coffee.

By the blue line, the referee in the Montreal Forum was handing out a penalty to Horton. On the sofa, my father had started breathing heavily, a bad sign. He bit into one of Sal's tarts without looking at her.

"A thank you would be nice, Doc Bradford," Sal said. "I baked them for you specially."

Morley grunted. As the camera zoomed in on the referee's

face, my father leapt to his feet. On the screen, the referee was escorting Horton off the ice.

"You no-good son-of-a-bitch! Beliveau started it!" He grabbed a second butter tart.

"Watch your language, Doc Bradford!" Sal cried. "And sit down! You're blocking our view."

"I won't sit down. That goddamn ref has it coming." Morley wound up like a baseball pitcher and the butter tart hit the television with a satisfying splat. Its juicy sauce slowly slipped down the glass. "You two-bit bum! You'll pay for that call!" My father threw another tart. Now large blurry smears of syrup and raisins covered most of the screen. We could no longer see the game.

His shouts brought Little Louie. Mrs. Pilkie was laughing, as if she'd seen men behaving like this before. My aunt looked aghast.

"Doc Bradford, that's enough," Sal said. "It's bad for your blood pressure." She nodded at me. I nodded back, although I hated sending my father outside during a game. But I went along, because Sal told me it kept my father from having a heart attack.

While my aunt and Mrs. Pilkie watched, Sal grabbed Morley by the arm and steered him like a resentful child into the kitchen where she made him put on his coat and hat. He didn't resist her, but he wasn't going to co-operate either. When Sal opened the back door and pushed him onto the kitchen porch, I wanted to stop her. But I couldn't make the words come.

"You stay outside 'til I say otherwise," Sal told him.

He dropped his eyes and said, "Mmm-hmm." I wasn't allowed to interfere. He and Sal had worked out a system. He had to wait out the game in the garage, warming himself with the space heater that was used to start the Oldsmobile on cold winter mornings. Sal and Morley's system didn't allow conversation. They used hand signals to communicate the score. The index finger on Sal's right hand meant a Leaf goal and her left index finger meant a goal by the other team.

After the Montreal Canadiens scored the next goal, Sal told me to put on my winter coat and tell my father. He sat waiting on an old lawn chair wearing his dove-grey fedora and dark winter coat. A plaid scarf was wrapped around his neck. How could he sit there with nothing except a space heater warming his toes? The air inside the garage froze me to the bone.

Shouldn't I spring him from his exile? And how would I go about it? I didn't have many options although I could always try scolding him in Sal's sternest shaming voice. *This is ridiculous behaviour for a grown man. Come inside before you catch your death of cold!* Would he come back if I pointed out that no sport, even hockey, was worth suffering over? But I already knew my father thought hockey was worth it. So I cleared my throat. Morley looked up hopefully; clouds of steam floated out of his mouth while I shook my head and held up the index finger on my left hand. The steamy clouds of his breath suddenly grew bigger and more dramatic.

That night, I held up my left index finger five more times inside the garage. My father's reaction never changed. Each time, he stared at me in disbelief, clouds of his breath billowing from his mouth. Each time, I waited for him to slump over, dead in his lawn chair. But nothing of the sort happened. And when I came back with news of another Montreal goal, he was still sitting upright wearing an expectant look as if he couldn't help hoping I was bringing good news.

No good news came. By the end of the game, the final tally was eight fingers on my left hand (for Montreal) and two fingers on my right (for the Leafs). George Armstrong, the gentlemanly Leaf captain, had a misconduct penalty for arguing a call, and the referee had handed out penalties to every player except the goalies. Sal put my father to bed with a hot water bottle and his electric blanket turned on high. Still in high spirits, Mrs. Pilkie kissed me goodbye. I watched her leave, and then I stared for a long while at the snow falling in the yellow glow of the street lamps.

THE NEXT DAY, MY AUNT and I packed our bags for our Christmas holiday. Morley drove us through the snowy streets to the train station. We said our goodbyes inside the freezing car, our breath fogging the windshield.

"Will you come down for Christmas?"

"I'll have to see, Mary." He helped my aunt and me out with our luggage. We walked over to the platform where the conductor stood, waiting to put us on the train. When my father was sure we were in good hands, he honked goodbye, and his red taillights slowly disappeared down the road. Did I mention the hopeless mood I fell into when Morley didn't come on my holidays? The hot, achy feeling was too embarrassing for words. I tried to push it down before Hindrance whispered, *See, Mouse, I told you. Morley doesn't waste time on pipsqueaks.*

PART FOUR

CHRISTMAS AT THE GREAT HOUSE

31

ON THE TRAIN, I MADE A LIST OF THE REASONS WHY I BELIEVED IN
John. There was no point holding back now.

The Case for John Pilkie

1. *Morley believes a concussion made John kill his wife and baby
   girl, and so do I. (It's a just a crying shame John didn't use his
   concussion for an alibi.)*
2. *The people who believe he's a killer (like Sal and Sib) are prejudiced.
   Sal wanted to marry him but he chose somebody else and Sib is
   jealous because Sal used to be engaged to John.*
3. *And there's another reason. Grown-up truth is different from
   plain truth because grown-up truth feels intimidating, like the
   way Morley looks in his white operating gown instead of the
   bright orange Bermuda shorts that Big Louie gave him for his
   birthday. There are so many interpretations of truth, after all.
   There's the stuff you read in old books and songs and newspaper
   stories pasted in my scrapbook, and long-ago epistles such as my
   great-grandfather's letters. And then there are the loving things we*

write on greeting cards and the dumb things we say to each other without thinking. So no matter what the newspapers report, John's truth will be different from what other people tell me.

4. *The last reason isn't obvious. John is always nice to Ben and me. If he is as bad as Dr. Torval says, I would like him anyway because when he is kind, he is kinder than anybody else.*

32

CHRISTMAS DAY WAS COLD AND OVERCAST. AFTER OPENING OUR presents, we.sat in the breakfast room eating steak and kidney pie while bottles of sparkling Burgundy cooled in the snow-banks outside. Nobody drinks the wine now, but in Big Louie's day it was a big deal.

"Is Morley coming today?" I asked.

"Maybe he's trying to come." My aunt left the table and dialled our number on the alcove phone. She waited a while before she hung up. "I can't get anyone on the line," she said, coming back. "Something must be holding your father up, Mouse."

"Something always holds Morley up," Big Louie said as she soaked her second helping of kidney pie with Willa's gravy. "That man's going to drop dead of a heart attack."

I felt myself flinch, but I didn't take up Big Louie's remark about Morley, the way I normally would. I guess I didn't think Morley would show in the first place.

WHEN EVERYONE WENT OFF FOR afternoon naps, I dialled our number. On the other end, the phone rang and rang until

Sadie, the town operator, patched me through.

"Doc Bradford's residence," a nasal voice said.

"Sal, it's me, Mouse. Is my father home?"

"He's at the hospital operating. Guess you heard about the Wongs on Highway 29? Well, their truck slipped on some ice. Mr. Wong bled to death on a snowbank."

"Ugh. That's horrible."

"The blood's still smeared all over the snow. Sib and I saw it yesterday. The Mackie girl had a head-on collision at Angel's Corners. Both cars are write-offs."

"Is the Mackie girl going to live?"

"If she's lucky. She's got a fractured skull, a dislocated shoulder, plus two broken legs. Your father was up 'til 5:30 this morning putting Lorraine back together. Did you get some loot for Christmas?"

I told Sal about the adventure book, *The Lennon Sisters and the Secret of Holiday Island* by Doris Schroeder, in my Christmas stocking. The Lennon Sisters were singing stars from the Lawrence Welk TV show. I didn't tell Sal that Morley took out one sister's gallbladder and that made the Lennon Sisters embarrassing as far as I was concerned. I didn't talk about getting new skates. Sal would say I was spoiled and maybe I was. It was hard to feel happy about my presents when Lorraine Mackie was broken into pieces and Mr. Wong had bled to death on the snow. Should I get Christmas presents while others suffer? I didn't know the answer and maybe Morley didn't either. Maybe that was why he worked so hard helping others.

CHRISTMAS DAY UNFOLDED WITHOUT MORLEY showing up. Before dinner on Boxing Day, Big Louie gave me a letter written by my great-grandfather and an heirloom brooch made of seed pearls and filigreed gold. She saved the brooch for last, because she didn't want the box getting lost in the Christmas wrapping. The brooch belonged to Big Louie's mother. Afterwards, I waited for my father to call me back. Finally, I gave up waiting and decided to write John and tell him how much I liked his letter.

Dear Mr. Pilkie:

I want to thank you for taking the time to read my composition. And I hope you had a good Christmas dinner at the Bug House. Christmas here was tons of fun and the snow isn't up to the windowsills the way it is at home.

On Christmas afternoon, we played the Fox and the Hare. First, my aunt helped Uncle Willie stomp down a large circle in the snow. Then Uncle Willie told me to be the hare, but my aunt said she would be the hare. She knows I could never catch anybody.

My aunt ran after Uncle Willie who pranced like a show horse along the tramped down paths. As soon as my aunt got close, Uncle Willie lay down in the snow and started moving his arms up and down. He told my aunt she had to make snow angels too so she lay down in the snow beside him, laughing and panting, and pretty soon all of us were lying on our backs moving our arms up and down in the snow.

For Christmas dinner, we ate two fifteen-pound hen turkeys because male turkeys are tough. Uncle Willie cut us slices while Big Louie shouted: "Start carvin', Marvin! I'm starvin'!" You would have been crazy about Willa's mashed potatoes, and her homemade bread sauce, not to mention her perfectly browned turnips. Willa put red carnations in our finger bowls and homemade bread inside our linen napkins. We dipped our fingers in the bowls and ate the bread with our turkey.

I hope your own turkey was juicy and the hospital cook didn't leave your roast potatoes in the oven until they turned hard as hockey pucks. After dinner, Uncle Willie produced a joke book. A dozen pardons for all the dirty words that follow. It started with Uncle Willie reciting a verse:

"This is the story of the bee whose sex is very hard to see. You cannot tell a he from a she but she can tell and so can he."

My grandmother finished it: "The bee is a very busy soul and has no time for birth control so that is why, in times like these, you see so many sons of bees."

Everybody laughed their heads off.

"Let's see if you can remember this one, mother," Uncle Willie said. "The farmer asks the young man, are your intentions toward my daughter honourable or dishonourable?"

"And the young man says, I've got a choice?" Big Louie answered. Everybody laughed twice as hard and Uncle Willie swore that my grandmother was the only woman who could tell the punch line of a dirty joke properly.

Maybe Uncle Willie's jokes will make you mad so please ignore the places where I have scratched the jokes out. Tomorrow we're going on a sleigh ride along Bear Creek and then we will visit my great-grandfather's grave. In case you forgot, he's the pioneer oilman. My grandmother toasts my great-grandfather's grave every Christmas with a bottle of champagne because my great-grandfather was a temperance man. And every year, my grandmother pours a glass of bubbly on his tombstone, and shouts: "Down with temperance, Dad!"

Well, I have to go now and read a letter my great-grandfather wrote. Big Louie says I will be very surprised by it, and she wants to talk to me after I finish. I hope you get to watch the Leafs game in the Bug House. By the way, it's not fair that you can't get a review of your case, and cross my heart I will do all I can to help you.

Your special friend,
Mary Bradford

P.S. I can't help wondering what you mean by special friend? That's how you signed your last letter. Not that I'm taking it the wrong way. I'm just asking.

33

ON DECEMBER 30, AFTER WILLA PUT ME TO BED, I SNUCK DOWN-
stairs and watched the Leafs play the Canadiens on the huge
colour TV that Big Louie had bought in Detroit. We couldn't
get colour TV in Madoc's Landing. Our reception was always
black and white, and as snowy as Christmas on the *Perry Como
Show*. I imagined Morley swearing a blue streak when the Pocket
Rocket fired a pair of goals to make the score 3–1. The Leafs lost
3–2 so I went upstairs to read my great-grandfather's letter. I
read it over and over, unable to believe my eyes.

Vergennes, Vermont
February , 1862

Dear Mr. Vidal:

*Me and mine do not appreciate you contacting us regarding
the news of our son Cameron nor have our feelings changed
since I wrote your aunt some twenty years before. We have no
evidence other than the word of your dead mother that you
are Cameron's issue. My son drowned when he was a settler*

at Maxwell, a utopian commune on the shores of Lake Huron.
He was nineteen when he died. In his memory I ask you to
refrain from all further communication. Neither myself, nor
my wife Isabella wish to hear from you in future.

With every good wish,
Bradley Davenport

When I found her, my grandmother was in her bedroom pinning brooches on her bedroom curtain; she liked to keep her brooches on the inside panel so they would be safe from thieves who were bound to be interested in her one-hundred-year-old porcelain cameos of women wearing leafy garlands and scarves.

When she saw my face she said: "So now you know about Dad."

"Why didn't you tell me Old Mac's parents weren't married?"

"Dearie, I had to wait until you were old enough to hear it. But it makes sense looking back. Old Mac was always proper and sometimes proper people are the ones with the most to hide."

"I guess nobody can say that about you."

"Now, now. I'm not criticizing Dad. It's just a shame he thought he had to keep this from us."

"You mean that he was a capital B-A-S-T-A-R-D?"

"Don't be naughty, Mouse. Children pop out everywhere. Who cares where they come from? It only matters that we love them." Giving me one of her perfumed hugs, she added, "Life is full of shocks, Dearie. We have to roll with the punches." Big Louie's words made my spirits sink. What was the point of working hard to get rich if you didn't have a father to love you?

Back in my room, I took out my letter to John and added a second postscript:

> *Maybe you don't remember but I told you my great-grandfather found his father and struck oil. I was wrong. Mac Vidal didn't find his father. By the time my great-grandfather came up here, his own father was dead and buried. As if this isn't bad enough, Mac Vidal was a capital B-A-S-T-A-R-D and his father's family disowned him. It's pretty humiliating. Anyway, I'm giving up on my composition. There is no point wasting time on something so babyish.*

PART FIVE

THE ICEBOX WINTER

34

AS SOON AS OUR TRAIN LEFT THE STATION, IT STARTED TO SNOW. It snowed all evening. When I told my aunt about my great-grandfather's letter, she said it was about time Big Louie told me that Old Mac was illegitimate. Men go around making babies all over the place without getting married, so it was no surprise to her. Then she said she was sorry she spoke sharply and I knew that she was thinking of Max, whose baby was expected anytime now. In the morning, when I opened my eyes, she was sitting by the foot of my train berth, reading "Can This Marriage be Saved?" in *Ladies Home Journal,* her expression as concentrated as a nun at her prayers. I recognized the magazine feature. Some nights after Sal finished with the magazine, I read it under the covers with a flashlight and I was always amazed at the solutions the magazine counsellor came up with for hopeless cases.

A moment later, Little Louie tossed the magazine aside and stared sadly out the train window. I guessed her mind was still on Max. Maybe she felt blue about returning to Madoc's Landing with me. I shut my eyes again and tried not to think about my aunt and her problems.

BY THE TIME WE STEPPED out onto the platform at Madoc's Landing, it had stopped snowing. There was no sign of Morley, and it was cold, icebox cold, just as Sal had prophesied. Tubby Dault, Sal's father, picked us up. He whinnied like a horse when he laughed and said that my father and the hockey team were snowed in good up in Owen Sound. But John Pilkie and the Rats had won their game. My aunt gave Tubby a long-suffering smile.

Tubby was a short, barrel-chested man who ran a bootleg taxi. When you saw him coming, you knew somebody in town was either out for a Sunday drive, or having themselves a party. So when he drove in our driveway, the neighbours peered out their front window. I pointed at our suitcases and our neighbours nodded and shut their curtains. On the kitchen table, my aunt found Morley's note: *I'm in Owen Sound with the boys and Sal is at the farm. The young Coverdale fellow has made a rink in our backyard. Morley.*

John's promise rushed back to me and I hurried over to the kitchen window. A broad rectangle of ice shone under the porch light. So he was a man of his word, after all. *John is your special friend*, I told myself as I walked up and down the living room, slapping my sides to keep warm. I had to do something. The house was frigid. "Something's wrong with the furnace," my aunt called as she fiddled with the thermostat. When she turned on the taps, no water came out. The pipes were frozen and it was too late to call the repairman. So she plugged in Morley's electric blanket in his bedroom and made me get under it while she built a fire in the hearth.

"The pipes froze because Sal wouldn't let Sib spread horse manure on them. That keeps them from bursting."

"It sounds like the cure is worse than the disease," Little Louie replied.

"Well, maybe, but everything's going to be fine," I said.

Little Louie laughed tonelessly as she crawled in beside me. "I'm the one who should be telling you that," she replied, putting her arm around me, holding me close.

IN THE MIDDLE OF THE night, I woke and found my aunt gone. I put on slippers and a dressing gown and went to look for her. The house was so cold I could see my breath. Her voice floated upstairs. I could tell by her tone that she was arguing with my grandmother. I wrapped the sleeve of my housecoat around the receiver of the hall phone and put it to my ear.

"Steel yourself, Louisa. I have news for you."

"It's happened."

"Max's wife had a baby boy. And he's happy about it. I warned you, Dearie. Men change when they have a son. Especially if the boy looks like his daddy."

"Well, that's your opinion."

"It's a godsend, Louisa. Max isn't husband material."

"I can't believe you're saying this. What about father? Was he husband material?"

"You know the answer, Louisa. I don't want you to suffer like I did."

"Somebody's on the party line," my aunt said coldly. "I'd better go."

"All right, I'm here if you need me. Goodbye, Dearie."

My aunt slammed down the phone.

35

THE ICEBOX WINTER UNFOLDED THE WAY SAL SAID IT WOULD. IT snowed so much it covered up our backyard rink. Sal wouldn't let me go outside. Luckily, the snow hid the new pink flamingoes on our neighbour's lawn along with the eggshells and rotting banana peels that Sal heaved behind our garage when she didn't want the bother of taking the garbage out to the sidewalk. As for Morley, he worked day and night. Little Louie worked hard too. Every day she visited the mental hospital, researching her story, and every afternoon she came home with weird information like her description of the Total Encounter Capsule that Dr. Shulman was building for the men at Maple Ridge. It was going to be a windowless, soundproofed room, Little Louie told me, eight feet wide and ten feet long. Its walls would be painted green and it would be empty except for a sink and a toilet. The guards would stick straws through the door so the men could sip juice, milk, coffee, and eggnog, because they were locked in for three days once the therapy started. According to Little Louie, television cameras would be trained through holes in the walls so the men couldn't get away with anything. But strangest of all, the men were going to be locked up without their clothes on because Dr. Shulman believed nudity broke down their defences. When I asked if John Pilkie would take off his clothes too, she laughed. She said he would do anything if it would get a review of his case. I worried for him. The closest I could imagine to being in such a mortifying situation was having the Bug House boys catch me peeing standing up, which is what I did in the maple bush when I was caught short.

Then, one grey January afternoon after school, an envelope arrived with the familiar curly letters and the two I's dotted with smiling faces.

To my special friend, M.B.:

Boy, have you got yourself in a funk! You sound so blue I had to sit down and whip off this letter. You are special, and that's why I used the word. You are also one heck of a letter writer and I would be lost without a friend like you on the outside. Nobody in this godforsaken dump understands and doesn't want to either. Even Jordie doesn't believe me when I say my concussion made me crazy. He says he does but I can tell by his smirk that he is just humouring me, the way he does the other nut cases. And it is not babyish to write a composition about your great-granddaddy. It is a grown-up thing to do. And who cares if your great-granddaddy's parents weren't married? I sure don't. I know you must be plenty upset or you wouldn't have used a swear word. Look here. Your great-granddaddy is your hero. And a hero doesn't get everything he wants although most of us can get a lot of what we want if we work hard and take ourselves seriously.

Now this may sound funny coming from somebody like me. I've made a mess of things. I know that. But I had some bad luck. Peggy used to say there is something in my nature that makes my bad luck. She understood me very well. That's one of the reasons I loved her. But I won't get into my troubles here. Don't you go giving up on your composition. Those old oilmen were an interesting bunch even if most of them were Yanks who didn't respect our Queen.

I'm glad you had a good Christmas. Your family are top drawer. Especially you, and your aunt Louisa. She's a fine figure of a woman and a career gal too. The Christmas holidays wore me down. I got into a little altercation with Sib Beaudry. Nothing serious. Doc Bradford said Mother Pilkie could bring me a turkey dinner but Sib wouldn't let her. And Dr. Schulman was in Florida. I sat with the rest of the nutcases and ate rubber turkey in the group therapy room. Afterwards, the cook from the main building sent over candy canes and little red candy Christmas trees. Then Jordie showed us It's a Wonderful Life *with Jimmy Stewart. Sib shut down the movie projector halfway through and made us go back to our cells. The things I could tell you about this dump. Never mind. You're too young and sweet to hear what goes on. Hey, Jordie tells me you are learning to skate. Keep up the good work!*

> *With fondest regards,*
> *John*

There was another letter in the envelope, under the first one. I read it as fast as I could and then I read it all over again, unable to believe my luck.

Dear Mary:

*At the Beaudry farm, I said I would tell you and your pal
about the old days when a has-been like myself started out.
Well, here goes: my daddy said I was born with skates on
so he didn't have to lace them for me. There was some truth
to my daddy's boast. I always wanted to play hockey. Right
from the start I wanted to fly down the ice, my blood on fire. I
loved the chilly air coming off the rink and the fans' screams
in my ears. When I was a tyke, my daddy would take me
to the Ontario Hockey Association games and tell me I was
going to be a star. He said I had the discipline or at least I did
until that so-and-so tripped me and I fell head first into the
boards.*

*If freeze up came early my daddy built a small ice rink out
at the Light. He would strap pillows onto his shins. I would
take shots at him until I fell down. Then he would pick me
up and set me down on my skates and we would go at it until
the sun set. In late fall, it was pretty bitter out on the water.
I never complained. Daddy Pilkie was a hard man. He was
always at me to check the bejesus out of the other team. So I
swung my stick like the best of them. Course, you never can
avoid roughhousing. That's the way the fans want it.*

*I went through the junior leagues playing in the finals
every Easter. In the summer I worked at Towonda Lodge
building guest cabins for Old Man Beaudry. By the time I was
nineteen, I wasn't scrawny any longer. I was tough although
I never grew much after I was sixteen. My specialty was speed
and ragging the puck. These skills got the attention of
Mr. Lewis the scout who came up to Madoc's Landing. He*

*found the best players north of Barrie, Ontario. Kids up here
have nothing to do except play hockey. Hockey brings winter
inside, eh? You could say hockey shrinks winter down into a
rectangle of ice so us players can charge across it like gods of
the timberland doing combat for our fans. It's a miracle the
way we can enjoy ourselves all huddled together under the
arena roof. Did you know hockey started in Brebeuf County?
Those braves used to play stickball. Sometimes their games
lasted for months. They got injuries that crippled or killed
them. I learned this from a museum.*

   *Do you know a poem by Poe called "Annabel Lee"? I
found it last week in the hospital library. One of its lines
reminds me of you because you have the brightest brown
eyes of any gal I know. "And the stars never rise but I feel the
bright eyes of the beautiful Annabel Lee."*

Yours truly,
J.P.

I was only half satisfied by his explanation of special friend
(i.e., I was glad he cared enough to write to me about what the
term meant to him, although I had something else in mind).
What did I want "special friend" to mean? That I was the only
one who understood him, and that my understanding would
make him appreciate me so much he couldn't help loving me.
That night I dreamt about marrying him.

Mouse's Dream about Gentleman Jack Pilkie

In my dream John looks exactly like Edgar Allan Poe, except
that he has on a Red Wings hockey sweater and John's cowlick

hangs over his forehead the way it does in real life instead of being brushed back into a mop of dark curls, which is how the dead poet wore his hair. John looks as sad as Poe in his old sepia-toned photographs because we can't live in our kingdom by the sea. And John never tires of calling me "Annabel Lee" and he says love always works out, although you have to try as hard as you can, which is what the counsellor tells couples to do in *Ladies Home Journal* feature "Can This Marriage Be Saved?" "Yes, I know, darling," I reply, resting my head on his chest and inhaling the hot fresh bread scent of his white shirt that I starched for him myself.

Naturally, we have problems like other couples, but we act quickly on the counsellor's advice since we love each other so much. *John was often away from Mary playing hockey but when she told him she was lonely, he was able to reschedule his games so they could have more time together. It was a successful resolution and our magazine considers this case closed.*

The next morning I wrote him back.

Dear Mr. Pilkie:

Thank you for both your letters and for explaining why I am a special friend to you. You are my special friend too. And thank you for the compliment about my brown eyes even though I know you are just trying to be nice. "Annabel Lee" is one of my favourite poems. I especially like the line that says Poe loved Annabel Lee with a love that was more than love. It must be amazing to have someone love you like that. Not that anyone would want to love me. I am too twisted and awful looking.

*Our teacher won't let us take Edgar Allan Poe in school.
She says he's too gloomy. But I think she dislikes Poe because
he married his cousin Virginia when she was only ·
thirteen. Anyway, I saw Poe's picture in a book about English
Literature and I couldn't get over how sad he looked, like
a man without a friend to call his own. I guess that pretty
much sums up his life because he died of drink and didn't get
famous until after he dropped dead.*

*I also want to thank you for getting Jordie to make an ice
rink for me. Morley is too busy to shovel it so Jordie came
back yesterday and Ben and I watched him spray the ice with
our garden hose. The ice froze even and smooth without the
little bumps the other backyard rinks get because their parents
don't flood their rinks enough. By the way, Jordie said he
would teach me the slapshot. He said every hockey player has
to know how to do it. I am still having trouble standing up
in my skates although I try hard because I want Jordie to tell
you I am doing my best.*

> *With the very fondest wishes,*
> *Mary*

*P.S. I hope you don't mind me signing off with the very fond-
est wishes. I wouldn't want anyone getting the wrong ideas
about our friendship.*

36 .

YEARS LATER, WHEN BEN WAS RESEARCHING A BOOK ABOUT THE
NHL, he sent me an old newspaper story about John. It had been
written by Malcolm Thomas, a reporter at *The Windsor Star*,
and I was astonished at how closely the story followed John's
account of his concussions. John may have told us some lies,
but the information about his concussions has been backed up
with fact. The reporter, too, was sympathetic to John's situation.
He said that John's second concussion had happened during the
second summer after the Detroit Red Wings won the Stanley
Cup. Nobody noticed when John fell into the boards in a practice game and struck his head. The team doctor didn't bother
to check out his injury. In the fall, John drove from Windsor to
Toronto to play the Leafs, and it was here that things started to go
badly for him. "Suffering from loss of memory, the result of injuries received several weeks ago in an NHL game, Pilkie was sent to
the Whitby hospital for observation," the *Globe and Mail* article
said.

According to the reporter, Malcolm Thomas, John was able
to recognize his friends and talk with the other hockey players,

but he often drifted into incoherent conversations. Twice he wandered from his room at the Royal York Hotel and came back minus his topcoat and wristwatch. He said he had given them to people he met on the street.

Things grew more serious when he jumped out of a car going forty miles an hour and got in another automobile travelling in the opposite direction. How he managed to pull this off is beyond me, although I had seen him do some extraordinary things. He must have opened the door and timed his jump like a stuntman and then raced across the highway and flagged someone down before the nurse who was driving the first car had the chance to turn around. The nurse had been taking John to the Whitby nuthouse hospital for observation. After he fled her car, he disappeared for a week until he remembered who he was and turned himself in. Two police escorted him to Whitby, where he was diagnosed as suffering from a nervous breakdown caused by the strain of the hockey season and his head injuries. A Canadian surgeon performed "a major brain operation" by cutting an opening through John's skull to relieve the pressure on his brain. But, when John tried to return to Detroit, even though a board of twelve medical examiners had given him a clean bill of health, he was informed by the United States immigration authorities that he would not be permitted to enter the country for a calendar year because he had been a patient at a psychiatric hospital.

John went back to Windsor. Six weeks later, the terrible fire happened.

I read Ben's newspaper story with indignation. It made me see all over again how unjustly John had been treated, and why he'd turned to a child like me for comfort. I believed in him, and he'd needed that. Of course, I didn't understand his feelings then. I was hoping that he would love me in the way I had begun to love him.

To my special friend:

First of all, you are not twisted and awful looking. You have the biggest, kindest eyes I've ever seen, and your long brown hair is pretty too. Second, learning to skate is hard for everyone, no matter who they are. So use your hockey stick to help you balance. You'll see. Skating is easier than walking once you get used to it. And don't you pay attention to what Jordie says about slapshots. Wrist shots may be slower but they're more accurate. Look, here are Gentleman Jack's rules for good hockey. Number one: Stick your elbows out wide. Number two: Make sure your elbows are the only thing the player skating behind you can see. Number three: Keep the blade flat on the ice and make sure it's in line with your body. Slide it back and forth in a straight line.

You follow my tips and you'll be okay. By the way, I have pneumonia. Us Pilkie men have bad lungs. So I am stuck in the Bug House infirmary, popping pills to keep my fever down. I caught the bug five days ago in the Collingwood Arena. Your daddy was none too pleased. Collingwood has the biggest, coldest arena around and I'll be darned if those cheapskates didn't turn off the heat. After the first period, our dressing room was like an icebox. We were all hot and sweaty coming off the ice so we got chilled and played badly. Your father chewed us out. I was shaking like a leaf and couldn't play the third period. Toby Walker and Kid McConkley scored a goal each, but we lost the game. Your father hasn't been in to see me yet. That's how I know he's mad. He expects a lot of us boys.

I was telling you about Mr. Lewis the scout. When Mr. Lewis saw me play, he phoned my daddy. Then he phoned the coach of the Maple Leafs. The next thing I knew I was off to hockey camp for a tryout. I didn't get a contract with the Leafs. I signed with the Oshawa Colts and that led to the Detroit Red Wings. Those years went by in a blur and players like me made more money than our daddies. So we lived it up, throwing money around and getting into trouble. Maybe you read about my hijinks, lighting cigars with hundred-dollar bills, that type of thing.

When I was playing for Detroit, I had the eyes of the country on me plus the attention of the towns south of the border. I was free but in another way I was not free at all. When I was a kid, it was only my daddy's expectations I carried. Then my daddy drowned when I was fifteen, and I had Mother Pilkie's expectations on me. When I was nineteen, it wasn't just her expectations but the expectations of the coach and the owner of the Wings weighing on me. I also had the expectations of my teammates and the fans. I didn't want to let anybody down. Then my hockey playing stopped after my own teammate took me down in a practice game. I don't know why. He tripped me and I fell into the boards. When I came to, I was seeing stars. I kept saying the same thing over and over: Don't tell the coach. That made my coach laugh. He said I'd had my bell rung. He held up his fingers and asked me to count them. I counted wrong so I had to go to the Detroit hospital.

The coach said my concussion was a badge of honour. He made me wear a helmet. It was just a few patches of leather tied together with an elastic band. I kept it on for a few games but my teammates called me a coward for wearing it so I threw it away and played bareheaded like the rest of the boys. Then I took a second hit. I had headaches for months after. I kept seeing lights feeling dizzy, that type of thing. The coach said he didn't want any malingering. As long as he was the boss and I could move my arms and legs, I was going to play hockey. I went up to Toronto for a game. My headaches got worse up there. The coach said I had mood swings. He sent me to the Whitby nuthouse for observation. The sawbones told me I was suffering from a bleed and they put a plate in my left temple. You can't see the scar because it's under my hair. That was the start of my problems. The coach wouldn't pay for my operation because my first injury happened in a practice. Then the American border guards wouldn't let me back into the States because I had been in the Whitby hospital. They said a crazy person couldn't play for the NHL. So Peggy and I moved to Windsor hoping I could play hockey with the Red Wings again.

You know what happened next.

A shrink from the Big Smoke is coming up to see me. If he likes me the doctors in Toronto will give me a review of my case. Mother Pilkie thinks it's a done deal because your daddy promised to talk to the Toronto shrink on my behalf. So maybe I won't be leaving here in a wicker casket like the rest of them.

There is something you can do for me. Mother Pilkie has a cold. So I'm missing the Medonte honey she brings. The Bug

*House jam can't hold a candle to it. Why don't you and your
aunt Louisa visit me in the infirmary and bring some along?*

> *Affectionately,*
> *Your special friend,*
> *J.P.*

37

ON THE SAME DAY THAT FRANCE TESTED ITS FIRST ATOMIC BOMB, the seventh blizzard of our icebox winter blew in from the Bay. Its flakes were as fine as grains of rice. As silvery and light as dust motes floating in sunlight. I put on my snowsuit and galoshes and went outside to wait for the Bug House van. By that time the flakes were coming down hard and fast, and it took me longer than usual to climb aboard and take my place by Ben.

"Snob, snob, Mary Bradford's a snob," the Bug House boys chanted as I sat down. Ben's shoulder pressed mine. "Don't listen," he whispered as we bounced up and down, anxious looks on our faces. It was bad enough that Hindrance caused me problems, but now that it was winter and we had to take the van, Ben and I were stuck with our mortal enemies. Groan. Sigh. I wished John could scare them off the way he did that afternoon at the icehouse, but there was nothing he could do now to stop Sam and his friends calling me names.

As soon as the boys grew quiet, I showed John's letter to Ben. He read it twice, his eyes popping. John had never signed off "affectionately" before. I told Ben about the "Annabel Lee" poem with its line, "And we loved each other with a love that was more than love." Did John love me, I whispered, with feelings stronger than love? I couldn't help thinking I was puffing myself up. Ben shook his head.

"He's crazy about you," Ben whispered. "You have to visit him, Mouse."

"You think I should?"

"He asked you, didn't he? I'll come with you."

"What if we get caught?"

"Now what are you two whisperin' about?" Sam surprised us, breathing down our necks.

"None of your beeswax. And it's 'whispering,' not 'whisperin'.'"

"Is that so, Peg Leg?" Sam said. "Well, I know who you're whisperin' about. Pilkie! He nearly killed one of the guards last week."

"He did not!"

"Did so! My dad told me, but nobody is supposed to know in case they stop Pilkie from playing hockey."

"Who was the guard?"

"Sib Beaudry. John choked him with a sheet when Sib came into his cell. My dad says Sib went out cold for one whole minute."

"Well, Sib was asking for it. He picks on John."

"John! She calls him John!" Waving his arms like a conductor, Sam chanted: "Mouse Bradford is sweet on the hockey killer!" The Bug House boys chanted in the same singsong voice: "Mouse Bradford is sweet on the hockey killer." They were still chanting after the driver dropped us off. I walked into the schoolyard, holding my hands over my ears.

In current affairs class, I talked about the Rats making the Pickering Cup semi-finals. While the Bug House boys blew raspberries at me behind the teacher's back, I explained how John had led the Rats to victory over the Orillia Warriors during his first game back with the team. Generally, the Warriors played so cautiously the other team went to sleep on their skates, but this time their shutdown brand of hockey didn't work. Instead of playing slower, John skated harder and faster until he was outskating every player on the rink. Reading from *The Chronicle*, I quoted Kelsey Farrow: "It was a cleanly played game with the referee handing out only eleven penalties." Before Sam could put John down for getting six of the eleven penalties, I repeated what Kelsey had told us at the Dollartown Arena: "A player who can't get physical is no use to his team." Everybody, even the teacher, grinned.

By noon, the snow was a solid white wall, shutting out the street. We had to be let out early. The hospital van was waiting near the front door. The chant started again as I struggled up its steps. "Mouse Bradford is sweet on the hockey killer." I didn't bother covering my ears. Our van crept along behind the snow-plow as we passed Dollartown Arena and the shops on the Main Street. In the falling snow, Maple Ridge was a yellow glow behind the skeleton shapes of the trees on Bug House hill. I imagined John all by himself in the hospital infirmary. Was he thinking about me? More likely, he was being bullied by Sib Beaudry. Sib deserved to be choked as far as I was concerned. I put Sam's story in a part of my mind where I didn't have to look at it.

When the bus dropped me off, I told Little Louie about John inviting us to visit him.

"Do you think they'll let us see him, Little Louie?" I asked.

She frowned. "Probably not, Mouse."

"But he's down in the dumps."

"Well, you're right about that. But there's nothing I can do."

"Really? Oh, can't you help us, Little Louie?" I cried. "I'll just die if I can't see him."

She stared at me, surprised. Then the muscles in her face relaxed. "I guess it wouldn't hurt," she replied. "A visit from you might do John some good. He's pretty wound up about getting a review of his case."

"Will we have to throw bedsheets up to his window? And then climb up them?"

She laughed. "Nothing so dramatic, Mouse. I'll sneak you in the next time I do research at the hospital."

She grinned at my astonished face. Then she pulled out her date book and marked two Fridays from now with a big "X" and the initials "J.P."

38

ON SATURDAY, TO PLEASE JOHN, I PUT ON MY SNOWSUIT AND my skates and met Ben outside. The wind was cool and damp on my cheeks and I had to talk turkey to get myself down the kitchen steps: *Come on, Hindrance. Do it for John, your special friend.*

Although Hindrance hurt like anything, Ben helped me over to the rink, where both legs slid out from under me and I went face down into the wet packing snow. Ben bent over me, apologizing as if it was his fault that I couldn't stand on my own two skates. The kitchen door burst open. My aunt rushed out and helped me up, brushing the snow off my hair and shoulders. She said she would put on some cocoa if Ben and I came back inside. I didn't need to be asked twice.

LATER, I TORE A CLEAN page out of my schoolbook and wrote: *John wants me to learn to skate and I am trying my best.* The sentence looked too long, so I crossed it out and wrote: *I can't skate very well.* Next, I crossed out *very well* out so the shorter sentence said, *I can't skate.*

The shorter sentence didn't feel right either so I crossed out *I can't skate* and wrote: *I am a failure.*

Then I took out some notepaper and wrote him a letter.

Dear John:

I would have written sooner except that I hoped I could say I have learned to skate. Well, I can't stand up not even holding on to the hockey stick you made me. I wish it wasn't true but there is no way around it. The more I try the more my leg hurts. The other night Ben tried to push me from behind but I went over on my ankles. Ben goes way too fast but then it might not matter how slow he went because I can't get my balance. This afternoon, I tried skating without anyone around to make me nervous and I fell again. Little Louie thinks I shouldn't skate in case I hurt my left leg.

Maybe I will do better the next time. I am very sorry for letting you down. You don't deserve to be treated this way when you are helping me learn what any ordinary kid can do without thinking.

> *With fond regrets,*
> *Your special friend,*
> *Annabel Lee (alias Mary Bradford)*

P.S. Do you know why fathers are so mean to their daughters in old stories? We have to write a school composition about Iphigenia, the daughter of Agamemnon. He sacrificed her to get a good wind for his ship. That started me thinking about fairy tales where the daughters get the lousy jobs. Sons in fairy tales don't have to do that, do they?

John's letter arrived three days later. Did he know how much
I wanted to wring affection out of his words? Or maybe he did
understand and pretended not to notice how eager I was for proof
that he had romantic feelings for me. He was gallant that way.
Or maybe he was just plain oblivious because he was becoming
more and more desperate. My father and I didn't realize what
was going on, although Little Louie knew. Yes, she knew but she
didn't let on she did.

Dear Mary:

*So you think of yourself as Annabel Lee. You have a
big imagination. But look here, I'm not disappointed in
you. I know you're doing your best and your best is better
than most people's. So don't blame yourself because you're
having trouble learning to skate. It takes more time than
you'd think.*

*As for daughters in old stories, I reckon their daddies
were only thinking of themselves and they didn't understand
how precious their girls were to them until it was too late.
Of course, daddies are hard on their boys too. Look
at your great-granddaddy who got his hopes dashed
because his daddy didn't marry his mother. I figure most
of us love our daddies, but one way or another we think
they don't love us. Take my daddy, for instance. I was
never good enough for him. I waited for him to say he
was proud of me. He never did. Your daddy is too busy
to play with you. It makes me feel bad every time I think
about it. And Sal's daddy has too much fun throwing
back beers to pay attention to her but don't tell Sal I
said that.*

Well now, I didn't mean to get serious on you. Here's hoping I'll be up and at it soon so I can play hockey again.

> *Your special friend,*
> *J.P.*

39

RIGHT AFTER JOHN'S LETTER, I GOT THE CHANCE TO SEE FOR myself how Sal's father treated her. Morley was throwing a party for his hockey team. To save money, Sal took me with her to buy bootleg beer. Afterwards, she wouldn't admit she had done anything wrong by taking me along. She was so used to men dropping by for their bottles of Zing that she didn't think my father would care. Maybe he didn't. It was a lapse she would conveniently forget, when she started drinking in earnest herself.

Sal Takes Me to a Bootlegger

Sal liked to call French Town "a den of iniquity," and I'd noted in my book of true facts that this was a term for an opium den. So I was surprised that afternoon when she drove me over in our station wagon. I knew that things had changed between my father and Sal; letting her drive my mother's old car was a sign of what would follow. And that day, Sal wanted to show off the station wagon to Tubby Dault. When we pulled in, Tubby was shovelling snow on his driveway. It was a cold day and the snowbanks rose above the top of his toqued head. Behind him stood the original cabin, which had been made out of big old wide, whitewashed logs with plaster between the logs. The Daults had lived in the log house since they paddled all the way to Madoc's Landing from Drummond Island after the War of 1812. In the early days, their ancestors had been French-Canadian voyageurs and later soldiers with the British army. In exchange for fighting on the British side, the Daults were given lots in French Town and the log cabin had been put up by Dault men in 1822, forty years before the poor, overworked delinquent boys laid the foundation stones at the Bug House.

As Sal helped me out of the car, Tubby took off his mitts, which hung like mine from strings that went through his coat sleeves. Bending over, he shook my hand, his lips pulled high above his gums like a horse when it neighs at you. "Sal, you should have told me Doc Bradford's girl was coming so I could clean up." He winked at me.

"You look fine, Mr. Dault," I said nervously.

He laughed. Putting his fingers between his teeth, he whistled shrilly. A German shepherd bounded up, carrying a bottle of Fanta in its jaws. He uncapped the glass bottle, and handed me the pop. He whistled twice this time and the German shepherd brought him a bottle of beer. I caught the label, Brading Ale, as Tubby handed the bottle over to Sal. They passed it back and forth while I sipped my Fanta, praying a police car wouldn't go by. Tubby didn't seem to care that it was illegal in Brebeuf County to drink on your front lawn. Or maybe it was so cold he knew the police wouldn't expect to see people drinking in the open air. From the cabin came the sound of a fiddler playing "Red River Valley," the song that John had played the day he laid sod on the hospital grounds with the work gang.

"Ed, eh?" Tubby tilted his head in the direction of the fiddling. "That's how he pays me. Well, girlie. Your suds are all set to go."

Sal looked pleased. Motioning with his bright pink, mittenless hands, Tubby led us into his log home. It was one big room heated by a wood stove. Inside, a fiddler was walking up and down serenading half a dozen men sitting on a sofa that looked like the ones in the Salvation Army store window. Shocked, I stared down at my galoshes. Some of the men had on nothing but their long underwear, and there were empty beer bottles on the table near them.

Tubby clapped his hands. The men by the wood stove jumped to their feet, and one of the men yanked a handle at the back of the sofa. There was a loud creaking noise as the sofa folded out into a bed — except that it wasn't a bed. The part designed to hold a mattress had been cut out, and in its place were rows and rows of beer bottles. Tubby took out some of the beers and handed them to the men. When every man held a bottle, the man in the long underwear folded the bed back in place so it was a sofa again. Tubby wiggled his fingers and all the men sat down and started drinking.

"So you've got a new sweetheart, eh?" Tubby winked at Sal. "Soon you'll be too good for us Daults."

"Hush up, Pop." Sal drew a finger across her mouth, and looked directly at me. Tubby's eyes followed hers. "Oh-oh. " He quickly sat me down on a chair away from the men and said he had a story to tell me about my father. "It was when I worked in the Bug House kitchen, eh?" He started talking in rapid French, which Sal quickly translated. As a young man, Tubby was big and strong so he often helped out on other jobs at the hospital. One day a patient died and he was asked to carry the body on a stretcher. It was forbidden to lift the blanket. But he found himself alone and he was curious. So he lifted the blanket covering the corpse, and my father was lying there, pretending to be dead.

By the woodstove, the men laughed.

"Her father likes to joke around, eh?" Tubby called. The men smiled and nodded. I nodded and smiled too, although nobody associated joking around with Morley now, so I guessed Tubby was talking about something that happened before I was born. I had heard about those days from Sal, who said every woman in Madoc's Landing ran after the young doctor who kept racehorses in a barn near the Dollartown Arena. There were old snapshots of my father and unknown women patting the muzzles of thoroughbred fillies. When he married my mother, Morley gave up racing horses, and put his passion into the Madoc's Landing hockey team.

"Do you want to hear another story?" Tubby asked.

"Yes, I do. Can you tell me about Sal getting engaged to John Pilkie?"

Tubby roared. "Maybe Sal should tell you that one." He nodded at Sal, who sat daintily sipping her beer. I expected her to say "no" but, instead, she motioned for me to come closer so the men by the woodstove couldn't hear.

The Heartbreaking Story of Sal and John Pilkie

Sal was going on thirteen when she fell in love with John. The Pilkies were Tubby's second cousins by marriage and after

Mrs. Dault ran away with a beer salesman, Mrs. Pilkie used to cook dinners for Tubby and Sal. When the Pilkies weren't at the Western Light, the two families were knit tight.

The winter John turned seventeen Tubby helped Mrs. Pilkie with the birthday party. By then, Roy Pilkie had drowned. Tubby found toboggans for John's guests and he made John a bonfire by the harbour after the kids had finished tobogganing down Bug House hill. While the other kids roasted marshmallows, John kept jumping over the flames. Sal didn't think much about it until John took her aside and asked why she didn't notice how hard he was working to get her attention. Sal had had a crush on John since grade one, but he was five years older. She felt touched when he admitted he felt the same way she did.

They started going steady, and they stayed sweethearts all the time Sal was in high school. After John was discovered by a scout his life changed. Sal said he began thinking highly of himself, although he still came home every so often to keep track of Mrs. Pilkie, who depended on John to pay her household bills. When John started playing for the Oshawa Colts, he and Sal got engaged. Sib was playing for the Colts too, but Sal wasn't interested in anybody except John. Then John started playing for the Detroit Red Wings; the next thing Sal knew, John was engaged to her schoolmate, Peggy Wilson. Sal had been the one to introduce John to Peggy, a quiet, brown-haired girl with buckteeth. Peggy had come down with polio when she was two; she walked with a limp, like me, and Sal hadn't considered Peggy competition. "No offence, Mouse, eh?" Sal asked. I said none was taken, because I wanted to hear what happened next. Sal wrote John demanding an explanation for his engagement to

Peggy. He wrote back that Sal had stopped answering his letters, so he gave up on her. Later, Sal found out that Mrs. Pilkie had picked up John's letters at the post office, saying she would give them to Sal. She never did.

In those days, Mrs. Pilkie worked at the post office. She thought Sal wasn't good enough for her son. The postman found out about Mrs. Pilkie hiding her son's letters and told Sal. For three years, Sal was too hurt to speak to Mrs. Pilkie. But the damage was done. John was already married with a baby girl on his hands. When John burned up his wife and child, Sal decided Mrs. Pilkie had done her a favour.

"But his concussion made him do it," I said.

"I know Doc Bradford feels different and I respect him for that," Sal replied, her voice low and confidential. "But John always had a temper. When he was mad, he was hopping. And he always liked fire, eh? Think of him jumping over that bonfire when we were teenagers."

I didn't try and argue. What was the point? If John did what he did by mistake, then Sal's whole life was ruined. Better to think of him as a bad man so she couldn't be hurt again.

40

THE DAY THAT LITTLE LOUIE HAD PROMISED TO SNEAK US IN TO see John in the Bug House infirmary arrived. It was two Fridays later. The day with a big "X" on it in Little Louie's date book. True to her word, my aunt drove Ben and me over to the Bug House after school. In our station wagon, Ben explained how we should act. In the "Old-Man-So-and-So" voice Ben's father used when he wanted Ben to listen, Ben told us not to say "the Bug House." We were not to call the hospital "the loony bin" either, or "the nuthouse," even though lots of people did. And we shouldn't gossip about patients howling at the full moon, because there wasn't a shred of truth to it. Nor were we to call the patients "inmates" or refer to them as "criminal lunatics." If a patient was a lunatic, he didn't know right from wrong, so how could he be a criminal lunatic? I'd heard some of Ben's rules before, but most of them were new as far as my aunt was concerned. Pretty soon she was laughing her head off at how seriously Ben was taking himself. Little Louie was only eight years older than me and I couldn't help thinking that my aunt was really a kid at heart herself. She acted like she was playing hooky from school although she looked the most grown-up I'd ever seen her. She'd trimmed her bangs, and she wore a short, colour co-ordinated skirt and blouse; the turquoise shade brought out the blue in her heavy lidded eyes. She had on a short Persian lamb jacket even though it was below freezing outside. The seams of her nylons were straight.

Like Ben, I wore my padded snowsuit. My hair was combed back into a ponytail under its hood. I'd daubed my lips slightly (well, ever so slightly) with Candied Apple, my aunt's Revlon lipstick. I was carrying our gift — the jar of Medonte honey I'd borrowed from our pantry.

The hospital infirmary was on the top floor of a brick farmhouse on the hospital grounds. We entered through its basement door, sneaking glances at the workshop where patients were hammering and sawing wood. Sib was in plain view, strutting back and forth like a bandmaster. The patients were making pews for the local church, Little Louie whispered as we peeked into the gloomy room. It was so dingy we could barely make out the hulking shapes of office desks and chairs piled up by the walls. The sight gave me the willies. What if I was one of them, and not the daughter of Doc Bradford? What if I had to slave away for no money in the Bug House basement? "There, but for the grace of God," as my father put it.

Upstairs, in the front hall, a nurse stopped the three of us. Ben and I smiled politely up at her. Little Louie said, "I'm with *The Chronicle*. These are my children."

"Oh, all right, dear." The nurse smiled back a little tentatively and walked away. When Little Louie was sure the nurse wasn't coming back, we crept up a flight of stairs and down a long hallway. The walls were hung with the same weird oil paintings that hung in our house. In every painting, people were paddling canoes on calm northern lakes but none of the paddlers had eyes or mouths.

Suddenly, Little Louie flattened her back against the wall and motioned for us to do the same. At the end of the hall, Chief Doucette was sitting at a desk, a billy club resting in front of him. A revolver bulged from the shoulder holster that criss-crossed his white shirt. Slowly, the chief stood up and stared in our direction with a frank, blind look. I realized he didn't see us, because he was thinking about something else. "Quick. In here!" Little Louie whispered and tugged us into an alcove. The sound of the chief's footsteps echoed past us down the hardwood floor. When the footsteps faded away, we hurried past a bedroom where patients lay in cots reading or gazing into space. An old woman without any hair cried, "What happened to your leg, little girl?"

"It's all right," Little Louie called softly. "We're on our way to see a patient." The woman sank back on her bed. Ben whispered, "Mrs. Gruen won't tell. She can't remember things." Little Louie nodded. Somewhere nearby, a man was coughing. The three of us stopped to listen. "John," I whispered.

Sure enough, John was in the last bedroom, lying in bed in striped pyjamas. Jordie was sitting nearby in a chair, flipping through a scrapbook. One of John's hands was handcuffed to the metal headboard. "Jumping Jehosephat!" he waved with his uncuffed hand. "Am I seeing things or have two beautiful women just walked in?"

He pointed at the edge of his bed. My aunt sank down gracefully on his mattress, crossing her long legs in their nylons and opening her jacket so John could see her pretty turquoise blouse.

Ben and I remained standing in our snowsuits. "We're on guard duty," I explained. John nodded solemnly.

"I don't know about you, Louisa, but the kids should scram." Jordie jumped up. "Chief Doucette will be back in a couple of minutes."

"No, you scram, Jordie," John replied. "Go distract the Chief, eh?"

"Okay, but make it snappy," Jordie said on his way out.

"Louisa, look what Mary has brought me!" John held up my jar of Medonte honey. "It's fresh too. Made this year, it says here."

My aunt smiled and my heart sank. The Candied Apple lipstick looked pretty against her big white orderly teeth. It did not look nearly as nice on mine.

"It was thoughtful of Mary, wasn't it, son?"

"Yes, Mr. Pilkie," Ben replied.

"John. Call me John, eh?" Without waiting for an answer, he pointed to the scrapbook that Jordie had been looking at. "Maybe you and Mary want to look at my pictures while Louisa and I talk." Ben picked it up, and we stared bug-eyed at a picture of a young John Pilkie in a dressing room with a bunch of toothless, sweaty men. Using an upended trophy, one player was pouring champagne into John's open mouth.

"That was taken the night we won the Stanley Cup. In those days I was somebody, eh? Not like now. Now here's Sib and me with the Oshawa Colts." John tapped a photo of two slim young men leaning over their hockey sticks. Ben and I didn't recognize Sib without his bald head and pot-belly.

"The Colts were a lot nicer than the Wings, I can tell you that." He coughed again, covering his mouth with a handkerchief. "Those NHL managers, eh? You're just a slab of meat as far as they're concerned. But forget I said that. How's the skating coming, Mary?"

"I ... I can't stand up very well."

"It's true, Mr. Pilkie," Ben said.

"Her balance will come. It's her posture, son. She needs to keep her head up. And bend at her knees and ankles, not from her waist ... Now what's that noise?" He cupped his hand to his ear. Down the hall, we heard Dr. Shulman's raspy chuckle and Morley's off-hand rumble. There was another voice, low and sarcastic. It was Dr. Torval, Dr. Shulman's friend.

"Quick now, Louisa, you hide in the closet. And Mary, you and the boy under the bed!" My aunt obeyed him, closing the closet door quietly while he lifted up the bedspread and we crawled underneath in our bulky snowsuits. Luckily, the bedspread hung almost to the ground.

"Gentlemen! What can I do for you?" John asked in a hearty voice.

"The boys have a few questions to ask you, John," my father said, and I imagined Morley looking down at John with his sad healer's eyes. "Chief Doucette's going to uncuff you. Then he'll wait in the hall until I call him. All right, chief?"

There was a clink of metal as Chief Doucette unlocked John's handcuffs, followed by the sound of footfalls leaving the room. "Okay, do your worst, eh?" John said.

Dr. Shulman and Dr. Torval talked in deep low voices, like Doomsday judges. "How do you feel when you think about your crime?" Dr. Shulman said. "Would you have done anything differently?"

"The day Peggy and baby Sheila burned up was the worst day of my life."

"Were you angry at the time?" Dr. Torval asked.

"I couldn't think clearly. My concussion affected my judgment, eh?"

"You walked off these grounds in June," Dr. Torval said. "Do you call that using good judgment?"

"Well, sir. No offence, but I can't agree with that. As I told Doc Shulman, I wanted to get attention for my case."

"And what's this about roughing up a guard?" Dr. Torval added. "Mr. Beaudry says you tried to choke him with a sheet."

"I was going to send you a note, Henry," Dr. Shulman said sounding embarrassed. "Sib admitted he'd been riding John pretty hard."

"Sib has never liked me, sir," John replied. "He wanted to play for the NHL, but he drank too much beer. He's held it against me ever since."

"You have an answer for everything, don't you, Pilkie?" Dr. Torval asked. "Well, you've got nerve. I'll say that. What I'd like to know is whether you're free of your fits of aggression."

"Tell them how you feel, John," Morley said.

"I save my anger for the rink, Doc Bradford. Then I let her rip. If you can't beat 'em on the rink then you can't whip 'em in the alley, am I right?"

"Try to be serious, son," my father said. "Do you feel fine? Is the hockey helping?"

"It sure is, Doc Bradford. I feel like a new man," John said.

"You feel differently now," Dr. Torval says. "What about your wife and child? Would you do the same thing today if your wife got up your nose again?"

We heard the rustle of covers being thrown off, and then the headboard moved sideways as a pair of bare feet smacked the floor. John's feet were so close I could touch his heels. I glanced at Ben and he put a finger to his lips.

"What did you say, Doc? Are you insulting my wife?"

"I was asking how you feel about your wife."

"No, you weren't. You were saying I murdered Peggy because she was a bitch."

Morley's black wingtips creaked closer until they rested by John's bare feet. "Get back in bed," my father said gruffly. "Now. I mean it, son."

"No way, Doc Bradford. Not until he apologizes about insulting Peggy."

"Calm yourself, Pilkie," Dr. Torval said. "Chief, get in here."

Footsteps pounded into the room. Suddenly, the bedsprings dipped so low the mattress touched our heads before it bounced up again. Terrified, Ben and I crouched lower. Above our heads, we heard a deep, wheezing gasp and then a man groaned in pain. A moment later, the groaning switched to an awful, choking noise that sounded like somebody being strangled.

"That's enough, chief," Morley said. The choking noises stopped.

"No more lip, okay, Pilkie?" Chief Doucette said. "Or next time I'll stick this down your throat and make you swallow it."

John mumbled, "Jesus Christ," and Morley said, "Thattaboy, son. You'll see. Everything's going to be fine. Just do what Chief Doucette says."

From the hall came the sound of squeaking wheels. "Sorry to interrupt, Dr. Shulman," a woman said. "I'm here to take John to hydrotherapy. He'll go in the wheelchair. But Chief Doucette has to cuff him to it."

"All right, Jeanie," Dr. Shulman replied. "We were just leaving. Goodbye, John. Stay calm now." The men said goodbye and the squeak of the wheelchair grew fainter, which meant John was leaving, too. When we were sure they'd gone, my aunt hurried out of the closet. She and Ben helped me up and we tiptoed down the hall so we didn't disturb the bald-headed woman.

Once outside, we couldn't stop talking about what Chief Doucette did to John. Ben thought the Chief gave John a Chinese wrist burn. I thought the Chief must have pressed his billy club against John's windpipe. My aunt hissed that John didn't do himself any favours by getting angry. That shut Ben and me up for a while.

41

TWO DAYS LATER, MORLEY GAVE A PARTY FOR THE RATS. THE cases of Brading Ale that had been hidden inside Tubby's sofa were stacked all the way up to our living room ceiling. On our dining room table, Sal had set out a coffee tray along with a baked ham with pineapple rings and cloves, the way my father liked it. John walked in with his mother and Jordie. Their eyes lit up when they saw the beer.

"Now that's a sight for sore eyes!" Jordie elbowed John, who gave everybody his big, grand piano grin. "Good to see you, Doc Bradford," John pumped my father's hand. "And you too, Mary ... Ben ... Louisa. Hey, it's been a coon's age, eh?" He winked, because we had just seen him in the infirmary.

"Are you ready for our big game next week?" Morley asked. Before John could answer, Mrs. Pilkie said, "You're going to get a review for my boy, aren't you, Doc Bradford?"

"We'll have to see, Georgie." Morley smiled. "Though you and I have been in tough situations before, haven't we?"

"So you'll go to Toronto to talk to the doctors?"

"Mother Pilkie," John said. "Not another word or you're going to jinx us!"

"I don't want to do that. Do I, doctor?" Mrs. Pilkie asked, but Morley had already moved off to greet another guest. As soon as my father was far enough away, I said, "Hello, John." And Ben said, "Hello, John," too.

"Well, now. John, is it? It's about time the pair of you called me that!" His smile grew bigger. He squeezed Ben's shoulder and kissed my hand in his old Gentleman Jack style. "Doesn't your niece look grown-up, Louisa?" He pointed to Big Louie's heirloom brooch pinned to the front of my Peter Pan blouse and he and Little Louie laughed when they saw me blush. "Is that the brooch you got for Christmas?" I took it off and the four of us examined it.

"Real pearls, eh?" He bent close and whistled.

"Little Louie thinks pearl brooches are too fancy for girls my age."

"Do you, Louisa? I think it looks downright pretty."

Secretly, I thought Little Louie was right, but I didn't let on. The four of us went into the kitchen where Sal was feeding coal into the stove that Sal called the old bugger behind Morley's back.

"So Sal," John said, shaking her hand. "Mary's going to skate for us tonight, eh? And you're going to give me a cig, aren't you, Sal?"

"Nope," Sal replied. "You take good care of yourself, John. We want the Rats to win."

"Sal's right. You shouldn't smoke," Little Louie said.

"Go on, the two of you!" John laughed. "Do you think my playing makes a difference, son?" he asked Ben.

"Yep," Ben said. "When I grow up, I'm going to be a defence-man like you."

Sal and Little Louie laughed like anything, my aunt's voice warbling high and girlish next to Sal's low, appreciative chuckles.

"Ben's right. We're all counting on you." Little Louie smiled at John, showing him her pretty white teeth. John winked as he took a cigarette from Sal. I couldn't help thinking how much had changed since the afternoon he came for tea with the other men from Maple Ridge. Kelsey Farrow no longer wrote about the death of John's wife and baby daughter in the newspaper. Nobody, Little Louie and Sal included, thought of John as a killer. He was the hockey star who was going to bring the Pickering Cup back to Madoc's Landing after twenty-five years.

"Okay, Mary." He tapped my bottom. "Away you go and get your skates. You too, son," he told Ben. I said okay, my heart in my mouth.

WHEN I RETURNED, CARRYING MY skates, Morley had left for Cap Lefroy's house with his doctor's bag. Nobody seemed to miss him in the living room, where the players were laughing and talking. I heard Sal asking if anybody wanted another Brading Ale. Coming down the front stairs, I almost ran into John and Little Louie in the front hall. At first, they didn't see me, and I stopped on the last step, waiting to be noticed.

"Somebody's making that up," John said. "Doc Bradford wouldn't let me down."

"Sssssh," Little Louie said, and put her hand on John's shoulder.

John spun around. "Well, well, we're here gabbing and you're all ready to go, eh?" He sounded slightly ashamed of himself.

"Mary, it's too late to skate now. Ben has gone home and John and I need to talk," Little Louie said. The fierceness in her tone took me by surprise.

"It's only nine o'clock," I protested.

"Maybe Louisa's right, Mary. Off to bed, eh?" He waved me away, and I trudged back upstairs. Now I didn't have to worry about looking dumb, except that I had got my nerve up for nothing. And there was something else. If Little Louie hadn't sent me to bed, he would have come outside and watched me skate. And even though I'd have made a fool of myself, I would have had him to myself. Well, almost to myself because Jordie would have come and Little Louie too. But John would know I was skating for him, my special friend.

It wasn't until the next morning that I remembered my brooch. It wasn't in the living room, or behind the potted plant by the kitchen window. It wasn't anywhere. Sal started to say something, but cut across it. "It'll turn up," she said. I hardly heard her. By then my mind was on something more serious. I was waiting for my aunt to wake up so I could ask for her help. "My friend" — which is what Little Louie called having a period — had come in the night. It was crazy to want something as icky as blood. Just the same, I had longed to get "my friend" so I could be a grown-up woman like Sal and Little Louie, instead of an N.B. And now here it was. Between my thighs felt sticky and the bottom of my pyjama bottoms was stained red, as if somebody had spilled tomato juice down there, the place that nobody spoke about.

42

AT ONE O'CLOCK IT STARTED SNOWING AND, PER USUAL, I FELT
the same lonely sensation I often experienced in a blizzard. As
if the snow was walling me in flake by flake. That week in *The
Chronicle*, Little Louie had written: "An icebox winter has led
to a jump in book borrowing. Already, residents in Madoc's
Landing have taken out 6,300 library books compared to the
total number of 3,227 by this time last year. For those of you who
hate winter, our library offers a ready-made escape."

As I put on my snowpants, the phone rang. Little Louie grabbed
it and covered the receiver with her hand. Her eyes widened and
her jaw dropped but, when she saw me watching, she rearranged
her face so she looked normal. Then she said "thank you" and
put down the phone.

"Who was that?" I asked.

"Just a nurse at the Bug House," my aunt said.

"Why would she call you?"

"She's helping with my research, Mary," my aunt replied,
her tone warning me not to ask more questions. Taking me by
surprise, she smoothed down the collar of my Peter Pan blouse

and asked why I wasn't wearing Big Louie's brooch. "Don't you like it?"

"You said it's too fancy for a girl my age," I answered, not wanting to tell her it was missing. Either I had lost it, or somebody had taken it, and I wasn't interested in considering those possibilities just now.

"Did I really say it was too fancy for you?" My aunt frowned and didn't press me. She seemed lost in some world of her own (i.e., she didn't do up her galoshes the way she normally did or put on her wool toque). When I handed her the toque, she stuffed it in her pocket. Looking slightly dishevelled, she helped me buckle on my brace, and we went out into the winter twilight. She wanted to drop a book off at the library and pick up her paycheque at *The Chronicle* before we met Morley at his office. The sidewalks were hip-deep in snow, so we tramped down the middle of the road. Every so often a car passed us by, very slowly, the falling snow muffling the noise of its wheels.

We stamped into the library, kicking the snow off our galoshes. I waited on the upper floor where I wasn't usually allowed to go because I wasn't old enough. While my aunt handed over her book, I stared at the middle-aged women in cardigan sweaters with jewelled clasps and the old pensioners in their hunting caps and boots. They didn't look studious, yet there they were hunched over books, the storm wind moaning outside the high glass windows. A moment later we were back outside and on our way to *The Chronicle*.

AT THE NEWSPAPER OFFICE, KELSEY Farrow was typing at a roll-top desk. He grinned at the sight of Little Louie coming in without a hat, snowflakes glistening on her loose blond hair. "What do you think of them denying Pilkie a review of his case?" he asked as he handed her the envelope with her cheque.

A frightened look passed across Little Louie's face. "Is it true? I hoped it was a rumour."

"Oh, it's true all right. Dr. Shulman told me himself. Pilkie's going to be plenty upset."

"I suppose you're right, Mr. Farrow." My aunt gripped my arm, and the two of us stumbled out of the newspaper office. I could feel the tension through her hand, and I knew Little Louie was more upset than she was letting on. I didn't blame her. If John was unhappy before, he was going to be miserable now. The thought filled me with dread.

Outside, the temperature had dropped. I told her to do up her galoshes and put on her toque and she obeyed me as if I was Sal telling her to mind her P's and Q's. Then I wrapped my scarf so tightly around my face that my breath left ice droplets on the wool. The streetlights didn't come on until we were in front of Morley's office.

WE HAD TO WAIT IN the front. Morley was at the back with a patient. Through the wall, we heard his voice reassuring them. I pretended to read *Ladies' Home Journal,* but I was hanging on his every word. "It's very hard, isn't it, Mrs. French?" my father asked. My father's kindly tone made the blood thud in my ears, and I wished that his big, sad, healer's eyes were showering me with hope instead.

A soft female voice said, "Yes."

"Don't worry about the operation. Percy will be fine. I'll see to that," my father said.

Now my father's voice grew louder, and suddenly, he was coming down the hall towards us. He wore his white doctor's coat. A woman followed him wearing a coat with ermine cuffs. She was obviously from the city and she was holding the hand of a small boy. I stared at his split upper lip, which was the pink shade of an earthworm before I remembered my manners and dropped my eyes.

"This is Mrs. French and her son Percy," Morley said.

"Nice to meet you." The woman gave us an embarrassed smile.

"Percy's going to look brand new when we're done, Mrs. French," Morley said. "Aren't you, Percy?"

The boy said "yep" the way Ben did.

At the door, the woman turned, as if remembering something, and said to my aunt, "I came all the way from Toronto just to have your husband fix Percy's cleft palate. He's the only doctor I trust."

My aunt didn't look at her. Instead she sat blowing smoke rings at her galoshes. The woman sighed and hurried out the door with her son.

Some Sad Facts about the Leafs

To impress Morley, I recited a few sad facts about the Maple Leafs. In the 1952–53 season, the Leafs were two points short and missed the playoffs. In 1953–54, after a one-year break, the Leafs went to the playoffs, but lost to the Detroit Red Wings. In 1954–55, the Leafs were one game short of making the Stanley Cup playoffs.

"Maybe the Leafs will do better tonight," Morley said.

"I hope so," I replied. "But the Canadiens have already won seven games — and the Leafs only two."

Encouraged by Morley's smile, I added: "Oh, I forgot. In 1956–57 the Leafs missed the playoffs again."

"Mary, please," my aunt said. "I'm too nervous for words."

"Little Louie's upset, because Kelsey Farrow says John Pilkie isn't going to get his case reviewed," I blurted out. "And I'm upset too."

"I heard about that, but John will still score for us tonight — you'll see. Everything's going to be fine." Morley cuffed my cheek with his large hand, trying to catch me up in his enthusiasm.

"I hope so." I felt bad all over again. How would John play tonight? *Oh, please*, I thought. *Don't let him mess up.*

43

LITTLE LOUIE, SAL, MORLEY, AND I REACHED THE PORT WALDIE
arena at six p.m. Grinning with excitement, Morley disappeared
down the passageway to the players' dressing room, and my aunt
and I headed to the food stand to buy popcorn and hot chocolate.
Outside, the blizzard had obliterated Port Waldie. I had written
in *M.B.'s Book of True Facts* that it used to be called the Chicago of
the North. It was famous for the Georgian Bay Trestle, the longest
wooden railroad bridge in North America. *A truly amazing feat of
engineering, the 145-foot span of Ontario red-and-white pine curves
across the 2100-foot stretch of swampy Port Waldie Bay.*

A half hour later, Morley returned, grim-faced and silent.
I wondered if he was worried about John. But it was too late to
ask him what was going on, because the Rats were coming down
the corridor in their gold and white sweaters. John was clomp-
ing along at the back of the line with Kid McConkley. I held up
his old hockey card and waited for him to grin and wave, but
instead he threw my aunt a wild, furious glance. She stiffened
as if she'd been slapped and threw him a sad look back. Then
he lowered his eyes and didn't glance our way again. I called

out his name. He still didn't look up, but there was a change in the way he was holding himself so I knew he had heard me. His face was pasty and he was wobbling as if he couldn't stand straight. I held my breath as he skated slowly around the arena, listing to the left and right like a boat bobbing around in rollers. Next to me, Morley sat pensive and silent, his eyes trained on the players. As John glided by unsteadily, Morley yelled, "Thattaboy, Gentleman Jack!" Ignoring us, John looked up at the empty scoreboard. Morley lifted his eyebrows in surprise. John always waved at Morley in the stands.

The organ started, "When the Saints Go Marching In." John cut his skates hard at centre ice, sending up a shower of spray. Per usual, he bowed to the crowd; then he took out his harmonica and played a few bars of "Roll Out the Barrel." The crowd broke into clapping. The clapping stopped and he surprised us by putting down his stick. For a moment, he waited, poised like a performer about to do a trick. "That man just loves grandstanding," Sal whispered. I didn't bother answering. A strange, wild mood was drifting through the arena. John bowed again. While we held our breath, he jammed his thumbs in his ears, waggled his fingers and stuck out his tongue, making the loony face he had for me in the sugar bush. Was this one of his jokes? Slowly, people started to laugh. John started skating around the arena, and now their laughter faded. He was baring his teeth at the shocked crowd, and waving his gloves like menacing paws. Around us people chattered nervously. A few of them shouted his name. He ignored their cries, and wobbled through a pirouette, his arms criss-crossed daintily across his chest. He stumbled coming out of his spin. Little Louie grabbed my arm and squeezed it when he caught himself. He took a few strokes on his skates and stretched out his hands, lifting up his leg behind him like a female figure skater, I covered my mouth to hide my giggles. Then I froze. I knew what he was doing. He was getting back at Morley.

"He's drunk," Little Louie whispered. My father nodded. A few people jumped to their feet and began to boo. Someone blew a bugle. Oblivious to the catcalls, John skated the full length of the arena again, his leg out behind him, his arms still uplifted daintily. As the organ switched back to "When the Saints Go Marching In," he tried to stop. Too late: he crashed into the boards and lay on the ice. A long sad "ooooh" passed through the crowd. The referee skated over and helped John to his feet. For a moment, it looked like he was going to fall again, but he held steady and waved apologetically at his stupefied team-mates. Morley was already moving down the aisle. The referee opened a door in the boards, and my father stepped onto the ice. He walked slowly towards John. Two referees followed my father, carrying a stretcher. My father put his arm around John's shoulder, and talked to him. John's face took on a humble expression as if he felt sorry for what he'd done. Or was he just pretending? Morley gestured at the stands, and John nodded, dropping his eyes. Morley waved away the referees carrying the stretcher and strolled off the ice. John skated after him, his expression troubled. Morley appeared unperturbed, although I was pretty sure that was not what my father was feeling. It was not what Little Louie and I felt either. Without John, the Rats would lose their advantage over the Port Waldie Icedogs. Our breath heavy in our throats, we watched Morley take John by the arm and lead him down the passageway to the dressing room.

44

THE FIRST PERIOD STARTED. KID MCCONKLEY TOOK JOHN'S place. We all cheered when Kid McConkley scored the first goal with an assist by Toby Walker. There were no more goals after that. My father's eyes drifted towards the dressing room door, but John didn't reappear. After a half an hour on the ice, Toby Walker and Kid McConkley lost their spunk. They, too, had expected John to skate onto the ice and help them. Who else could pass the puck at exactly the right moment so the forwards could score?

In the third period, the Icedogs took four goals and my father grew morose. Sal whispered encouragement. Morley ignored her, his eyes on the referees, as if he was getting ready to smash one of the officials in the jaw. Sal must have been worried about him doing something like that, but the game finished without my father punching anybody. The Rats lost eight to one. It was a humiliating defeat, their worst of the season.

We were halfway down the aisle when an announcer said over the loudspeaker, "John Pilkie has escaped. Please disperse as quickly as possible and let the police do their work." The fans stampeded for the exit. Cursing John's name, they streamed around my father, who stood gazing down at the people rushing by; he was too big for anybody to push out of the way, although some in the crowd threw him dirty looks. Not that it mattered; he didn't seem to care if he was being jostled. He stayed frozen to the arena floor, looking all for the world like a broken down dam trying to hold back the rapids. Little Louie and I tried to push our way over to him, but too many people held us back. There was nothing to be done. Breaking my father's trust, John had walked out on his team and ruined their chances for the Pickering Cup.

OUTSIDE THE ARENA, THE FAINT red gleam of taillights broke the darkness as the cars left the parking lot and crawled along the main road. My aunt and I tramped over to the Oldsmobile, using Morley as a windbreak. "Nobody can predict what John will do," Sal muttered as we got into the car. "He's not right in the head. You said so yourself."

"I never said John was crazy," my father snapped. "I said he had a problem with authority. The NHL gave him a bad shake. But Rob will fill us in." He pointed at Dr. Shulman headed our way across the parking lot.

"Morley, will they find John?" Little Louie asked.

"Let me talk to Rob for a minute, will you?" Morley said in the same irritated tone. Little Louie tucked her head into her collar, looking as if she might cry. I reached over to squeeze her hand and she lowered her eyes and moved her hand away. As Morley started the engine, Dr. Shulman leaned his head in the window and explained that the referee had found Jordie tied to a bench in the dressing room. John had taken Jordie's twelve-gauge shotgun. Holding my father's eye, Dr. Shulman said, "Pilkie found out you didn't go to Toronto to argue his case."

Morley frowned. "You know why I couldn't. A clerk died in the town hall fire that day. He died." Clearing his throat, my father added, "John promised to sober up and come back on the ice. He was on his third cup of black coffee when I left him."

"I know, I know," Dr. Shulman replied. "It's just bad luck, isn't it? For all of us." There was a quaver in Dr. Shulman's voice, and I thought of what my father had said about how John and his hockey playing would help Dr. Shulman with the town. Now that John was gone, things would be a lot harder for Ben's father.

"Okay, Morley, we'll talk about what to do in the morning." Head down, Dr. Shulman hurried off.

"John didn't mean to let you down," I cried. "He was just too sad to play."

Morley gave me a white-faced look. Nobody said a word as we drove off. The snow was coming down too fast to see the divider line on the highway. Sal turned on the radio. The newscaster said the Toronto Maple Leafs had beaten the Montreal Canadiens three to one.

"Well, that's good news," Sal said.

"I don't care about those bums," Morley replied. We lapsed into silence again. The snow kept falling wild and thick, the wind driving it at the windshield of our car.

I thought of John's face as he followed Morley off centre ice. He and Mrs. Pilkie had counted on Morley to persuade the Toronto doctors to undertake a review. But Morley had had a crisis on his hands; he couldn't take care of everybody at the same time. Nobody knew that better than me.

BY THE TIME WE REACHED Madoc's Landing, the snow had stopped. The plow hadn't come yet so Whitefish Road was impassable. My father shut off the engine and a car slowed down to see if we were in trouble. Morley gave the driver his Morley wave, his right hand floating up from the wheel, his index finger shooting out. Then he started up the car again and turned off the road. It took me a moment to realize what he was doing. He was going to drive down the snowy meadow between the guards' houses and Whitefish Road. While we watched horrified, our car started down the hill, its fender throwing up mounds of fluffy snow that poured in waves across the hood and up over the windshield. "You're going to hit something," Little Louie cried. Sal didn't speak. She knew there was no point asking Morley to stop.

"We'll be fine. You'll see." My father pressed his foot on the accelerator, and we ploughed on, bouncing over the ruts hidden under the snow. My aunt hid her eyes, while I sat dumbstruck. Nobody talked as the Oldsmobile rolled on down the hill until at last it burst through a snowbank and we came to a full stop, a few houses down the road from our home.

My father shook his head. "I gave John a second chance. How could he let me down?"

I waited for Sal to say "I told you so" but she stayed quiet.

"John is a no-good bum, just like his old man," Morley said, answering his own question. Then he got out of the car and the three of us waded through the snow to our house. I wanted to tell Morley how mistaken he was, but I knew better than to argue.

45

THE NEXT DAY THE *CHRONICLE* HEADLINE JUMPED OUT AT ME: "THE Houdini of Brebeuf County Escapes Again!" I had to force myself to read Kelsey's description of John leaving Jordie Coverdale "tied up like a pig in the poke." The idea of John turning on Jordie filled me with grief because Jordie liked John, and John liked him back. The quotes from Dr. Shulman made me feel even sadder. Dr. Shulman said John's success playing hockey had led to "a marked improvement" in his psychological health, but the failure to get his case reviewed destroyed Pilkie's trust in the hospital staff.

"He felt he had nothing to lose," Dr. Shulman was quoted as saying. Kelsey also quoted Dr. Torval, who said Pilkie's behaviour showed the characteristics of a full-blown persecution complex. "Pilkie has no ability to identify with the needs of others," according to Dr. Torval. "He's unable to value the feelings of anyone other than himself."

The photograph of John on his old hockey card appeared beside the article. He was gripping his hockey stick menacingly and wearing his Red Wings sweater. The caption underneath read: "Pilkie Lets the Town Down."

The next day, *The Chronicle* ran an editorial about John. It said that Pilkie should be kept locked up for the rest of his life because he had betrayed the town's trust in him. When nobody was looking, I tore up the editorial and stuffed the shreds into the coal stove in the kitchen. Scowling, I watched the coals flare; then I went up to my bedroom, and sat on my bed, turning John's old Detroit Red Wings card over and over in my fingers. A strange, flat sensation settled over me as if the meaning had gone out of things. I stowed his hockey card carefully away in my jewellery box, put a pillow on the floor to cover the crack under the door, and cried as hard as I could.

FEAR TOOK HOLD OF MADOC'S Landing. The cruel urges and malicious notions that lurked in every home now belonged solely to John. It was as if the town had gathered up all the evil in the world and deposited it in his person. John may have frightened some people before, but now he was the bogeyman on everybody's tongue and a handy way for mothers to get their children to do what they said. "Come straight home from school or the hockey killer will get you. Don't go out at night in case you meet the hockey killer in a dark alley."

Our neighbours cancelled their bridge parties and stayed in their homes. They said John had double-crossed them. He made them believe in him again, and it was hard to know what was worse: their fear or their shame about being fooled. Two days after his escape, the mothers of the Bug House kids lobbied Dr. Shulman to put a police officer on the hospital van that took us to school. Every morning, the policeman politely helped me up the van steps. Inside the van, the Bug House kids couldn't stop talking about John. Sometimes they said they saw him in the schoolyard wearing his ankle-length raccoon coat and carrying Jordie's shotgun, or they claimed John was living in a shed behind the guards' houses. Or they spotted the hockey killer up on the top of Bug House hill howling like a wolf at the full moon.

In the hospital van, Sam whispered: "My dad says Pilkie has a cousin in Vancouver. So he's heading west. Nobody will know him out there."

"You mean he isn't famous in Vancouver?"

"Maybe Pilkie's a big shot to you, Mouse," Sam snorted. "But he's just a no-good killer to us."

I turned my back on Sam and pressed my face as hard as I could against the iced-up window. Somewhere outside our warm bus he was shivering in the cold and I wanted to feel as if I was freezing, too. Closing my eyes, I ran my mind back over what had happened. When did John decide to walk out on his team? When he drank his coffee in the dressing room? Or did he plan it days before? I imagined him stealing out the arena door and then stopping to listen to the game inside. He must have had his doubts before he walked off into the storm, floating away into the falling snow as only he could.

After school that day, I pulled out John's old hockey card and placed it next to a lighted candle on my bedroom window. Slowly, carefully, I drew a circle in chalk around the hockey card and chanted Old Man Beaudry's rhyme, "One for the mouse, and one for the crow, one to rot, and one to grow ..." But the words sounded dumb, like something made up for babies.

46

TWO WEEKS, ONE DAY AND NINE HOURS AFTER JOHN WALKED OUT on Morley, Ben burst in on Little Louie helping me with my homework in our kitchen. Ben said he had something important to talk over, and the three of us trailed upstairs to my bedroom where Ben handed over his father's file on the patient called J.P. Little Louie and I read it together:

February 20, 1960. Met Ptn again in my office. Told Ptn the committee had turned down his request for a review, and he became extremely agitated. He said Dr. Bradford, one of our local doctors, had promised his mother that he would get a review of his case. Pointed out that one man couldn't deliver a review since the outcome depended on the judgment of several doctors, not just one. Ptn asked if Dr. Bradford had met with Dr. Torval. Said that Dr. Bradford had been unable to make a special trip to Toronto to speak on Ptn's behalf. Ptn grew despondent.

Ptn was reminded of his episodes of aggression. One, with the guard Sib Beaudry, who reported Ptn had tried to strangle him after Ptn asked to go for his TB X-ray. Second incident involved a flare of temper with my colleague, Dr. Henry Torval. Ptn became withdrawn, refused to answer further questions. After several prompts, he informed me that his wife had thrown the match on the floor of their bedroom, causing the fire. Ptn said she thought he was going to leave her. Ptn claims he had been hard to live with after his head injury. Reported his wife had mistaken this behaviour as indication that he had lost interest in her. He was unable to convince his wife otherwise. Wife had suffered postnatal depression following birth of daughter and found Ptn's lack of attention devastating. Ptn reports he had neglected his wife due to money worries and concern over hockey career. Am recording this conversation in approximate fullness at Ptn's request.

"I'd like to be able to use your notes when my request for an appeal is heard," he said. I complied. His request was reasonable given his report of events that led to the charges against him:

R.S.: Your wife was the one who threw the match?

Ptn: She was angry with me for drinking beers with an old teammate, and said that I left her with the baby when she wasn't well. I told her my injury had set us back financially, and we couldn't make our next payment on the mortgage.

R.S.: How long had your wife been upset with you?

Ptn: Since the baby was born. Peggy got polio when she was a kid. She never was strong like other women. She did all the looking after of the baby while I sat around. I didn't lift a finger.

R.S.: What prompted her to throw the match?

Ptn: I called her a bitch. She lost control of herself and threw a lighted match on the floor. There was a boom, like a firecracker going off. The flames spread through our bedroom. Peggy wouldn't let me near the baby. She screamed that I was going to pay, and she picked up little Sheila and locked herself in the bathroom ...

R.S.: Didn't you say you were in the bedroom?

Ptn: There was a bathroom off the bedroom. That's where she went. She wanted to get away from me. She didn't mean to kill our kid.

(There was silence while Ptn struggled with his feelings.)

Ptn: Peggy was one of the kindest people I know. But the baby ... didn't sleep very well. Peggy had a hard time soothing her.

R.S.: What happened next?

(For several minutes Ptn was unable to speak. Ptn was in tears.)

Ptn: Peggy wouldn't open the bathroom door. I went outside to get a stepladder. There was another explosion. The top floor of the house went up in flames. Peggy had sprinkled more coal oil in the hall to get rid of the bugs and that made our house a tinderbox. I called the fire department at our neighbour's home. He said he heard Peggy shouting I was going to pay for what I did.

R.S.: Are you suggesting that what your wife said led to your guilty conviction?

Ptn: It made my lawyer think I should plead guilty to a count of insanity because I was known for roughhousing.

He said my history of hockey fights was against me, and that I would be locked up, and possibly executed if I told the truth. He pointed out that nobody was going to believe a young mother would burn up her own child and herself with it.

R.S.: And now you're in here, paying for a crime you didn't commit. Is that correct?

Ptn: It sure is. I am boxed in. My lawyer didn't tell me that mental cases were locked up for life. I trusted him and did what he said.

R.S.: I understand your feelings and I will look into this for you.

Here Ptn bowed his head and fell silent, and I was no longer able to coax him to talk.

Dr. Shulman's report ended with these sentences: "Two days after our last interview, Ptn escaped while playing hockey at the local arena. At present, his whereabouts is unknown."

I IMAGINED DR. SHULMAN'S ROUND, kind eyes as he tried to comfort John, and John bowing his head while he took in the bad news.

"What are we to going do?" I asked my aunt.

"You know it's too late, Mouse. We can't do nothing, " Ben said. "We can't do anything."

Ben threw me a look. He turned to Little Louie. "Can you write about it in the newspaper?"

"They let me go." Tears slid down Little Louie's cheeks.

I patted my aunt's shoulder and told her everything was going to be fine.

"Oh for God's sake, Mary. You sound just like your father," she said and laughed. Then she started crying all over again.

PART SIX

THE AGE OF ACHING

47

NOW IT'S TIME FOR ME TO GET TO THE PART OF MY STORY WHERE I learn what I needed to learn all along: most of the truths we seek lie in the extremes and although we have to travel to that rugged place to feel them in our bones, the extremes are no place to live. Three weeks and twelve hours after John walked out of the arena, leaving Morley and the Rats stranded, I inform Hindrance that I don't want to talk with her anymore. I also give Ben my book of true facts. Then I write a three-page letter to Big Louie explaining that I will soon be a teenager so I'm changing my name to M.B. Bradford. My grandmother phones me immediately.

"Congratulations, Mouse. You're about to reach the age of aching," Big Louie says. "Let's hope your aching doesn't last very long."

I don't know what to say to such a strange birthday wish, so I tell my grandmother how much I like the two-hundred-and-fifty-page history of oil in North America that she sent up, especially the chapter on my great-grandfather titled, *Mac Vidal, Oil Baron of Canada West*. She tells me that next year I will be going to a girls' boarding school in Toronto. It's time I left home and saw the world beyond Madoc's Landing.

My grandmother gave me this startling news three weeks and three days after John walked out into the blizzard, although my family doesn't talk about John anymore. Not Little Louie or my father, and especially not Sal. Nobody wants to hear her say she was right about him. Maybe Sal doesn't want to hear herself saying it either.

A few days later, Little Louie and I go with Morley on his Sunday calls. Ordinarily, my aunt would stay at home to work on a newspaper story. And, ordinarily, I would play my old guessing game in which I close my eyes and try to guess where my father's car is on the road. I would know by the racket under the car's wheels that we were crossing the wooden bridge outside town and the engine's throaty hum would mean we were climbing up the headland overlooking Madoc's Landing.

Now I sit watching the snow-covered trees and meadows flash by with new appraising eyes. One day soon, I'll be leaving Madoc's Landing. And then, I won't go on boring drives in the countryside, or live in a place where it snows half the year. In the fall, Big Louie is sending me away and I'll never go through another icebox winter again.

From the backseat of our car, I can see the frozen bay. I can also see the road across it that the shore people have marked with dead Christmas trees. After freeze up, everybody takes their cars on the ice, or they use scoots, the flat-bottomed boats with steel runners that can sail on both ice and water. Occasionally, people go by snowmobile, a new invention that looks like a bobsled on skis. No matter how you travel, the

Christmas tree road stops you from losing your bearings and, if the cold weather holds, you can safely travel across the ice until early April.

My father pulls into the farmhouse lane. After he tramps through the snow to the farmhouse, I get out of the car to look for signs of spring. There are one or two: the March sun is hot on my face and I'm sweating inside my snowsuit. Dirty icicles drip from the wooden trim on the farmhouse gables. The snow-banks near the barn are burned with deep, yellow pee-holes left by the farm dogs. I turn my eyes north, hoping for a telltale line of blue on the horizon. But the Bay is a solid sea of white all the way to the horizon. Near Towanda Lodge, where Old Man Beaudry lives, there are still icebergs by the shore. So it looks like Sib can keep on driving his snowmobile over the ice without worrying.

Disappointed, I climb back in the car. My aunt doesn't glance up. She didn't get out to look at the view the way she did in the summer when she was seeking a better understanding of things. Instead, she sits in the front seat, smoking her head off and frowning. For her, the Bay is something to avoid; while for me the Bay is a giant clock that measures the way time slips through our lives. Today the clock says spring is just a piece of nonsense dreamed up to keep us going.

MORLEY'S NEXT CALL IS TOWANDA Lodge. Two cottages away, the car's engine conks out and we have to walk down the old lumber road to the lodge. I'm soon thirsty and hot inside my snowsuit, because it's hard going. The temperature is above freezing, and the thick, mushy snow is pierced with small holes where water droplets have fallen from the trees.

Outside the lodge, I spot fresh boot prints in the melting snow. "I guess Old Man Beaudry's had visitors," I exclaim. Morley nods, and my aunt lights up a Sweet Cap. The quick, nervous way she smokes suggests she's keyed up about something. "Louisa?" Morley says. She hurries after him while I hang back to examine the tracks. Some of them go down the small incline that leads to the storage space under the lodge. It occurs to me that the basement would be a good place for somebody to hide. What if John's there? If he was, I can tell him I know about his wife throwing the match.

There's a knock at a window. Behind the glass, my father is signalling for me to come inside. I do as I'm told. Away from the March sunshine, the lodge feels dank and chilly, although its thick walls should keep out the cold. It was built when the land was logged for white pine, but maybe Old Man Beaudry is too sick to stoke the woodstove. In the kitchen, my father shows us how to work the hand pump and then he disappears down the hall. Through the pine board walls we can hear Old Man Beaudry complaining about his stomach. It sounds like my father is going to be here a while.

My aunt pumps us cups of water. "Mary, I want to go outside and look around," she says, tossing her drink down. "You stay here and rest."

"I don't want to sit here by myself."

"You won't be alone. Your father's down the hall." She tips her head towards the sound of voices coming through the wall. Unexpectedly, the lodge falls silent except for the noise of a door banging outside in the wind.

"Can I come too? This old place gives me the creeps."

"No. Not this time."

I freeze. Somewhere in the building, there's the low, hollow sound that makes me think of a rubber plunger going into a human chest. The noise repeats itself.

"John's here! I heard him cough."

"Don't be silly," my aunt says. "He's probably miles away from here by now."

"It's him. I know it is. And I'm going to find him." I hobble off and she lets out an exasperated sigh and follows me down the hall.

OUTSIDE, THE AFTERNOON SHADOWS ARE deepening to a dark powder blue, as if somebody has been painting the sky on the half-melted snow. It's a trick of winter light at this time of year. At first, I can't see well in the refracted glare, but I find the tracks again. Little Louie and I follow them down to the storage space under the lodge. The boot prints are the size of a man's foot. "What if they belong to John?" I ask, imagining the pleasure in his dark, pop-out eyes when he sees us. Little Louie purses her lips and shakes her head. "But I heard his cough," I insist.

The footprints lead to a door in a high, latticework wall. The hinge squeaks when we step into the basement, which smells of rotting canvas and sawdust. Rows of overturned sailboats have been laid across wooden horses, and nearby, water trickles from a bust pipe. Then, somewhere in the gloom, a man coughs again. This time Little Louie hears it too. "Be careful," she hisses. I'm too revved up to listen. The noise is coming from behind a plywood partition. I hobble over, my eyes adjusting to the dark, and peek in the door. Inside a narrow room, a man with wild black hair and a beard sits smoking on a cot. When he sees me, he glares as if I'm part of the world that wishes him harm.

"Mary?" He jumps up, a muscle in his cheek twitching. "What in tarnation?"

"Mary heard you coughing." My aunt comes up from behind and puts her hands on my shoulders. Why isn't she surprised? Or is Little Louie trying to stay calm for my sake? A small, wet smile spreads across his face. "By golly, you two are a sight for sore eyes." He butts out his cigarette, his eyes burning with an emotion I don't understand.

"Are you going away? Please tell me! Where will you go?"

"Hush, Mary," Little Louie says. "Let me talk to John for a minute, will you?"

He nods in the direction of the door. "We'll just be a minute. Okay, Annabel Lee. You stand guard, eh?"

"It's my birthday tomorrow!"

His smile widens. "Well now, many happy returns! Can you be a nice girl and keep watch for us?"

Reluctantly, I do what he says. I don't understand why he has to talk to her alone. I'm his special friend, I tell myself while I keep my eye on what's going on outside the latticework door.

THE ROAR OF AN ENGINE shreds the air. John and Little Louie hurry over. "Don't tell on me, okay, Mary?" he whispers. "Specially not your little pal, eh?" I can feel myself tremble as I nod yes. "When will I see you again?" I whisper. He puts a finger to his lips and pushes me towards the door. "Get going now." His hand falls away. When I turn to look, he's disappeared into the shadows. I trudge outside with Little Louie. On the road, Sib's snowmobile is speeding towards Towanda Lodge.

"Saw Doc Bradford's car." Sib stops his machine and calls. "Thought I'd come by and check."

"We've had some trouble with the engine," Little Louie yells back.

"Want me to take a look at it?" Sib asks.

"Would you?" Little Louie asks. A door bangs overhead, and Morley rushes outside. He must have heard the noise of the Ski-Doo from inside the lodge. "Sib, can you take us back on that thing?"

I consider telling Morley about John, but everything happens too fast, and I promised to keep my mouth shut. Sib jumps off his machine and runs over.

Little Louie climbs onto the front seat of the snowmobile. Morley and I get in its large caboose. My father grips my shoulders with both hands so I won't fall out. After seeing John, my father's presence confuses me.

48

SAL IS IN THE KITCHEN BAKING ME AN ANGEL FOOD CAKE. SHE stops when she sees me enter, covered in snow. Using a broom, she brushes it off my galoshes and helps me out of my soaking wet snowsuit. A snowball fight with the Bug House boys has ruined the home perm I got for my birthday. Sal gently tugs a bedraggled clump of my hair. "I guess those bad boys fixed your Toni. Shame on them, eh?" The warmth in her voice takes me by surprise. Before I can stop it, the urge to confess overpowers me. "I saw him yesterday, Sal." Sal studies me. "Saw who, Lady Jane?"

"He was hiding under Towanda Lodge."

"Is that so? You saw a man there?" She waits while I nod. "What did he look like then?"

Should I tell Sal about John when I promised I wouldn't? I've never told on him before, and it comes to me that my friendship with John has been full of secrets from the start. First, there were our pen pal letters, and after that, weeks of me learning to skate for him and finally, our visit with him in the hospital infirmary. And there's something else. If I tell, I'll get myself and Little Louie in trouble because she's keeping his secret too. But it will be worse for him because he'll be stuck behind bars for the rest of his life. He'll never be released, not after defying Morley and Dr. Shulman. In that respect, he's as good as dead.

"I couldn't see very well. But he was ... around John's age."

Sal's eyes hold mine. "Did you get a real good look at his face?"

I drop my eyes. "I think so."

"Well, then. Don't go scaring me like that. Remember Petrolia, eh? You thought you saw him stealing your granny's car. Plenty of drifters stay at the lodge to help Old Man Beaudry with his chores. You must have seen one of them bums."

Suddenly, I'm too giddy for words. When she notices me smiling, Sal sucks her teeth. "For a minute there, you had me fooled." Turning her back, she starts to work on my birthday cake again, whipping up the icing, using margarine instead of butter.

WHEN MORLEY FINISHES HIS SECOND helping of my angel food cake, he gets up to leave. Outside, another snowstorm has blown in.

"Are you going out on a night like this, Morley?" Little Louie points at the dining room window where white powder, like thick sprays of Sal's icing sugar, sticks to the pane.

"It's Cap Lefroy. He won't last the week." Morley picks up his doctor's bag, cuffing my cheek. "We had a nice birthday tonight, didn't we Mary?"

Morley waits while I compose myself. I feel a horrible weightless sensation, as if I'm circling earth in a capsule like Laika, the Russian dog who was shot into space with no hope of coming home. When my answer doesn't come, Morley pulls on his coat and walks out. I watch him go over to the Oldsmobile, the snow coating his shoulders like fluffy dandruff. Per usual, he's scraping off the windshield, inside and out. When he notices me at the window, he waves. I don't wave back. After I can no longer see his car on Whitefish Road, my aunt says in a low, serious voice: "Alice used to find it hard too."

Puzzled, I fix my eyes on her face.

"It broke your mother's heart the way he put his patients first. Didn't you know that?"

"No."

"Well, it's true. She died angry." Before she can say any more, I hump myself out of the dining room, the angel cake thick as sand on my tongue. Little Louie rushes after me. "Listen. It's not true what I said, Mary. Your mother didn't die angry. She never complained. It was me who was mad. I thought your father should have paid more attention to her."

"Are you telling the truth?" I ask.

"Of course, I'm telling you the truth. I wouldn't lie to you." When she says the word "lie," her face changes. I don't think anything of it. I throw myself against her chest, sobbing. And I am hers, as if she is my mother, and not my mother's sister who chews gum and leaves her room in a mess.

A Girl Talks about Goodness with Her Father

The father, a large man over six-foot-five and his thirteen-year-old daughter are discussing Montaigne. Their conversation is not in his office, where he dispenses pills and cough medicines dressed in a white coat, but during an afternoon walk. It's a habit with them, to hike in the countryside while they explore Montaigne's ideas.

The going is rough on the old lumber trail near the Bay, and the father takes his daughter's hand to make sure she doesn't stumble.

"Montaigne thought to do good was the proper duty of a virtuous man," the girl says. "How do you feel about this, father?"

"When I come into the hospital in the morning and see the patients smiling in their beds, I know I have done my duty."

"When I try to be as good as you, I feel angry. As if too much is expected of me," the girl answers.

"If you do good every day, you will learn to ignore those thoughts. I have no resentment now. I just set a course and follow it."

They stop by his Oldsmobile and the father gets in. He motions for her to get in too. The girl hesitates. Then she starts running as fast as she can in the opposite direction. Suddenly, she stops. What has she done? She shouts for her father, but by now his car has turned into a speck on the country road.

IT STRIKES ME NOW THAT the story I wrote after Little Louie put me to bed was based on a recurring dream. In the dream an old 1950s car is travelling down a country road. A large, menacing stranger wearing a fedora gets out and asks me to get in. I can't see who it is because the man's face is hidden under the brim of his hat but I know he is my father. All the same, if I get into the old car with him, I will end up dead. At first, I don't understand the dream's meaning. I think it's warning me not to get into cars with older strangers. Years later, I understand: the dream isn't about strangers. It's about my will taking me over. It's about the danger of falling into my father's habits until I work myself to death like he did.

49

AROUND NOON THE NEXT DAY, AN ENVELOPE WITH FAMILIAR handwriting arrives. It's postmarked with the stamp of a village near Towanda Lodge, but Little Louie's name is on it instead of mine. Sal is preoccupied with boiling up tomato soup for lunch and she doesn't see me grab the envelope and put it inside my satchel. I disappear upstairs to read it:

Dearest Louisa:

Don't think yours truly has given up. If all goes as planned we'll start a new life far away from this two-bit town.

All my love, John

P.S. The thought of you keeps me going. Thanks for giving me hope again.

"All my love?" He signed my letters "affectionately," meaning what you would think affectionately means (i.e., he has fond, affectionate and all-round serious feelings about me). He could have signed off with "best regards." Did "affectionately" mean nothing? And how could Little Louie love him? Not long ago, she had Max and now she has John, too. Humiliating thoughts crash around inside my head: *He wouldn't love you, no matter how much somebody paid him. You are too scrawny and twisted-looking, even if you have become a bleeder.* To steady myself, I try breathing slowly, and reread his postscript. It still says the same thing: "the thought of you keeps me going" and I get mad all over again. There's not a word about me, his special friend. A big fat zero. His compliments were meaningless toss-away things. I was dumb enough to think he cared for me when all the time he was saving his real love for her. "Thirteen is the aching age," Big Louie said. Well, I'm filled up with aching and somebody better make it go away. Yes. Why didn't I think of it before? Something is owed me by John and Little Louie and I have to get that owed thing before I ache myself to death in Madoc's Landing where the big empty spaces between the houses will make you go wild with loneliness.

When I get myself calm again, I call down that I don't want any lunch. Sal comes upstairs and stands outside my room, muttering as she dusts the hall furniture. The fake chirping of her voice suggests that she hopes I'll stop sulking and come out and talk. I stay where I am. Later, when Sal is gone, I put John's letter back in its envelope, glue its edges shut with LePage glue, and leave it on the hall table.

THE NEXT MORNING, SAL HAS to wake me because I slept in. It's Saturday and she reminds me that it's Scooterama, when everybody in Madoc's Landing comes out to see the scoots race each other up the Bay. The race is later this year because the Department of Lands and Forests wanted to enter its new fibreglass scoot built by the Department of Lands and Forests. The scoot wasn't ready in time so town council postponed the race until the end of March. Thanks to our icebox winter, the ice is still thick enough to give the crowd a good show.

Scooterama has never interested me before, but a front-page story about the new fibreglass scoot in *The Chronicle* starts me thinking. The scoot has a closed-in cabin, and a giant half-moon-shaped rudder, and it outruns the older, wooden models, which are heavy and hard to steer. Most of the scoots on the Bay are hand-built and resemble wooden motorboats, except that an airplane engine and a propeller mounted on the stern drives them. The new fibreglass scoot works on the same principle only it's bigger and sleeker.

There's a picture of it on the front page along with a newspaper diagram that shows the position of its steering wheel, foot-feed gas pedal, and the storage compartment under its bow, which has lots of bunk beds, the newspaper says. Its driver plans to take it north to the town of Kilarney to demonstrate how much farther and faster it can travel than other scoots.

I go upstairs and pack some clothes into my school satchel. I stick in my Scholastic notebook and my grandmother's history of southwestern Ontario, too, and leave my hockey cards behind. Then I write my goodbye note.

Mouse's Note to Morley

Dear Morley:

I have decided to start a new life elsewhere because you don't have time to love me and the one person I thought

cared about me loves somebody else. I know you may be sad
after I go but you won't stay sad for long since Sal is there
to cook for you even though she leaves lumps in her mashed
potatoes. I am giving you back my Lone Ranger cowboy
hat so you will have something to remember me by. I know
I ought to have been easier to look after (i.e., not get sick
with polio) when you have so many patients to cure
although I don't think healing people makes you better
than anybody else. I think you look after the sick because
you like to do it and I'm sorry to have to tell you this but
your selfishness has pressed like a big pile of granite rocks
across my heart. Now that I'm striking out on my own, the
pile of granite has lifted off my chest and I don't have to
worry anymore about being second best. Maybe you don't
want me to feel like second best. And maybe you never did
but that's how I felt. Anyhow, I'm changing my name to
M.B. Bradford. Don't try to look for me. I won't be back
this way again.

> *Love, your daughter M.B.*

I put my note on Morley's dresser and go downstairs for
breakfast. My father is still in the kitchen working on the
soft-boiled eggs that Sal cooked for him. I stare sadly at the back
of his head. *You will never see him again,* I tell myself. *You will*
never see the thick iron-grey hair that matches his fedora, or his sad,
deep-set healer's eyes, or feel the rough love tap of his hand against
your cheek when he says hello. You will never sit by his chair and
keep people from disturbing him when he naps after supper, or write
things for him that he doesn't read. And he has no way of knowing

that you are going out of his life forever, and Sal doesn't either although she'll be glad to have Morley to herself.

As we put on our winter coats, Morley trains his eyes on me. "Are you all right, Mary?"

"I'm not 'Mary' now," I reply. "I want to be called 'M.B.'"

"What's wrong with 'Mary?'" he asks, trading a look with Sal over my head.

"You named me after a dog," I reply.

He reels back. Then he asks in a false, jolly voice, "You didn't believe Sal's story that you were named for my old spaniel, did you? Your mother always wanted a girl she could call Mary."

I look at Sal for confirmation and she nods; suddenly, it's way too much: having to say goodbye when they don't know I'm leaving and then finding out that I wasn't named after a springer spaniel. But it's too late to change plans now. I just smile like anything and follow Morley and Sal out the door.

50

AT THE TOWN DOCK, MORLEY STOPS THE CAR AND SAL AND I GET out. To my surprise, he keeps the engine idling and watches me walk off into the crowd. He smiles and flaps his hand at me and I flap mine back, willing him to go before I lose my nerve. After a few minutes of watching me from his car, he drives along the line of people waiting to see the scoots. I feel as if he's following me, until the crowd parts to let his car through and then there's no sign he was there at all. Morley won't be back for ages. He's on his way to the hospital and there's no telling how long he'll be gone. So when Sal goes off to talk to Kelsey Farrow, I tell her I'm meeting Ben at the Dock Lunch stand, and I'll find her in a couple of hours. "We'll watch the scoot race together." Sal, the fool, takes what I say as gospel and when she says goodbye for the last time, she doesn't know it's her final chance to tell me to watch my P's and Q's or call me Lady Jane, a name I hate more than apple juice in baby-sized glasses.

Ben isn't coming to Scooterama because he's visiting his grandmother so I'm not worried that he'll show up and wreck my plans. The only fly in the ointment is Mrs. Pilkie, who is standing next to me in the lineup to see the new fibreglass scoot. I have to make an excuse about why I'm by myself and not with Sal. Then we all file aboard and admire the scoot, which is twenty-eight feet from stem to stern. But I don't get off with the rest. While the next group of people line up to get in, I duck into the storage compartment and lock the door. The compartment isn't as big as *The Chronicle* claimed, and oil drums are stacked on some of its bunk beds. There are oil drums on the floor too, but why sweat the small stuff? I check my watch and lie down on the empty bunk. In two hours and forty minutes the race will start, and I'll be flying over the ice faster than John Pilkie can skate. Nobody can stop me now. I'll go like the wind without even trying. And then because I'm worn out from getting ready to leave my old life behind, I close my eyes and dream that John and I are flying down the Beaudry hill on a toboggan. Exhilarated, I press my face into the fur of John's raccoon coat, feeling the strength of his back muscles. *He wants me, and for that, I will stand by him through thick and thin, and nobody will catch us because John is too fleet of foot.*

WHEN I WAKE UP, THE scoot is rattling and shaking like a tin can. Scoots vibrate when they travel over ice but inside the compartment, the vibrations feel worse than usual because I am up against the fibreglass side. The next thing I notice is that my bed isn't as comfortable as my bed at home and there are the oil drums all over the place and then I remember I am running away because John loves Little Louie and Morley is too busy with his patients to care about me. Then the vibrations stop. I can't hear anything except the whining sound of the wind outside.

Somebody tries to push open the door of the compartment. Before I can react, there's a horrible splintering noise as the wooden door breaks and a man pokes his head in. At first, I don't recognize him. I'm not used to his face with a beard, although his big pop-out eyes and cowlick are the same. I burst out: "I didn't tell on you! I mean, I did tell but Sal wouldn't believe me." He takes a wheezing breath as if pneumonia is rattling his lungs. "Mary, you're too damn honest for your own good, eh?" Giving me a wink, he sticks his head outside and calls: "Sweetheart, we've got a stowaway. Come see for yourself."

Little Louie pokes her head inside, and now it's our turn to stare although I turn away as soon as I see it's her, and she cries in a low, sad tone: "Mary! Dear God!" She must see the look of pure hate on my face because she adds in a shamefaced whisper: "John didn't want me to tell you."

"That's not true!" I shout. "You're a big, fat liar!"

"Mary, I didn't mean to hurt you!" She tries to come in, but he gently pushes her back outside. "Let me talk to Mary, darling." He sits down on the bunk beside me. "How did you get here, Annabel Lee?"

"I'm running away to start a new life." My voice comes out in a whisper, because I still love him — but not in the way I used to before.

"You and me both. And Louisa too." He smiles slightly. "But we've got a few people right now who want us back in Madoc's Landing. Like to have a look?"

I'm not sure I do, although I let him take my hand and we go up on deck. My aunt is there, gripping the gunnels and staring at the mainland where five small black dots spouting rooster tails of snow are speeding across the ice.

"They're coming after you?"

He nods. "They won't catch us. Not if I can help it. Right, Louisa?" He grins and she smiles back reluctantly. For the first time, I notice she isn't properly dressed. She's wearing her expensive Persian lamb jacket and her cloche hat. Plus her nylons, of all things, and a new pair of high leather boots that I've never seen before. John has on his raccoon coat and choco-late-brown fedora. The two of them look like they're dressed for church, or maybe a honeymoon, but I'm too cowed to ask how they got on the scoot or why they are wearing clothes like that.

HALF AN HOUR LATER, JOHN stops the scoot and takes an oil drum from the storage department. While Little Louie and I watch, he fills up the tank, looking apprehensively out the door of the cabin. He can see the engine and giant propeller. He can't see much else, however, because large flakes of wet snow have started falling around us. It's one of those freak snowstorms that happens in late March when the weather is changing. The damp wind blowing through the door is making me shiver and I well up, thinking of Sal making hot cocoa for me in the safety of our kitchen and warning me about the cold: "You have to stay dry, bundle up, keep warm, stamp those feet of yours, get the circulation going." Well, Sal can't help me now.

Soon we can't see the mainland or the scoots, which grow tinier and tinier before they vanish altogether behind the falling snow. They're there, though. They have to be, and I consider throwing myself over the side and striking off in their direction, but I'm wearing my brace and I wouldn't survive in a blizzard if they missed me, so I just stand there shaking and wondering how I feel about being stuck in a predicament with John and

Little Louie. To be honest, it couldn't be worse since now I have to see up close how much he loves her and how little he cares for me.

"What are you making that face for, Mary?" he asks in a soft voice.

"I want to go home," I whisper, surprising myself, and he nods as if I have said something sensible and important.

"I wish you could, but it's too late to change horses now." He points at the distance. "We can't see them, but they're there, eh? When the wind blows the sound our way, I can hear their engines. Go sit beside Louisa. She'll keep you warm."

I do what he says, although I don't want to. My aunt smiles and puts her arm around my shoulders. I allow her to pull me close. I hold myself as stiff and straight as a board. It doesn't take me long to notice that she is shaking worse than me, and then I remember how much she hates the open water so her shaking has to be from fear. I don't say anything to make her feel better. I don't even try.

ABOUT FORTY MINUTES LATER, JOHN has to fill the tank again. He grumbles about a leak. Then he realizes he's scared us, and he gives us one of his dimpled grins and says there is lots of oil so we don't have to worry, even with a leak. He gets out the second oil drum, while Little Louie and I sit huddled together. She has her head down between her legs, and she's shivering worse than before, because it's colder in the scoot now. The floor is vibrating crazily under our feet. At least I'm in my winter snowsuit and not a coat you'd wear to church. Then, in the distance, there's a noise like a jet plane. At first, I think I'm hearing things. Little Louie jumps up, peers out through the cabin door and I do too. The noise grows louder and louder until a round dot trailed by a feathery spray of snow slowly emerges out of the solid white curtain. It's alone. The other scoots aren't following behind it. Whistling softly, John studies the scoot through a pair of binoculars and hands them to Louisa. Louisa looks through the glasses. Finally, it's my turn. I must be seeing things. Morley's dove-grey fedora and broad shoulders are visible behind the windshield. I'm shocked at how vulnerable he appears in the flimsy scoot, engine exposed to the open air. It doesn't have a cabin, just a windshield, and a wedged bow that curls up off the ice like a rounded pie cutter. The propeller blades, slapping the air like giant paddles, could slice your head off if you stood too close. I have seen these kinds of scoots before; they're used to jump over snow mounds at winter carnivals and their design emphasizes speed, not comfort. Only a northerner like my father would drive such a quixotic contraption.

Morley's come after you, I tell myself. *You, M.B. Bradford, who ran away from home.* Shame burns through me. And other feelings that have been so deeply buried they seem like part of my muscles and bones: first, shock over the way I have underestimated my father. And a sense of wonder because he loves me more than I thought; me, of all people, who has just done something undeserving of love. And now more strongly, the conviction that I have been at fault, as I always am, for not doing a better job of things, and most of all, for running away without thinking of the pain I would cause. I feel physical sensations too: the freezing cold, and the pulse in my throat and the pins and needles in my fingers, which means I'll get frostbite if I don't watch it.

My father's large, anguished eyes rake our deck. Suddenly,

he spots me. He waves. The propellers of his scoot churn the air as he comes in close enough for us to hear him. "Are you all right, Mary?" Morley calls. I wave my hand with its freezing fingers and he shouts: "John. Give me Mary. I'll let you go!"

John pulls out the shotgun from under his seat. He looks over at Little Louie. She says in a whispery voice: "Oh, John, no."

I think of him trying to strangle Sib with a twisted-up bedsheet. "Are you going to shoot my father?" I ask, a tremor in my voice.

He snorts. "Not if I can help it, eh?" He fires a shot in the air and waits. Morley keeps on coming. John fires another shot and the bullet hits the ice near the bow of Morley's scoot. Immediately, my father slows down his machine and cups his hand around his ear.

"Sorry, Doc Bradford. No deal!" John avoids my eyes as he screws the lid back on the gas tank. For a moment, he hesitates as if he's having second thoughts; I wait, too, hoping he'll change his mind and do what my father asks. Instead, he turns the key and the scoot's engine splutters. "Bugger double bugger," I swear under my breath. "Let it conk out." No such luck. John fingers the choke, and the motor kicks over and we take off again, the noise of our engine and the whirling propeller creating a terrible racket. The sound of my father's scoot grows fainter. I cross both sets of fingers inside my mitts hoping Morley won't give up.

51

UP AHEAD THE SNOW IS FALLING SO FAST THAT I DON'T SEE THE dark stretch of water.

"Sit tight!" John shrieks. "We're going across!" He guns the engine, and the scoot makes a long skidding turn to get into position, then we fly across the open water, cold spray burning our faces.

I close my eyes. Will it sink? Of course not. It's built to go on water as well as ice. It sails across the open patch as easily as one, two, three. Now the icy sprays of water stop and we're on solid ice again. "Dad, Dad!" I wave frantically at his scoot. Behind us, it's swerving in a wide arc, getting ready to approach the open stretch.

"Hey, you're blocking my view!" John pulls my arm down. There's a loud splash, and Morley's scoot is submerged up to its gunnels. What happens next flashes by in an instant: Morley's scoot sails across the open water and its engine conks out as soon as it reaches the other side. Morley jumps off the scoot and drags it onto the ice, but the scoot is heavier than ours and its wooden bow cracks the ice near his feet. John pushes the gas pedal to the floor and Morley vanishes.

Just past the Île au Géant, John turns off the road of Christmas trees and onto the unmarked bay. He glances back to see if my father is following us. A thrill shoots through me. Once more a dark speck is visible in the distance. Once more John stomps on the accelerator and my father's scoot disappears. We're way out in the shipping channel now, miles and miles from shore. My hopes of Morley catching us begin to fade. I press myself against Little Louie, whimpering. She puts her arm around me and calls out to John.

"What's the matter?" he yells.

"Mary's leg hurts."

Over the noise of the engine, he shouts that he will take off the brace at the Western Light. So that's where we're headed. Nobody else would be desperate enough to go out there when the ice is getting thin.

SOMETHING'S WRONG. SMOKE BLOWS INTO our faces; heavy and oily, like the smoke from a diesel engine. John makes Little Louie hold the steering wheel and goes out through the cabin door to see where the smoke is coming from. Morley's scoot is too far away for us to smell its fumes. There is nothing behind or in front of us except cold air and ice. Then we see what's causing the smell: the icebreaker steaming up the Bay from the east. Purposeful, it surges towards us, accompanied by an earsplitting ringing like the noise of a million drink glasses shattering. On its bow the words *St. Brébeuf* have been painted in white. Our scoots are directly in its path. I watch horrified as Morley's scoot zigzags helplessly back and forth ahead of it, trying to stay out of its way. High up in Wheelhouse, the captain won't expect to see scoots out here. "Holy shit!" John cries. He rushes back into the cabin and points our scoot west across the solid ice, heading away from the icebreaker.

It keeps on moving towards my father's scoot as if a magnetic force is drawing it forward. Now it's almost on top of Morley. My father's fedora sits on his head, as if fixed in place by the same magnetic force. And then, just as the icebreaker is about to run my father down, it makes a slow arc in the other direction and steams off. We watch, our mouths gaping, while Morley's scoot rides up a gigantic wave like a toy that has been tossed overboard and disappears behind a wall of lake water. I listen for its engine. The vast frozen stretch is silent; there isn't even the cry of a seagull. We are way out in the open, the most dangerous stretch of the Bay. Here there are no islands or peninsulas to act as buffers against the wind. A moment later the scoot floats back up again. Morley isn't at its wheel.

"My father's fallen overboard!" I cry.

John stops the scoot. He and Little Louie rush to the stern to look. When they come back, Little Louie's face is ashen. She shakes her head without meeting my gaze.

"My God. I'm sorry," John says.

I start sobbing. "Maybe he's still alive. Can we go back?"

"We'd only drown."

"No, no! We have to rescue him!"

"Are you crazy, Mary? No way."

"But we can't just leave him!" Little Louie says.

"Shut up both of you. For Christ's sake!"

My aunt starts sobbing, too. John's big black eyes soften. "Look, girls. I'm sorry. We have no choice. Tell me, Mary — is your leg still hurting from that thing?" He bends close, trying to make me look at him, but I avert my head, tears still trickling down my cheeks.

"It's all your fault!" I scream. "I hate you!"

"I guess I'd better take that darn thing off Mary," he says, ignoring me, and he tells Little Louie to help me out of it. Silently, she and I undo the buckles and pull it off.

"Okay, you two, we have to keep moving," he says. "It's getting dark." He points at the sun sliding down under the clouds on the horizon. Little Louie and I stare miserably at each other, and she reaches over and takes my hand. This time I don't hold myself back because I'm stiff and cold. I bury my face in her chest and she puts her arms tight-tight around me. In the next second, our scoot takes off, leaving Morley behind. *Morley is gone*, I tell myself. He was your father and he came after you, Mouse Bradford. I think of how sorry I felt for myself in the morning, watching him eat his soft-boiled eggs and pretending I would never see him again. I hate myself for being such a baby. It was me and my dumb ideas that caused him to drown. He wouldn't have come after me if I hadn't run away. And now the worst has happened. Numb with misery, I don't react when John points at some snowbanks.

"See, girls! We're almost there." Through my tears, I see he's right. Up ahead the tower of the Western Light rises out of the snowy twilight.

AFTER JOHN DRIVES US OVER the last stretch of ice to Double Rock, he helps Little Louie out of the scoot; then he lifts me over the gunnels and carries me across the shore ice. It shudders under his feet, spongy as meringue. Little Louie stumbles alongside, walking with difficulty in her fancy city boots, her head down against the wind.

"I want to find my father."

Cupping the back of my head, he pushes my face into his chest. "Listen Mary. Don't go causing trouble, eh?" The roughness in his voice surprises me and suddenly I don't believe his story about his wife throwing the match. Fear rushes through me. Now anger. How could I have loved him? It was Morley, Morley, my father I loved. Heaving with sobs, I flail my arms trying to hit John's face. He sets me down, and together the three of us plod up the slippery wooden ramp to the house. It's hard for me to walk in my soggy wet snowsuit, so he picks me up and carries me again. This time, I don't fight back. I'm too exhausted. When we reach the lighthouse, he kicks open the door and lifts me across its threshold. Its shambling rooms look unchanged from the summer, except for the snowdrift beneath the living room window. On a shelf in the living room, the Snakes and Ladders game is still there along with the old guidebook, *How to Survive in the North*. He carries me into the kitchen and sets me down on a wooden chair by the Franklin stove. Little Louie follows us, looking around as if she can't believe what she sees.

"A good thing we made it, Annabel Lee." He taps the windowpane as sheets of rain mixed with snow come shuddering towards us, leaving shimmering rivers on the glass. "It's not fit for man or beast out there."

"Don't call me 'Annabel Lee.' That's stupid."

"Hey, you don't mean that, eh? I know you don't."

"I hate you. And my name is M.B. Bradford."

"Well, okay, M.B. Look — I'll have you girls fixed up in a

jiffy." The slight alteration in the way he's holding his head lets me know I've shocked him. He breaks up an old chair into kindling and fills the stove. Soon there's the crackle of burning wood, and its fierce warmth fills the kitchen. He pulls up a chair and tries to massage Hindrance. I pull my leg under the table where he can't reach it. When Little Louie glares at him, too, he jumps up.

"Oh, it's going to be like that, eh?" He sucks his teeth disapprovingly and retrieves a flashlight from his coat pocket. He aims it on a trap door in the floor. "There's always pork and beans in the root cellar. Wish me luck now."

Neither Little Louie nor I say anything. He opens the trap door with another exasperated sigh and climbs down the stairs. I force myself to stand up and look out the window. It's raining more now and the wind has come up the way it sometimes does after sunset. A line of red light glows along the horizon. If Morley had hung on, the warmer temperature might have saved him.

LITTLE LOUIE AND JOHN HAVE disappeared upstairs to talk over our situation. They don't want me to hear. Or maybe John doesn't want me to hear him trying to coax my aunt into a better humour. But I can hear the troubled sound of their voices rising and falling like the wind outside the lighthouse. "I should never have gone with you, John," Little Louie moans. "We're going to die out here." John shouts that they're going to be all right, and my aunt starts to cry. Now his voice drops, and he says imploringly, "Louisa," and then some words I can't make out. But no matter what he says, she keeps on weeping and talking about how we're going to die. She sounds scared to death, like a schoolgirl. And for a moment I feel pangs of terror too, but then why should I care? Morley is dead. I might as well die myself. Besides, she took John from me. John wouldn't let me leave the scoot. Why wouldn't he let me go with my father? Why couldn't he set me down on the ice near Morley? John had the faster machine; he could get away in time. Maybe he didn't trust my father. Maybe he thought Morley was still mad because John walked out on the game and they lost their chance to win the Pickering Cup. The whole situation is so hopeless I start to sob again.

52

OUTSIDE, A SHUTTER BANGS IN THE WIND. THE NOISE COMES from somewhere in the living room. Farther away, there's a sound like the knock-knock-knock of a hard object bumping against wood. It has to be a large object to make a noise so loud. When I look out the window, a boat-like shape is being blown around on the ice, although it's difficult to make out what kind of boat it is in the rainy twilight. The harbour is dark with shadows. Now I see the impossible — what is beyond any sense of how things work back in the world of the mainland. Morley is steering the wheel of the scoot and the wind is catching the blades of its propeller and blowing the scoot in half circles. The scoot bumps against the boathouse dock. Without warning, it stops spinning. My father heaves himself off its bow onto the ice. He picks himself up and begins stumbling towards Double Rock. I knock on the windowpane although he's too far away to hear. He staggers up over the rocks and lurches along the slush-covered walkway. His frozen hair sticks up in pointy grey tufts, and he's weaving from side to side. The front door of the lighthouse rebounds off the wall with a crash. In the living room, there's another crash. Morley has upended the couch and he's peering under it. Why is he looking for me there? Then it hits me: he's looking for my body. I drag myself to the kitchen door, and call his name, but he's making too much noise.

"Where is she, John. Goddamn you!"

"Here," I manage to croak. At the sound of my voice, he puts down the couch. "Mary," he says tenderly. "Thank God!"

I steady myself against the doorframe. "You came after me."

"Sal found the note," he replies. "Mrs. Pilkie said you got on the scoot and didn't get off." There are steps behind me, and my father's face darkens.

"Don't come any closer, Doc Bradford." Next to me, John lifts up the shotgun and sights it.

"No! No!" I scream. I must have blinked because I don't see Morley rush past me and grab John's gun. I didn't know my father could move so fast. He sticks the gun into John's chest. "Now I'm going to kill you, you son of a bitch!" he says.

"Go ahead," John cries. "Finish me off, Doc Bradford!"

Immediately, John begins coughing, and I'm startled by how sick he sounds. His wheezing cough has turned into a phlegm-choked rumble.

The sound takes my father aback. He puts down the gun. With his foot, he pushes it under the couch and then he grabs John by the throat.

The two men hit the floor, making the kitchen walls shake. His hands tighten around John's neck until the veins stand out on John's forehead.

"I didn't run off with John! Tell him, Little Louie! Please!"

Her voice comes out small and whispery. "John and I got trapped on the dock. So we took the scoot." She hesitates. "We didn't know Mary was on board."

Morley's gaze locks mine, his eyes burning as if he's willing me to understand something. Then he slumps to the floor, his hands dropping from John's throat. We bend over him.

Gingerly, I touch my father's cheek. It's blue and cold. "Is he dead?"

"He's got hypothermia," John says, rubbing his neck where Morley was choking him. "It makes you sleepy. Let's get him warm. My daddy taught me what to do."

I nod my head and Little Louie does too.

He looks at us, and points at the kettle hanging from a nail on the kitchen wall. "Get some snow from outside and boil some water and we'll put hot cloths on his chest and forehead. The arms and legs don't matter." Little Louie and I retrieve snow and heat it up in the kettle as John grabs my father's ankles and drags him closer to the stove. He removes Morley's duffel coat and plaid shirt and massages my father's chest. Little Louie pours hot water over the rags I've found behind the stove. John applies a hot rag to my father's face and spreads a larger one across Morley's chest. We all listen to Morley's breathing. At first, it's hard to hear any sound but Morley's chest is still moving up and down. John runs his hands across my father's face and chest; then he says under his breath: "Please, Doc Bradford, please." He looks towards the window, popping his fingers against his palms. Outside the sky is a rainy void, and I think of the Pilkies' name for their island: "Little Alcatraz."

"It's not working." John sounds genuinely disappointed.

"He's alive. You have to save him."

"Don't look at me like that, Mary. I tried, eh?" he cries, his big eyes glowing with hurt. "I brought you girls out here for nothing. I'm good for nothing. Crazy, too." He sits down with a loud crash at the kitchen table. "You know it's true, eh? Nutty as a fruitcake." He bangs his forehead on the table. It makes a horrible sound against the wood. Little Louie shouts at him to stop, but he keeps right on doing it. The sound is terrible. "We know your wife did it!" I burst out.

He stops banging his head. Immediately his coughing starts up and he pulls out a plaid hanky and blows his nose. "What in hell are you talking about?"

"Little Louie and I saw the file. My friend Ben stole it. You told Dr. Shulman she did it."

He looks at me first and then at Little Louie. Their gaze holds for one, two, three, four seconds. Overcome, he drops his head. "I'm not good enough for you, Louisa," he says in a hoarse voice.

"Oh, John," she says softly.

"I was punch-drunk, eh? I can't remember. Maybe I killed them. Peggy was going to leave me and take the baby, too. I let people down. That's what I do. But I wouldn't hurt either of you. Do you believe me, sweetheart?"

Fear is bright in my aunt's eyes, and I know she's thinking the same thing. What's he going to do to us? "Well, you can't disappoint me," I pipe up. "I have been disappointed by life already."

"A girl like you?" He cackles hysterically. "You think you've been disappointed?" But when I pull up my left pant leg so he can take a good, hard look at Hindrance, he stops what he's going to say and sighs.

53

I SUPPOSE I WAS CRAZY TO THINK HE WOULDN'T HURT ME, BUT by then I realized I was in no danger. Each of us knows one or two people who give us a sense of who we might become, even if no one mentions the possibility out loud. Maybe we've sensed it in ourselves from the beginning and all we need is someone to reflect that possibility back. As long as a few people see our potential we can hope that someday we might become the person they think we are. I was that person for John Pilkie and for a while he had been that person to me.

So in a version of Sal's meanest, shaming voice, I told him we couldn't waste time. He and Little Louie watched while I dragged myself over to the bookshelf, pulled down the old guidebook, *How to Survive in the North*, opened it to the right page and shoved it under John's nose:

> If nothing else is available, a rescuer may use his own body
> to warm the hypothermia victim. Some Eskimo tribes place
> the victim, naked, in the arms of another naked tribe mem-
> ber until the body heat of the rescuer revives the victim.

"You want me to get skinny with your father?"

"Yes."

"I'm not a goddamn Eskimo."

"Eskimos know more about cold than us. Please. Just try it and see."

He turned his back to us for a moment, but when he spoke again, his voice was contrite. "All right, Mary. I'll do it for you." Shaking his head, he began pulling off my father's trousers. Morley's eyes flew open. Grumbling and muttering, he held on to his belt and wouldn't let go.

"It's all right," I whispered in Morley's ear. "We're doing this to keep you warm." I remembered what Morley had told me about pain. So I said, "It's not that you aren't cold, Morley. It's that you don't mind if you're cold. Pretend you're tossing the cold away. You'll see. You'll warm up." My father's eyes closed. He began to snore.

John wrapped a scarf around my father's head. "To keep the heat from escaping, eh? Now turn the other way, and let me get my clothes off."

"I won't look," I said. "Please save my father."

"That's what I'm aiming to do." He grabbed my hand. "Do you forgive me?"

I didn't say "yes." Instead I wiggled out of his grasp. For a moment, I thought he was angry again.

He dropped his eyes to the floor. "You're going to make me work hard for that, aren't you?"

I still didn't answer. Not until John climbed under his raccoon coat with my father. Then I whispered, "Yes," but I don't think he or Little Louie heard me.

Out on the Bay, the wind had picked up again, and it started to rain, hard and fast, drops that shook the old windowpanes of the lighthouse. The wood stove was throwing off more heat than before, and every so often, my aunt or I woke up to stoke it. Through the kitchen window, the sky was black as pitch, as Sal would say, although Sal seemed a million miles away now, and I knew the girl who used to listen to her was gone for good.

SEVERAL TIMES DURING THE NIGHT I dreamt John and my father were rolling over and over on the floor, locked in each other's arms. Sometimes my father was on top strangling John with his bare hands, and sometimes John was on top holding a pillow to my father's face. Once he wasn't on the floor at all but standing over my father holding Jordie's shotgun.

When I woke up, it was late morning. The stove was keeping the room very warm, and Little Louie was cooking up the cans of pork and beans that John had found in the root cellar. My father was fully dressed. He sat in a chair, drinking hot water from a tin mug. He stood up slowly when he saw me, and I put my arms around his hips and placed my cheek on his stomach. He patted my head over and over without speaking. I guess we looked pretty funny, but I was glad to be close to him, glad and thankful to be like any girl with her father after a disaster, knowing there is more to be said and not sure where to start. Then Morley shifted his weight slightly and I could feel the rumble of words starting in his chest.

"Are you all right, Mary?" he asked.

"Yes. Are you okay?"

"I'm fine."

I took an anxious breath because I didn't know if Morley

would believe me. "John saved you. He made you warm last night."

"John made a mess of things. He could have killed you."

"But he didn't."

"Thank God for that." The anger in Morley's voice subsided slightly.

"Where is he?"

"Gone. He left that for you." My father pointed at a note on the kitchen table. It had been written in the familiar curling script:

To Mary:

I figure with your leg and my bad luck we had more in common than you might think, but you and Louisa are better off without me so I'm on my way. I told her to stay and look after you. You'll find your brooch in the pocket of your snowsuit. I took it to help your aunt and me start a new life out west but we don't need it now. I wish I had done better for you and Louisa and Doc Bradford.

Love,
J.P.

I retrieved the brooch and held it in the palm of my hand, and it struck me that one day soon Big Louie would come up to visit, and I would wear the brooch for her and tell her everything, well mostly everything that had happened at the Western Light.

"He's gone?"

"He's in the old dory," my father replied.

Little Louie came outside with me. During the night, the ice had gone out, and in every direction I saw a broad reach of shiny dark blue water. Then I spotted the dory. John was rowing it out into the shipping channel where the late morning sunshine, filtering through the clouds, lit up large, floating chunks of ice. He had walked eleven miles in a blizzard and hid himself in the basement at Towanda Lodge, the place he had worked as a teenager, and now he was setting out on the Great Bay, a sick man in a small boat who would need all his strength to row to the nearest harbour. But he had grown up in the wilds of the open. If anybody could make it to land, it was John.

"You didn't go?" I asked my aunt.

"No," she said as if she wished otherwise.

In soft, halting words, Little Louie told me how John had stolen Sib's truck from the Beaudry farm. He was to pick her up at the dock, because the road by the harbour is the only way out of town. But as soon as John arrived, things went haywire. Sib had reported the truck stolen and a police officer spotted them in it. So my aunt did what she'd told my father they'd done, they fled the truck and got on the Lands and Forest scoot because John knew it was the fastest one. She cried and apologized: "I guess I wanted someone who needed me more than anything." I replied that I understood perfectly, although I didn't really understand — not for years and years.

Then we fell silent. To the north, the sky had clouded over and a band of watery pink light glowed beneath ragged-looking thunderheads. We saw a zigzag of lightning, followed by a loud cracking noise. John put down his oars and unfurled the dory's sail. My breath caught in my throat as he steered the dory into the wind, and I thought — as I have thought during all the special times in my life — that I must not forget the moment presenting itself to me, because I wanted the experience to stay in my memory, maybe not exactly the way it was but as a symbol of all that had happened and could be remembered, to be turned over again for new meanings until I could certify it as part of the experiences that have made me who I am.

Out on the Bay, the hull of his dory was turning as black as India ink under the storm clouds. The figure of John had darkened too and the dory grew smaller and smaller until it was a smudge on the horizon. We waited until it was out of sight.

Little Louie took my hand and we went back into the house, where Morley was serving up the pork and beans. We ate to the raucous, communal sound of seagulls diving for fish.

54

I NEVER SAW JOHN AGAIN. KELSEY FARROW CLAIMS THAT SOME-body told him John is playing hockey for an important team in Chile. My father and Little Louie are sure John drowned in the early spring thunderstorm that blew up around noon. We went home that afternoon on the coast guard boat after a seaplane noticed smoke coming out the chimney at the Light. Below deck on the coast guard, we had been protected from the hail and high winds, but a small-craft warning had been issued. John would have found his journey long and difficult.

I preferred Kelsey's story of John playing hockey in South America, and I was beginning to understand my right to my own interpretation of things.

As we sailed home on the coast guard boat, we told Morley that John couldn't remember who started the fire, even though he told Dr. Shulman that his wife did. Morley knew Peggy as a child, and he said that Peggy was quick to expect the worst from people. She'd been treated unkindly by her family and school friends, and Morley could imagine Peggy riding John hard until he lost his temper; but he didn't think Peggy was the type of woman to set a fire. Morley said John had a father who beat him and then he couldn't play for the NHL after his concussion so there was plenty of reason for John to take his bad luck out on somebody. Of course, anything is possible, Morley said, and that's when he told me that people are unpredictable, and he meant it was true of him too.

THAT SPRING, THE MONTREAL CANADIENS won their fourth straight Stanley Cup, defeating the Toronto Maple Leafs. A day later, Big Louie drove up in her new tomato-red DeSoto and picked up Little Louie to take her back to Petrolia. Years later, my grandmother died at eighty-six, although she had lived long enough to see Petrolia put up an oil museum, which exhibited Old Mac's letters. My aunt went back to her reporting job at *The London Free Press*. A few years afterwards, when Max divorced his wife, Little Louie married him without my grandmother's blessing. My aunt kept working at the paper and she and Max raised their three children plus the son Max had with his first wife. My aunt and Max also helped Ben when he started out as a cub reporter. Now Ben is an anchor on one of those sports channels on television.

Sal had good luck, too. The summer after Little Louie left, Morley explained that he needed a wife to help him look after me and he married Sal, who had no doubt that Morley was the man for her.

I never did learn to skate very well, but on June 15, I stood before my classmates at the Regent Street School and read them my composition on my great-grandfather. Standing on the school stage, I finished with the following conclusion:

In closing, I want the reader to know that I have my own
reasons for admiring Mac Vidal. No matter what anyone
says, my great-grandfather was a seeker who found more than
he sought and I intend to borrow hope from his success ...

Following my recital, I was awarded first prize in the Georgian
Bay School District competition. Sal sat in the front row beside
Ben and the Bug House kids. They all clapped politely while I
accepted a check for twenty-five dollars. Morley came in afterwards, so he didn't hear my talk, but Kelsey Farrow quoted from
my speech in *The Chronicle*. Morley read it aloud at the breakfast
table. When he left for work, he was grinning like anything.

As for Morley, he spent the rest of his life working the way
he always did. Socialized health care had come in by then, but
it arrived too late to help my father. Sal said you couldn't teach
an old dog new tricks, and a few years later, when he was dying
of heart disease, and I was called back to Madoc's Landing, no
one was surprised. During his final hours, most of the town
showed up on the hospital hill, carrying lighted candles; I lit
a candle too and went out to stand with his well-wishers who
stayed on the hill far into the night. Sal made Morley get out of
his hospital bed to look. He had shone his light on them for
decades, and now we were shining some of that light back on
him, and he was pleased and surprised to realize what he'd
meant to people.

As for me, I still don't know what goodness is, but it feels
more mysterious than evil, although few of us are bad in the
way we've been taught to think. Most of us are too busy to notice
what we have to offer while some of us, like John Pilkie, are
afraid we're going to be abandoned by the ones we love so we

leave them before they can leave us. In any case, I've made my peace with Morley, and with John, who was the boy Morley saved at the Western Light and the man who sailed off from the lighthouse for the last time while I stood and watched him go. The next year I was shipping out myself, heading for the city and boarding school, away from rugged weather and lonely stretches of water and pine islands and men like John and my father, starting a new life for myself in the world that I hoped was waiting for girls like me.

ACKNOWLEDGEMENTS

THIS NOVEL WAS INSPIRED BY MY FATHER'S LIFE, ESPECIALLY BY the story of him helping a lightkeeper save his son when the lightkeeper's family was trapped on a remote lighthouse on the Georgian Bay. But my book is a work of fiction and I purposefully didn't make the landscape identical to Midland, where I grew up, although there are a great many similarities. So readers shouldn't look for mistakes of fact in the novel's geography. *Hansen's Handbook to the Georgian Bay* is a fictitious text, for instance. And so is the other text mentioned in the story, *How to Survive in the North*. I've also taken liberties with some of the earlier practices at the Waypoint Centre, as the psychiatric hospital in Penetanguishene is now called. As far as I know, no leashes or guns were used at the hospital then. However, I've tried to be accurate about cultural events in the 1950s.

I owe my largest debt of gratitude to my editor Marc Côté who believed in me at a time when I needed a champion. Another debt is owed to my friends on the Midland, Ontario — Then and Now Facebook page for helping me remember those faraway times.

And I am especially grateful to Sylvia Sutherland, Gayle Hamelin, Barb Rutherford-Ivory, Catherine Dusome-Hayward, Roger Attridge and others who kindly read an earlier draft of this book. Thanks also go to York University, the Canada Council of the Arts, and the Toronto Arts Council who gave me assistance in the early drafts, and to John Fraser at Massey College who provided me with a place to finish my book.

I also want to thank Paul Gross for reading an early draft of my novel and very special thanks go to my mother, Jane Swan, for her generous help with my research as well as Charles Fairbank and Patricia McGee, who provided invaluable information about the early days of oil in southwestern Ontario. In addition, I'd like to thank Bonnie Reynolds, Midland librarian; Vincent Lam, author; Janet Iles, researcher; and Robert Duff, sports columnist for *The Windsor Star*, who helped me with my research into head injuries suffered by hockey players in the 1950s and early '60s. Particularly valuable was his research into the case of Jack Gallagher, a Canadian player who suffered from post-concussion syndrome while playing for the Detroit Red Wings. After the injury, Gallagher was confined to an Ontario mental hospital. I've borrowed some facts from Gallagher's tragic life such as the decision by American border guards not to let Gallagher back into the US after he'd been confined in a psychiatric institution. As a result, his career with the Red Wings was over.

THE SHAMEFUL TREATMENT OF HOCKEY players like Gallagher by their managers is a stain on our national sport, and deserves more attention than I was able to give it in this novel. I am also deeply indebted to Robert F. Nielsen, who wrote *Total Encounters*, a history of Waypoint Centre in Penetanguishene. Nielsen's research revealed hospital practices going back to its early days as a boys' reformatory and also directed my attention to the Bug House kids, the children of the hospital staff who enjoyed a freedom on its grounds that would be unthinkable today.

MANY OTHERS HAVE CONTRIBUTED TO this novel. Thanks to many of the staff at the Waypoint Centre: Dan Parle, Waxy Gregoire, and psychiatrist Russ Fleming. Some of the historical information about the Waypoint Centre has been conflated for dramatic purposes. My story also borrows from the life of Mel Wilkie, a mental patient who was incarcerated there for murdering his wife and child in a fire. Wilkie escaped many times, trying to draw attention to his case, and when I grew up in Midland, Ontario, he was notorious for his "elopements," as they were called, and a bogeyman to children and parents alike. While I was never a Bug House kid myself, my father, a local GP, operated on its patients if they were sick and I sometimes drove through its grounds when I went on calls with him.

FOR HELP WITH MY RESEARCH, I would also like to thank the former executive director of The Writers' Union of Canada, Deborah Windsor, and Toronto writer and producer Geraldine Sherman. Thanks also to Canadian editor, Ellen Seligman; American editor Lorna Owen and especially to my daughter, the literary agent Samantha Haywood, who read numerous drafts, as did writer Katherine Ashenburg, and my patient partner, editor Patrick Crean.

The final debt is to my father Dr. Churchill Swan, who didn't live long enough to see my portrayal of the working conditions of small town doctors in the 1950s in this novel. Although he formed the basis of the character known as Dr. Morley Bradford, the other characters aren't autobiographical. The aunt and grandmother of Mary Bradford are fictitious inventions as are the Shulmans and the rest of the figures who appear in this book.

Some parts of this novel appeared in *Exile* magazine Volume 30, Number 4. An essay about my father used as research for this novel appeared in the anthology *The First Man in My Life*, edited by Sandra Martin, Penguin Canada, 2007.

ABOUT THE AUTHOR

SUSAN SWAN'S CRITICALLY ACCLAIMED FICTION HAS BEEN PUB-lished in fifteen countries and translated into eight languages. A former chair of The Writers' Union of Canada, her impact on the Canadian literary and political scene has been far-reaching. Swan's previous novel, *What Casanova Told Me*, was a finalist for the Commonwealth Writers' Prize, Canada and the Caribbean Region; it was named a top book of the year by *The Globe and Mail*, *Calgary Herald*, *NOW* Magazine, and the *Sun Times*. A final-ist for the *Guardian* Fiction Prize and the Trillium Prize, Swan's third novel, *The Wives of Bath*, was made into the feature film Lost and Delirious, shown in thirty-two countries. *The Biggest Modern Woman of the World* was a finalist for the Governor General's Literary Award and the *Books in Canada* First Novel Award. Susan Swan is a graduate of McGill University and has taught at York University, Humber College, the University of Toronto, and the University of Guelph. She lives in Toronto.